Lost & Found

A Mystic Meteor Tale

ELLE HYDEN

Lost & Found

Two lost souls are on a collision course. One searching for a life partner while the other mourns the loss of hers.

Selina is at a crossroads. No job, no home to call her own, and no partner. She has to turn her life around, but in which direction? Returning to her Native American roots, she seeks mystical aid from the spirit world, to find the life she hungers for.

Rea has been able to find a measure of solace after her wife's death but longs for the crack in her heart to heal. Sighting a falling star, she sends her wish out into the universe, where it's heard by the most unlikely allies.

Selina and Rea's paths crossed many times in the past, but they'd never connected. Now they are being inescapably drawn together by fate, desire, and a touch of the mystical. Will love and trust prevail over loss and fear, so they can have their shot at being found forever?

Join them on their souls' journey through the Lost & Found.

Copyright © 2019 by Elle Hyden

ALL RIGHTS RESERVED.

This book contains material protected under International and Federal Copyright Laws and Treaties. Any unauthorized reprint or use of this material is prohibited. No part of this book may be reproduced or transmitted in any form or by any means, electronic or mechanical, including photocopying, recording, or by any information storage and retrieval system without express written permission from the author / publisher, except by a reviewer who wishes to quote brief passages in connection with a review written for inclusion in a magazine, newspaper, blog, or broadcast.

This is a work of fiction. Any resemblance to real persons, living or dead, is purely coincidental.

Acknowledgements

Although this is technically not the first novel I wrote, it feels like it is. That one now resides in the Twilight Zone and will probably never see the light of day. During my two-year hiatus from writing, fellow author, Ocean Coco, encouraged me to start again. If not for her, I wouldn't have typed the first word in this book, much less finished it. Then there are all the authors in the Lesfic Sprinters group on Facebook that egged me on every step of the way. A big thank you to Fletcher DeLancey, because I read her books over and over and over again, wanting to emulate her ability to create memorable stories and characters. This kept me trying to improve my writing every day. She also personally took the time to tweak some of my scenes and showed me how to enhance them. I know I still have room for improvement, but I've been told by many other authors to just keep pounding away at it, and I'll get better. I want to offer my sincerest thanks to my beta readers: Annette Mori, TR Lynch, Kim Dyke, Ocean Coco, Tammie Lynn, and finally Gerda Gregersen, for their willingness to read my book and help me fine-tune it.

I want to thank my awesome cover designer, May Dawney, for visually creating what I think captures the key elements of my story. Not to mention the exemplary work done by my line editor/proofreader, Ashley Ward.

And last but not least, I'd like to thank the readers, because, without them, there would be no reason for writers to write at all.

~~~ In Memoriam ~~~
Suzanne M. Harding
1947-2018

I met Suzanne at the GCLS con in July 2017, and we hit it off immediately. We spent that time talking about writing, and as a wannabe writer, I listened intently to everything she said. By the end of the con, she practically ordered me to send her my WIP so she could mentor me along. Unfortunately, we lost her before she even read my first word. I have no doubt that this book would have been worlds better if I would have been able to take her up on her offer.

I got the idea for this book right after she passed away, and maybe, just maybe she was whispering in my ear at the time. And if my metaphysical beliefs hold true then somewhere, somehow, Suzanne knows she had a hand in this book.

TABLE OF CONTENTS

PROLOGUE	1
CHAPTER ONE	3
CHAPTER TWO	13
CHAPTER THREE	23
CHAPTER FOUR	34
CHAPTER FIVE	46
CHAPTER SIX	54
CHAPTER SEVEN	67
CHAPTER EIGHT	76
CHAPTER NINE	86
CHAPTER TEN	100
CHAPTER ELEVEN	112
CHAPTER TWELVE	123
CHAPTER THIRTEEN	137
CHAPTER FOURTEEN	149
CHAPTER FIFTEEN	159
INTERLUDE	165
CHAPTER SIXTEEN	167
CHAPTER SEVENTEEN	177
CHAPTER EIGHTEEN	187
CHAPTER NINETEEN	197
CHAPTER TWENTY	208
CHAPTER TWENTY-ONE	219
CHAPTER TWENTY-TWO	229
CHAPTER TWENTY-THREE	239

CHAPTER TWENTY-FOUR	248
INTERLUDE	255
CHAPTER TWENTY-FIVE	257
CHAPTER TWENTY-SIX	269
CHAPTER TWENTY-SEVEN	279
CHAPTER TWENTY-EIGHT	292
CHAPTER TWENTY-NINE	300
CHAPTER THIRTY	308
EPILOGUE	317
GLOSSARY	321

Prologue

The three entities coalesced into shimmering shapes that stood out brightly against the swirling white background. Inside their forms, sparkling pieces of energy from different soul connections danced about like fireflies. In each of them, one spark glowed more brightly than the others. It was those two souls that drew them together now.

"The time is fast approaching, the wheel of time is turning, and Selina is on the move," Lily advised the two women beside her. "Nita, you will be showing yourself to both of them before their first contact, to start the proverbial ball rolling," the old woman relayed. "Selina will be easy, but Rea won't understand what is happening. However, the encounter will have an impact that will leave her questioning what she experienced."

She then turned and spoke to the other woman. "Sherry, your task is more onerous, since you have only been able to connect to Rea's emotional center empathically, but that will be critical as well. She has to want to move on, which you already know will be one of her big issues."

Lily's form seemed to grow brighter. "Mine will be the most challenging, but I've been gathering the energy required to affect the physical universe and divert the path of one of the Lyrid meteors that are passing through earth's orbit now."

If an entity could sigh, Lily would have. "The future is still unwritten. It will be up to us to step in to nudge, poke, and prod our loved ones if their paths seem to be diverging. So, we might need to meet again." The two women nodded at her in agreement.

A current of energy eddied around Lily, prompting her that it was time to leave. "Let us go, and may the power of the fates go with us."

With that, their diaphanous forms wavered, merging back into churning whiteness, from whence they came.

Chapter One

A Wish and a Prayer

Driving south toward Bell Rock, the inky black of the night sky was giving way to the deep indigo of twilight in the east, drawing Selina's eye. She sped up on the deserted highway. It was imperative she reach her destination before sunrise.

The wind whipped through the open window, whisking around loose strands of hair from her braid, tickling her cheeks and ears. She took a deep breath of the cold crisp desert air, reveling in the scent. The familiar aroma of bear grass, agave, yucca, and juniper that managed to thrive in the arid soil, permeated the cab of her dusty pickup.

Glancing into the rear-view mirror, Selina could barely make out the shape of her Pop Pop's vintage motorcycle. It was snuggled in between all her other possessions, as she never owned more than she could pack into the bed of her truck. Maybe there was a bit of gypsy blood somewhere in the family tree, Selina mused. She'd never settled down, always moving from job to job, and one relationship after another.

Her fingers flexed on the steering wheel, a soft sigh escaping her lips. She was a bit depressed to find herself single again. There'd been a string of girlfriends since Selina had finally acknowledged at fifteen, that she was a lesbian or a two-spirit, as her Grandmother Lilakai—her Amá sání—had called her. At least among the Diné, it was understood and accepted, but it wouldn't have been in her conservative hometown of Lampasas, Texas.

Selina had known Bran wasn't "The One" but hoped they might make a go of it, until she'd come home to find all her stuff packed in boxes, and a large duffel bag full of her clothes sitting beside the door. The only explanation Bran offered was that things just weren't working between them anymore—a lame excuse used by one's partner to end things without disclosing the real reason for the breakup—and it hadn't been the first time she'd heard it either.

When Selina thought about their last month together, she suspected Bran might have met someone new. She'd stayed out late multiple times, supposedly at business dinners, but had been vague on the details. Probing for more information had made things worse. Bran had pushed back irritably with claims that Selina didn't trust her, and it put a wedge between them that continued to widen until everything broke apart. So here she was, at forty, closing the latest chapter in her woeful love life.

The high beams of her truck illuminated a road sign, indicating the turnoff she needed to take was one mile ahead. Selina was almost there. The diffused light from the moon setting in the west was mirrored by the barest hint of dawn in the east, their celestial bodies hidden behind the rocky buttes. Most of the ambient glow in the night sky was coming from the Village of Oak Creek to the south of Bell Rock.

The hum of the tires on the road was the only sound intruding on the tranquility of the desolate landscape. A new sign warned her the turnoff was two hundred feet ahead. Slowing rapidly, Selina flipped on her blinker, then turned left, crossing the highway, and drove into the empty lot. She parked at the back, close to the trail she intended to take, rolled up her window, and shut off the truck.

Selina opened the door and slid out of the cab. Feeling a bit stiff from the drive, she put her hands on her hips, arched her back, and rocked gently from side to side to work out the kinks. Directly above her, the heavens were an inky black canvas, with pinpricks of light in varied sizes and brightness, moved along the sky on their predetermined paths. Unexpectedly, multiple bursts of streaking lights flickered across her vision before disappearing from view. *Meteors!* An auspicious portent in Selina's mind.

She turned back to her pickup, grabbed her bulky backpack from the passenger floorboard, then locked the door. After slinging the bag over her shoulder, Selina leaned over the side of the truck bed and fished out a flashlight. Switching it on, she headed over to the sign marking the start of the Baby Bell trail.

Selina swept the flashlight from side to side as she made her way along the path, the beam catching the reflection of red eyes peering out at her from the safety of a desert bush. The critter froze for a moment, captured by the shaft of light, before fleeing back to some hidden burrow. A slight shuddering of the surrounding vegetation marked its silent retreat. Then she heard the yip of a coyote, the trickster, off in the distance, followed seconds later by the bark of another. Selina wondered if it was a signal some prey had been sighted or an alert that she had traversed into their territory. Luckily, they sounded like they were heading away and wouldn't cross her path; she didn't need any bad luck this morning.

This brought to mind the many stories told at the gatherings Selina attended in her teens after her mother died, and she went to live with her grandparents. The elders of the tribe had passed on to Selina, the rich cultural heritage of her people. It was there she'd learned to love and care for the land. Being in this place, where her ancestors once roamed free, was what drew her here now. At a mere one hundred fifty feet in elevation, Baby Bell was ringed in by towering buttes, so Selina never felt she was breaking the Diné taboo about high places.

This was where she'd first experienced the transcendental part of her being. Selina had felt a power calling to her, so she'd climbed the summit, sitting for hours in quiet contemplation until everything faded into the background, and a vision took her away.

Selina found herself working in a garden, digging a furrow for seeding. As she turned over the soil, the trench filled with blood. Unconcerned, she sowed it with corn kernels then covered them with dirt. Tender shoots breached the earth, then grew tall and green, swaying gently in the breeze, sprouting sweet ears of corn.

Moving over a few yards, Selina began a new row. When she turned over the soil this time, it was filled with thick white worms. She had no way to get rid of them, so she planted the kernels anyway. Selina watched in dismay as the stalks struggled to grow, but with no way to nourish them, she moved on. After all, she thought, it was only one row.

Selina dug furrow after furrow, and they were all fouled by grubs, but in desperation, she kept planting. By the time she finished, all but the first row of plants had wilted, turned brown, and died because their roots had been eaten. Selina fell to her knees, crying because one row of corn would barely feed her family with none left over to share with the community.

The sound of growling reached Selina's ears, and she looked up. There in front of her sat a ghostly white wolf. As she watched, it went to the first row of withered plants, digging them up, exposing the ugly grubs in the soil. Then turning around, the wolf pulled a thriving stalk of corn from the ground. Blood ran from the roots, like veins from a beating heart, filling the tainted row, drowning the grubs. Next, the wolf removed an ear of corn from the stalk. Grinding the cob in its teeth, it walked along, sowing the trench with new kernels. As it covered them with dirt, healthy shoots sprouted, where once the dead plants had stood.

Tears of joy filled Selina's eyes for the gift of the wolf's teaching, and she busily followed its example, replanting every furrow. Now the garden was a sea of flourishing green plants, the stalks heavily laden with corn. Enough to feed not only her family but many others as well.

At that point, Selina's awareness had returned, but in her mind's eye, she still saw the wolf. It seemed to be smiling at her. Finally, it turned and faded away.

When Selina had relayed everything about her vision to her Amá sání, looking for answers, she'd explained that a spirit wolf had chosen to be her guide. She'd also counseled that its meaning might not be immediately understood, but at some crossroad, it would make perfect sense, and it had when it came time for Selina to choose what to do with her life. After that, the wolf showed up whenever her life was in flux. The last time it appeared to Selina had been after her grandmother died five years ago, and this is where that encounter had taken place.

She snapped out of her musings, when the thinning scrubland along the trail gave way to the dark, salmon-colored, craggy dome, rising before her. Selina paused, studying the multi-leveled terrain delineated against the twilight sky, yielding to the blue-gray hues that heralded the advent of dawn. Choosing her path to the summit, Selina's sturdy hiking boots gripped the rugged sandstone surface, securing her footing on the rocky slope. After a fifteen-minute climb, Selina arrived at the semi-flat top. She shut off the flashlight, shrugged off her pack, and set them both on the ground.

Raising her arms to shoulder height, palms down, Selina closed her eyes, absorbing the energy emanating up through the ground. The unseen power of the vortex filtered through her system, filling her body until it vibrated. Selina centered herself, sensing all the scattered pieces of her soul align. Once she felt completely serene, her eyelids fluttered open. The beauty of the blushing pink and orange tints adorning the low clouds in the east filled her vision—it was almost sunrise, so she needed to get started.

Selina unzipped her bag, removed four painted rocks, and a bundle of cedar sticks. Pulling out her phone, she opened the compass app, so she could accurately place the stones in their proper positions. Black in the north, yellow in the west, turquoise in the south, and finally the white one in the east. Selina slipped the phone back into her pocket, untied the sticks, and laid them out until they formed a small circle just big enough for her to sit inside of. She removed two more items from her bag, a woven sweetgrass mat, and a leather pouch, which Selina placed within the circle.

Lastly, she pulled out a sage stick along with a Zippo lighter. With a quick flick of her wrist, the lid popped open. Thumbing the striker wheel against the flint, it sparked, igniting the wick, and the tiny flame wavered in the slight breeze. Selina held it under the blackened stub and waited until it began to smolder. She closed the lid against her jean-clad thigh, then slipped the lighter into the pocket of her hoodie.

Selina held the smoky torch out in front of her, moving slowly around the outside of the stone circle, clockwise, cleansing the area. Once she'd made a full circuit, Selina swirled the sage over her body, smudging herself. Finally, she brought the stick closer to her face waving her hand over it—filling her lungs with its purifying smoke.

Now she was ready.

Selina snuffed out the sage stick against the ground and entered the circle. Sitting crossed-legged on the mat, she faced the east, hands resting on her knees, palms facing up. Selina raised her chin, tilting her head back slightly, closed her eyes, and waited for the first rays of the sun to breach the barrier of Courthouse Butte. Selina hummed a quiet prayer chant, hoping the power of the vortex would carry it into the spirit realm and find its way to her Amá sání.

A point of light bloomed softly behind her closed lids, indicating the life-giving rays of the new day had made their appearance. Selina opened her eyes, stood, and picked up the leather pouch from the ground. She worked the ties loose and removed some shredded unprocessed tobacco from inside, then facing north, cast it out. Turning right, she repeated the offering ritual at each of the other three directions. Once she finished, Selina again sat in the center facing east. She lowered her forearms to rest on her thighs, gripped her hands together, lacing her fingers, and spoke softly in prayer.

"Amá sání, I have somehow lost my way. My life hasn't turned out the way I thought it would. I've been drifting through life from place to place with no real home or partner to anchor me.

"I've loved and been loved, but no one has truly captured my heart. I've learned to be content, even happy at times when living alone, so I know I can do it if I must. But oh, Amá sání, sometimes the loneliness is unbearable—so my wish and my prayer is—I won't have to. My soul aches to find an all-consuming connection with another…to find my home in them, so I will feel whole and complete.

"Please, Amá sání, hear my plea. Help me find the path that will lead me to my dream."

Selina's eyes drifted shut as a deep peace settled over her. The corporeal world around her seemed to peel away, and she thought she felt the impression of soft lips pressed to her forehead. A sense of comfort suffused her, and she knew her Amá sání was near.

Breathlessly she waited, hoping to hear some whispered words of wisdom, so she would know what to do next. Selina felt the stirrings of power start to rise up, then suddenly the morning stillness was shattered by the sound of car doors closing, and voices calling out to each other in the distance.

The spell was broken, and the energy dissipated. Selina opened her eyes, angrily looking around, pissed that her temporary haven had been invaded by hikers. She'd lost her tenuous connection to her grandmother's spirit—now there was no getting it back. *Why couldn't I have had just five more fucking minutes?*

Selina's lips gradually lifted into a grin, as she remembered being admonished by her Pop Pop—*If wishes were horses, beggars would ride*—when she'd protest about the way something had turned out. Then he would send her out on one, to contemplate whether there was anything she could do to change it. In this instance, there wasn't, so Selina would simply have to trust that when the time came, she'd recognize the path she was meant to walk.

The sun had risen, and the activity below her picked up—it was time to go. Selina rose, quickly packed her stuff, then headed down the dome, retracing her way back to the parking lot. She was thankful not to encounter any of the hikers along the trail, or she might have punched them—still annoyed at their interruption.

Arriving at her truck, Selina stowed her gear, and pulled a bottle of cold water out of her cooler, drinking half of it in one go. She opened the cab door, slid inside, and started the engine. Selina closed her eyes for a moment, contemplating her next move. When she opened them again, Selina inhaled sharply, surprised at the ghostly image of a white wolf sitting calmly, not twenty feet from her. Its icy-blue eyes pierced hers, while its tongue moved in and out in a gentle pant, waiting for Selina's acknowledgment. Then the wolf rose, slowly turned its head to the northeast, its profile now appeared to be that of a woman. A moment later, it turned back, its wolfish gaze boring into her, then it melted away into the brush, heading north.

With that, Selina knew where she needed to go. She threw the truck into gear, drove out of the parking lot, and turned back toward Flagstaff.

Chapter Two
This Too Shall Pass

Rea wrapped her hand around her coffee mug as she carefully lowered herself into the wooden rocker on her back porch. Once she was settled, her best friend, Patches, lay down over her feet. If he'd been a cat, he would have been considered a calico, but because Patches was a dog, he was considered a mutt. There was no way to tell what breeds made up his mixed heritage. Since the day Rea had found the pup, a few years back, abandoned in a dumpster, Patches had become her loyal protector, and he was as smart as a whip. On a morning like this, he also made an excellent foot warmer.

Although it was mid-April, it was cold enough to see steam rising from the brew in her mug. They still had frost on the ground occasionally, so they weren't ready to start planting yet. Rea loved the crisp, clean air here, so different from California's central valley, and savored it along with the rich aroma of her favorite Kona coffee blend.

The morning serenity was fading away with the darkness as the hens started clucking softly from their nest boxes inside the chicken coop. Rory, the rooster, took his cue from the ladies, crowing out his rise and shine announcement. Not that Rea needed an alarm anymore. After two years here, she didn't think she would ever sleep past sun up again. Her internal clock had been reset from the more normal seven a.m. wake time of a nine to five day, to the four a.m. start of a dawn patrol on the farm.

Rea usually spent the first two hours after waking in her home office doing paperwork. If she were diligent about it, as she had been this morning, then she'd reward herself with a brief respite before starting the physical part of her day.

Rea had come a long way over the last few years, from the total devastation of her wife's death to a place where she felt she could build a peaceful, satisfying life. Her mother's favorite saying had always been—This too shall pass—and it was passing. It was one reason Rea had decided to move back to Colorado after Sherry died. Colorado was home. Here she'd been able to find a little bit of the happiness she'd lost.

At least Rea wasn't depressed or vengeful anymore. She'd gotten her pound of flesh out of Excologen, hitting them where it hurt the most, in their corporate coffers. Rea had signed their nondisclosure agreement and bided her time.

The things Excologen cooked up in their research facility to increase crop yields, like genetically altering seeds, and using carcinogenic chemicals in their pesticides and weed killers, caused significant health issues. The big wigs at the top were aware of it, but their plan was to export those products to third world countries, where environmental regulations were practically nonexistent. They'd received the reports from their own scientist but continued the development anyway. Their careless disregard was why Sherry had gotten cancer.

Her oncologist found high levels of a banned chemical in her tissues and documented it. The aggressive form of non-Hodgkin's lymphoma that Sherry had been stricken with spread rapidly through her body and had resisted chemo. They'd only given her six months to live, but Sherry had waged a valiant battle, surviving almost two years. Her brother, Dan, an attorney and California State Representative, explained they couldn't use those stolen reports legally. But Dan used Sherry's medical history, threatening Excologen with a highly public court battle, knowing it was the last thing they wanted and had made them bleed greenbacks.

Some of Sherry's friends who still worked for Excologen gave Rea a heads up that some of the sensitive data had made its way outside the corporation, and people were starting to ask questions. It was what Rea had been waiting for and anonymously sent out the smuggled developmental reports to several environmental watchdog groups. When those were exposed, new lawsuits would follow, and Excologen would be paying out many more billions in settlements.

The last few months before Sherry died, they'd talked about all the things they found unsettling in society. Once upon a time, when they had been young and idealistic, they thought they could change the world. Sherry, through science, and Rea, through social work, but it hadn't turned out the way either of them thought it would. Sherry's final wish was that her death would at least improve the lives of some people. So, with the two-hundred-million-dollar settlement, Dan had wrung out of Excologen, Rea purchased as much land as she could around Moirai, Colorado, to start Agnatural Farms.

She didn't know who named the town Moirai, probably some hopeful homesteader way back in the eighteen hundreds when they'd settled here. But Rea felt the same way since she'd seemed fated to relocate here herself, bringing significant changes right along with her. At first, she'd faced opposition from some of the locals, but had taken the time to set up Town Hall meetings to lay out her plans. Rea had also offered them a way to financially benefit from joining her cooperative. She'd built a state-of-the-art warehouse for distribution of their produce, then made some low to no-interest loans to promote additional growth. They now had a decent-sized grocery store, some other new shops, and even a café. All this had pumped dollars into the local community, bringing other investors to the area as well, so the town was growing.

Things were coming together nicely, but she needed to add one more important piece to her organization. Rea needed a botanist willing to move here that could help them cultivate the best organic produce for their farms.

Rea submitted a detailed employment description with hiring criteria to several major online job search sites, and received half a dozen resumes from qualified people, but none of them seemed to fit her idea of the perfect candidate. Rea was staying in email contact with the two best applicants but hadn't made either one an offer yet. The little voice in her head was telling her to wait, and since Rea wasn't in a big rush, she'd give it a few more weeks before making a choice.

Finishing off the last of her coffee, Rea rose and went back inside. She loved her little hundred-year-old farmhouse with its wrap-around porch. When she bought the place, it needed extensive work done to restore it. The elderly couple who'd owned it had no progeny to help with the house or the farm, and sadly, it had gotten run down over the last several decades.

There hadn't been much of the original farmstead left anyway, as they'd sold off sections as they aged. But they had managed to hold onto almost four hundred acres, fronting the river with an enormous orchard of mature apple, cherry, pear, and plum trees. The property still had a big barn along with a few other outbuildings that had once held machinery. They'd needed some TLC, but fortunately, the structures had been salvageable. Next, Rea had proceeded to buy up the surrounding land, plus additional parcels here and there until she'd acquired nearly three thousand acres.

After rinsing out her mug, Rea put it in the dish strainer then went into the mudroom. She pulled on her jean jacket, stuffed a pair of worn leather gloves into the left pocket, then stopped and picked up a long-range walkie talkie from its charging station. Out in the boonies, cell service was sketchy, so she provided them to all of her managers.

Rea turned it on, tuned it to channel two, then keyed it. "Flash, this is Wonder Woman." Soft static filled the silence. She waited a moment then tried again, "Flash, this is Wonder Woman, come in please."

A second later, a woman with a heavy Hispanic accent answered. "*Hola, Cariña. Mateo is down in de cellar. He bring up jars of stewed tomato for me. He be back in a flash,*" she said and let out a hearty laugh. "*Ju know dat is why ju give him de name.*"

"Morning, Mama Mia. Yes, you would know best. The man never slows down. I could have called him Speedy Gonzales, then we would have had a whole Looney Tunes thing going on. That may have been more appropriate, given this crew," Rea offered with a laugh of her own.

"I wanted to let Matty know I'm off to check the filter on the orchard irrigation pump. I noticed yesterday the water pressure seemed low. I want to make sure it's clear of debris. I have a feeling the issue is with the float, so I'll probably be making a trip down to the river as well. Just let him know and tell him I'll catch up with him later."

"*Okay, Rea. Call him if ju need any help, an come by later. I make big pot of Caldo for lunch.*"

"Now there is an offer no sane person would turn down. I'll see you later then."

Rea had been pleasantly surprised when both Matty and Mia expressed their willingness to move to Colorado. They were a vital link to the old life she'd led in California, and Rea would have been so lonely without their familiar presence here.

Shoving the radio into a holster, Rea clipped it to her belt and grabbed her ball cap from its peg. She stepped out onto the porch, pulled the door shut, and settled the hat on her head. Rea stood there for a few seconds, admiring the swirls of orange and pink colors gracing the clouds to the east. She never got tired of gazing out over her land, knowing the money Sherry had paid for with her life was fulfilling their dreams.

Rea stepped off the porch, slapped her hand against her leg, and whistled before calling out, "Hey, Patches, are you coming with me today?" A minute later, he tore around the corner of the house, stopping at her feet, sitting at attention. Patches' tail swept the ground, creating a mini dust cloud above the dirt, and his lips pulled back, exposing his teeth, giving her his version of a canine grin.

"It looks like you have been up to something." Reaching out, she stroked his head. "Were you over at the hen house riling up, Rory?"

He lowered his head, his tail freezing in position, signaling his guilt. "I would have thought you'd learned your lesson by now. Are you looking to get spurred again?" With his body hunched, he lifted his head just high enough to give her a repentant look. "Well, come on then. Let's go before Rory finds a way out of his pen, and comes after you."

Patches padded along beside her as she left the house. Looking down, she asked him, "Should we saddle up Dolly or take the ATV?" Patches took off in a hurry, heading straight for the barn. "Okay then,"—she laughed—"I guess I have my answer."

Rea had learned to ride when she attended Girl Scout camp. She started as a Brownie riding in front of an older girl. Over the years that followed, she learned to saddle, groom, and care for the horses. Eventually, Rea became a Senior Scout, passing on all she'd learned to troops of youngsters.

Her last summer at camp, before leaving for college, they'd obtained the use of some prime horseflesh from a rancher who loaned them ten well-trained horses. When they'd arrived, Rea had offered to help with the unloading, but the rancher waved her off, saying his granddaughter could handle it all by herself. She'd never forgotten doing a double-take, as a beautiful tawny skinned girl, backed each one out of the trailer by their mane, mounted, then rode them bareback to the corral. The lithe figure moved with the horse as if she were a part of them, her blue-black hair billowing out behind her. But what Rea remembered most was the girl's startling light blue eyes, gracing her stark, angular features that spoke of Native American heritage. She'd definitely admired the young teen's beauty, not to mention her skill with the horses.

Rea shook off the memory as she approached the barn. Patches sat on his haunches, waiting patiently for her near the entry. She threw the bolt back then pulled open the heavy wooden doors, one at a time. The familiar smell of fresh dung, sawdust and hay drifted out. A faint rustling could be heard from the shadowy interior, followed by a soft nicker. Turning to the control panel, Rea slid two of the dimmer switches up, and light filled the space. A pronounced rattle of metal against wood greeted her. Rea paused at the stall on her right, and looked through the bars, watching as Jupiter nosed his grain bucket.

"Good morning, Jupe, you must be ready for your breakfast."

As Rea approached the stall door, he backed into the corner, still extremely shy of her. He was another one of Rea's rescues, a beautiful Appaloosa stallion, which had been found with a group of other horses on a repossessed ranch. All of them malnourished, with signs of physical abuse evident. She hoped in time to win his trust.

Rea spoke soothingly to him, "Are you hungry, Jupe? How about if I give you some yummy corn and oats first, then turn you out into the corral this morning? I'm going to be taking your girlfriend out for some exercise, however, so you will have to do without her company for a while. One of these days, I hope you will let me ride you, but there is no hurry, I'm the patient sort."

She opened the door and pulled the bucket from its holder then backed out before closing it again. On the opposite side, a pretty red filly waited good-naturedly for Rea to come to her.

"Hey, Doll, you're such a good girl. Can't you convince Jupe not to be such a scaredy-cat? Or maybe you just don't want to share me with him." She gently stroked the soft neck stretched out over the door. "Do you have a thing for girls too?" When Dolly nodded her head, Rea laughed. "Well then, let me give Jupe his breakfast, and we'll spend some quality time together."

She raised the lid on the grain bin, measured out the feed, and returned the half-filled bucket to Jupiter's stall. Rea edged around him carefully then opened the outside door into the paddock for him before exiting. Rea entered the tack room, and stopping at a five-gallon container, she worked the lid loose. From it, she removed several treats for Dolly and stuffed them in her pocket.

Rea ordered them from a specialty feed store that baked them for horses. They were made with oats, carrots, apples, and molasses. The shop also made a line of homemade dog biscuits she purchased for Patches too. She couldn't give Dolly any breakfast until they got back, but a treat now and on the trail wouldn't cause any issues.

Next, Rea went to the wall rack where several blankets hung. Pulling one off, she threw it over her shoulder then grabbed her saddle and Dolly's hackamore from its hook. Back at the stall, Rea set the saddle and blanket on a stand, then went inside and buckled Dolly into her headgear. Rea led her out, then gave Dolly one of the treats to munch on while she saddled her. Once she was done, Rea guided her out of the barn and mounted up.

Patches stood at the fence line, his body coiled and ready to spring forward, waiting for her signal to take off. "Come on, gang, let's go. Daylight's a-wastin." Patches streaked away with Dolly hot on his heels.

Chapter Three

Homeward Bound

The drive back to Flagstaff took a little over an hour. Selina spent the time singing along to tunes by The Queen of Soul—or Miss Ree—as her own family called her. Aretha Franklin's music connected to her emotional center as no other artist did. But when the opening strains of "Natural Woman" came on, Selina thumbed the control on her steering wheel and skipped over it to the next song. She couldn't listen to it right now since her own soul felt lost.

Selina remembered the first time she slow danced to the song. She'd arrived in College Station a few days before, and decided against her better judgment, to attend one of the freshman mixers. She'd let her pushy floormate, Dani, badger her into it. Selina had dressed all in black, hoping to escape notice in some dark corner. It had worked, for the most part, and she'd flown under the radar most of the night. But just as Selina was getting ready to slip out, she'd caught an alluring blond woman checking her out. The woman cozied up to her, introduced herself as Chris, and asked Selina to dance.

They swayed together on the darkened dance floor, lost in each other's arms until some asshat had started making sexist and racist remarks from the other side of the room. They'd decided to leave before things worsened and were almost to the door when they heard a woman yelling. Selina had looked over her shoulder, but could only see the back of a short, muscular woman, with spiky red hair, giving the prick a piece of her mind. It had escalated into some pushing and shoving, so they'd made a hasty exit.

She and Chris remained a couple all through college. Selina had thought she'd found the person she was supposed to be with. Unfortunately, after graduation, their lives went in different directions, and the long-distance thing had finally killed it. It had been the first in a long string of pairings that hadn't been strong enough to create the kind of lasting bond Selina craved.

Now she was at a crossroad. She didn't have a job, but with her savings, Selina didn't need to worry about that yet. Her truck was paid for, and she could always stay in the guest quarters at the ranch if she needed to. It would be less stressful to skip the ranch altogether, thereby avoiding any questions from the family about her messed up life. For now, Selina had all the gear she needed packed in her truck to camp out in the canyon. She planned to stay there for a few days anyway while she figured out which direction to head in next. Selina was convinced after this morning, the guidance she was counting on would be forthcoming soon.

Reaching the outskirts of Flagstaff, her stomach growled loudly, reminding Selina she hadn't eaten since yesterday afternoon when she hit a McDonald's drive-thru for a burger on her way through Vegas. By the time she'd gotten into town, around midnight, Selina had decided to check into a Motel Six for a few hours of sleep. She'd set her alarm for four a.m. to get to Bell Rock before sunrise, and hadn't taken the time to stop and eat. So, it wasn't surprising to find that she was starving.

Selina decided it was as good a time as any to fuel up and get a quick bite, so when she caught sight of a sign for the Little America Travel Center, she exited Interstate 40 and pulled in. Stopping at the pumps first, Selina looked around as she gassed up, playing the license plate game with herself. She'd just reached four when a lavish motorcoach rolled in towing what Selina considered to be a toy car behind it. Maybe she should consider buying something like that, then at least she'd have some type of home, even if it was on wheels. When the pump clicked off, Selina squeezed the handle a few more times till it read an even seventy dollars, which was a decent amount, she thought, for topping off both tanks. Now, her own tank needed filling.

Her next stop was the café, where Selina backed into a parking space that faced the windows, so she could keep an eye on her stuff from inside. She entered the busy eatery then headed straight to the bathroom to pee and wash her hands. When Selina exited, she found an empty booth along the front wall and slid across the bench seat.

The clink of cutlery against plates and the hum of voices filled the eatery. Selina's stomach rumbled to life again, when the aroma of cooking bacon escaped the kitchen through a set of swinging doors, as a middle-aged waitress backed through them. She hustled toward Selina, carrying a full pot of coffee in one hand, with a cup and saucer in the other. A black apron was tied around her ample figure, and her chestnut hair was up in a loose bun with a pencil protruding from it.

She plunked the saucer holding the cup down on the table without asking, held the pot aloft—waiting for a signal to pour. Selina nodded her head, and the woman filled it with the hot black brew.

With quick efficiency, she pulled out a set of utensils wrapped in a napkin from her apron pocket, placed it next to Selina, then launched into her greeting. "Hi, hon. I'm Tammy. I'll be your waitress. Would you like anything else to drink? Water or perhaps some juice? If so, I will bring it back when I take your order."

"Not right now, thanks."

"Okay, I'll give you a few minutes," she said, then bustled away, stopping at tables here and there, to top off other diners' coffee.

Plucking a menu from its holder at the end of the table, Selina gave it her full attention. She loved breakfast and could eat it at any time of the day. It always seemed to be especially good at these roadside diners serving mostly long-haul truckers. Sure enough, one of the menu items was called—The Big Boy Combo—which Selina thought was a little sexist. It had three eggs with hash browns or grits, ham, bacon, or sausage, toast or biscuits with gravy, and a short stack of blueberry or buttermilk pancakes. They also had a Rancher's Combo, which was identical to the other, except it offered a steak instead of a pork entree.

After perusing the endless choices, Selina made her selection then stowed the menu back where she'd found it. Unrolling the napkin, she removed the spoon, then added sugar to her coffee from the canister, stirring it before taking a sip. Selina savored its excellent flavor. That was another thing these restaurants got right; they always served a first-rate brew.

The ever-alert Tammy must have seen her put the menu away and hustled right over to the table. She pulled a pad from her apron pocket, then plucked the pencil out of her bun and asked, "You ready, hon?"

"Yes, ma'am," Selina said. "I'd like the Rancher's Combo. Eggs over medium, hash browns, steak, medium rare, toast, and the buttermilk pancakes. But could you please bring me the pancakes first, along with a large glass of cold milk?"

"Sure thing. It'll be about ten minutes on those pancakes, then another ten or fifteen minutes, on the rest of your breakfast." With a twinkle in her deep brown eyes, she gave Selina a sexy wink. "Smart move getting your pancakes first…that way, everything stays…hot."

Selina smiled, her often pathetic gaydar started pinging, and figured Tammy played for her team. "Yeah, it's not my first rodeo," she flirted back.

With an arch of a dark brow, Tammy responded, "Didn't think so, but it's good to know."

Tammy turned and walked away, adding a little extra sway to her hips, as if she knew Selina would be watching. She stopped briefly at an empty table full of dirty dishes, scooping something off the corner—probably her tip. Selina noted Tammy still had a firm ass under her jeans. Must be a benefit from all the walking she does in this job, Selina thought.

Managing to pull her eyes away from Tammy's lush derriere, she took her phone out of her back pocket. Selina thumbed the on button, and the screen came to life. No missed phone calls or messages, but then again, she hadn't expected any. Next, she pulled up her browser typing in the address to her Monster account. Selina had updated her resume a few days ago but hadn't looked to see what positions were available. Although she didn't have to go to work right away, it wouldn't hurt to start her search now. Her field was rather specialized, so it tended to take longer to find a new job.

Selina's last two employers had been cannabis growers since several states had gotten smart, passing either recreational and or medical marijuana laws. As a part of her graduate program, Selina had worked in one of the university labs, growing Psilocybin mushrooms, which were being used in research studies, as a possible treatment for severe depression and anxiety. Growing them had been a pleasure, because it fell in line with her belief that the best medicines were found in nature, versus being cooked up from chemicals by pharmaceutical companies. While Selina had never been into shrooms or peyote, she did occasionally enjoy a little of the—wacky tobacky—so to speak. As a matter of fact, she'd brought some of the best with her from Oregon, all of which were strains she'd personally developed.

A listing for a botanist caught Selina's attention. It had posted three weeks ago, and it was probably too late to secure the job. More than likely, they'd narrowed their choices down to a few candidates by now. But it was still up, so it was worth a shot, as the position seemed tailor-made for her.

The posting was from an organic farm in Moirai, Colorado, looking for a botanist to oversee crop choices, planting rotations, and soil conservation. They wanted to minimize the use of fertilizers, and all farming would be done without chemicals of any kind, including pesticides. It offered housing, along with a generous salary, and health insurance. Selina would need a primo cover letter to grab their attention.

She tapped her way into her Google docs account, opened her introduction template, and went to work on crafting what Selina hoped was a unique synopsis of her qualifications. Her fingers flew over the keys on the screen, as if possessed. Selina finished in record time—saved it as a pdf—then attached it along with her resume and submitted it through Monster.

Selina had never heard of Moirai and thought the name was unusual, so she googled it. When she typed it in, the first thing to pop up were references to the three Greek goddesses of fate. Selina read a little about them, then added Colorado to the search bar to bring up the location. The place was just a blip on the map, but she preferred small towns. Smiling to herself, Selina hoped the name was prophetic, and the Moirai would intervene, so she'd get the job.

Selina jumped when a glass of milk was thunked down in front of her, followed by a plate of pancakes, and looked up to see Tammy smiling at her.

"Here you go, hon. Hot off the griddle." Which was obvious, as a big round pat of butter was melting all over the top. "What kind of syrup would you like for those? We have maple, blueberry, strawberry, and butter pecan?"

"Actually, I would prefer honey if you have it. If not, I'll have the maple."

"Of course, we have…honey," she said with a shit-eating grin. "I'll be right back."

Selina didn't respond to Tammy's last salvo; she was too busy spreading butter on her pancakes.

When Tammy returned, she set a familiar little honey bear on the table. "I checked on your steak and eggs. They'll be ready in about eight minutes, so the timing should be perfect for you to finish those up." Tammy sashayed away as Selina dug into her food.

The pancakes were so light and fluffy that she savored every bite. In between, she washed them down with gulps of cold milk. By the time she'd finished both, Tammy was heading her way again, balancing a tray of food along one arm, with a pot of coffee in the other hand.

Selina pushed her empty plate across the table as Tammy arrived and set everything down. She also refilled her coffee cup then asked, "You need any more milk?"

"No, I'm good. Milk just seems to go with pancakes in my book, but coffee goes with everything else."

"Well, unless you're lactose intolerant like I am, then you miss out on quite a few of the best things…cheese, real butter, yogurt, and ice cream," Tammy lamented with a frown. "For me, giving up cheese was the hardest. So many of the most delicious foods have it in or on them. Oh, well. Why don't you check the steak and see if it's done to your liking?"

Selina pulled out the serrated knife held down by the thick sirloin adorning her platter, and cut into it. The outside of the steak was perfectly seared, the juice from its hot red meaty center—which Selina considered the only way a steak should ever be cooked—leaked out onto the plate.

"It's exactly as ordered, Tammy. Give my compliments to the chef. Not everyone can get a steak just right."

"If Buddy can't grill one properly after thirty years, there is no hope for him. You need anything else?"

"I could use some ketchup for my hash browns if you please?"

Tammy plucked a red squeeze bottle off an empty table behind her and put it down. "Here you go. Enjoy your breakfast. I'll be back to check on you and freshen your coffee in a bit," she said, then bustled off again.

Selina added a dash of salt and pepper to the top of her eggs, then took her fork and poked at their soft centers, until the bright yellow yolks ran over the top of the perfectly fried whites. Grabbing a triangle of buttered toast, she stabbed at the eggs until the bread was coated then bit off the corner. Selina hummed happily to herself as she chewed. She simply adored breakfast.

In no time, she had consumed everything on her plates and groaned as she rubbed her belly. Selina wondered if she popped the button on her jeans if her jacket would hide the evidence—she was that full. Tammy approached the table with the ever-present pot of coffee in her hand.

"You want any more coffee, sweet thing?"

Selina noted the change in address and gave the woman a smile. "No, just the check, please. I need to get on the road," letting her know she was only passing through.

Tammy pulled a pad from her pocket, flipped through a few pages, before stopping and tearing off a ticket. She placed it face down on the table and slid it toward Selina. "Safe travels, hon. If you ever head back this way again, make sure to stop in. We aim for customer satisfaction," she said with a gleam in her eyes.

She wouldn't be back, and Selina had never been into one-night stands either, but it wouldn't hurt to let Tammy know she found her attractive. "Oh, I will…if I pass this way in the future." Giving her a wolfish grin, Selina added, "There are definitely some delectable items here that I wouldn't mind sampling."

She knew her mission was accomplished, as she watched Tammy stroll away, fanning herself with her ticket pad. The bill was thirteen eighty, but Selina left a twenty on the table. Tammy's excellent service was worth a forty percent tip.

Selina left the restaurant, hopped back into her truck, and headed west again on Highway 40. Glancing at the glowing red numbers on her dash, she calculated she'd reach Holbrook by late morning. She planned on stopping to pick up ice for her cooler and maybe grab a can of stew or some chili before heading to her special spot, bypassing the ranch for the time being. Selina hoped she might find the answer to her pilgrimage there. If the appearance of the wolf was a harbinger, she would.

Chapter Four
Seeing Things

Rea always enjoyed the mile-long ride to the river. It was picturesque, with a quarter of the trail running along the orchard fence, and was much more scenic. The other trail cut through an old hayfield, which was nothing but a sea of grass, with an occasional shrub thrown it to break up the monotony. In a few more weeks, this would become a beautiful ride when all the trees erupted in blossoms. In one corner, the cherry trees were already covered in a riot of white flowers, and the others showed the bumpy texture of buds preparing to break through the protective skins of their branches.

The faint sound of buzzing was carried on the breeze, emanating from one of the wooden hive boxes Rea had placed strategically throughout the grove. Bees were not only a vital, irreplaceable resource for pollination here but also produced what she considered to be the nectar of the gods. She had other boxes, some with active colonies and some empty, spaced systematically all over her land. Rea even offered them to the surrounding farms, free of charge. She recognized the decline in the number of healthy bee colonies was one of the greatest threats in the world today, along with climate change, and could spell the planet's doom if it wasn't arrested. Pollution, along with the widespread usage of pesticides and herbicides, had already reduced their population to dangerously low levels. She hoped in her own small way to make a difference.

Her furry friend, Patches, was sitting at the corner of the back fence panting from his run. Rea stopped next to him, dismounted and looped Dolly's reins onto the post. Patting the horse's neck, she offered her another treat.

"Give me a minute, girl. I need to check something here."

Rea approached the shed with its solar windmill off to one side, turning slowly in the slight breeze. It kept the batteries charged for the pump and timer that ran the sprinkler system. She stepped up to the door, took the padlock in her hand, thumbing the tumblers until they read, zero-six-two-six. Rea opened the lock, and slipped it free, then hung it on the hasp.

Flipping the light on, Rea peered inside, looking for any field mice or snakes that seemed to enjoy the dark interior the pump house provided. She shuddered at the thought, but the coast was clear, so she entered. Along one side was a wall of shelves. Racks of batteries filled the top two tiers, and the lower ones held sprinkler repair parts along with spare metal filters. Making her way over to a rectangular box, she pulled up the lid then slid out the messed screen. Yes, she'd need to head to the river next. There had to be a problem with the float with this much silt clogging it.

Rea pulled a clean one off the shelf then swapped them out. Picking up a soft-bristled brush, she went to the outside faucet and turned it on. She ran the brush over the filter, washing out all the debris, then waved it back and forth, flinging droplets of water everywhere.

Going back inside, Rea put the cleaned one on the shelf, then changed the sprinkler timer to manual. With a whirring sound, the pump came on, and she stepped outside, waiting for the system to spring to life. A hissing stream ejected from the head, followed by the ticking of the metal arm slapping back and forth against the water jet as it moved in a broad semicircle, indicating the sprinklers now had good water pressure.

Rea reset the timer but decided to add an extra thirty minutes of run time to the cycle since the ground looked pretty dry. It would sure be nice to get some rain to soften up the fields for plowing, she thought. For the most part, her crops were irrigated with water they pumped from wells or cisterns, and those sources were analyzed regularly for any possible E. coli contamination. She'd procured some thousand-gallon tanks to hold river water, should it be needed, but they were also subjected to testing. The quality of the water used on crops was critical, and Rea didn't want to take any chances. Rea wasn't worried about using water directly from the river here in the orchard, but using it on the fields was another matter entirely.

Locking up the shed, she was startled when a huge grasshopper sprang from a clump of grass, landing on the sleeve of her jacket, causing Rea to shriek. Hearing her, Patches came running and watched as she flapped her arm and danced around, trying to dislodge it. His head shifted back and forth, fascinated by her wild gyrations.

Rea didn't want to use her bare hand to brush it away, but it was stubbornly staying put. Finally, she remembered the gloves in her pocket, so Rea pulled them out and used them to flick the critter off her arm, where it hopped unharmed back into the grass.

"Shit! I hate those damned things. They have such sticky feet. Oh, and crickets too. If it ever looks like we're going to have an infestation of either of those, I'm buying a flamethrower." Patches tilted his head to the side once again, as if questioning Rea's sanity.

Shaking her head as if it would dispel the irrational fear, she turned and said, "Now that I've entertained you, let's go."

Rea shoved the gloves back in her jacket while Patches took off down the fence line ahead of her. She walked over to Dolly, pulled the reins loose, then hoisted herself back into the saddle. Turning away from the fence, Rea gave Dolly a gentle kick to her side, and they headed in the direction of the river.

Patches disappeared down the trail, so she tightened her knees, leaned forward, clicked her tongue, and Dolly broke into a trot. As she picked up speed, Dolly's hooves kicked up puffs of dust along the dry ground. Rea's butt slapped against the leather saddle in a rhythmic cadence as she bobbed along humming—Wild Horses—her favorite Rolling Stones song.

It was a beautiful spring morning, and Rea was enjoying being outside instead of being stuck in an office all day. The life she was leading now was abundantly better than her old one, except for missing Sherry, whose death had made all this possible. Today was one of those days Rea felt the loss keenly. Nearing the river, she slowed Dolly down to a walk. Tilting her head back until she could look up into the sky, Rea spoke aloud.

"Sherry, I'm doing the best I can down here, and I think I've pretty much carried out all of our plans. Things have really come together in the last few months, but I still need a few more people for some key positions. My last stroke of fortune was scoring us a young doctor who'd just finished her residency." Rea smiled to herself. "We were lucky she was willing to relocate here. Of course, the enticement of paying off her student debt, accompanied by a decent salary, in exchange for signing a five-year contract with us, is what did the trick. She's originally from Zimbabwe, and I have high hopes she might stay on when her contract is up." Rea chuckled. "It didn't hurt that her girlfriend is an RN, and I gave her the same deal. So, we can finally have a clinic here instead of having to go all the way to Denver, Greely, or Loveland for care."

The smile slipped from Rea's face, and her lips turned down as she gave voice to her real concern. "I could use a good botanist. I sure wish you were still available. I'll simply have to find the next best thing. So, I'm doing okay," she said earnestly. "I'm happy most of the time. And yes, some days I am lonely when I have five minutes to think about it. But for those times, I live vicariously through the characters in a good lesbian romance book, and…if the earth moves me, I always have my shower massager. So, don't you worry about me," she stated emphatically.

Rea's voice softened. "I know I promised I would date again, but there hasn't been anyone who even caught my interest. Also, there are no unattached lesbians around, and I'm not about to go searching for any on some dating websites, either. But you have my word if one crosses my path, and I'm attracted to her, I'll give it a chance. If that doesn't satisfy you, then I'll have to leave the rest up to you." Rea could almost envision the mutinous pout that would cross Sherry's expressive features with that statement. A grin creased her face as she said, "Besides, I'm sure by this time you have some pull with the woman upstairs and could persuade her to send a cute little lesbian my way."

It wasn't the first time Rea had spoken to Sherry this way. It always seemed to ease the ache in her heart. It was so hard for her to imagine being with anybody else. Rea had the great love of her life, and the chances of finding someone as amazing as Sherry seemed improbable.

They'd been together for just over twenty-four years managing to avoid the pitfalls, that torpedoed other people's relationships—issues like career conflicts, finances, fluctuating libidos, and infidelity. Rea knew from her psychology studies that the last two were connected. If a couple didn't communicate to work through those times when one partner or the other might not feel the need for sex, it could lead to cheating. They'd acknowledged those times in their relationship without blame or pressure, continued to cuddle, and, if needed, indulged in masturbation without shame. Sometimes that led to a resumption of sex. Was there anything hotter than watching a partner pleasure themselves? It usually made one want to jump in and finish them off.

Rea was snapped out of her contemplation when Patches ran back up the trail, legs dripping wet. He twirled, then headed away again as if he was just making sure she hadn't gotten lost. Rea laughed at his antics. She loved her mutt, and he was great company.

A hundred yards ahead, there was a copse of mixed trees. Cottonwoods, willows, and scrub oaks that lined this area of the South Platte bordering her land. Pulling up on Dolly's reins, Rea dismounted then led her over to another shed almost identical to the one near the orchard. Except this one housed a vacuum pump, that was controlled by a pressure switch, instead of a timer. When the psi in the lines dropped below fifty, the pump came on and opened an inlet valve, pulling water up from the river. She didn't bother going inside yet. Instead, she walked to the back, following the inflow hose, checking it for leaks.

As Rea approached the river, the roar of rushing water drowned out the sound of the pump. Reaching the bank, the sight of the sagging line confirmed her guess that the float was missing. When one broke loose, the weight of the vacuum head, or what she called a slurpy, pulled it to the bottom, so it sucked up dirt along with the water. It was also a common occurrence during the heavy spring runoff, which is why they kept spares in the shed.

Rea felt a nudge in her back and turned to Dolly. "Hey, girl. Need a drink? I gotta get this line fixed, so let me get you situated, and then I will get it taken care of."

She took Dolly a few yards upstream where it was level, let her have a good long drink then urged her back away from the bank. Rea led her to a grassy stretch and secured the reins to a small tree. "Okay, Doll, you're all set. You have some nice spring grass here to munch on while you wait. I won't be long." Dolly bobbed her head up and down, softly nickering as she blew air out between her lips as if saying—Okay, you can leave now.

Rea patted her rump then walked back toward the shed. She wondered where Patches had run off to—but wasn't worried—he wouldn't go far without her. When Rea reached the door, she thumbed the tumblers on the lock, and once again, inspected the interior before entering.

Like the other shed, there were tiers of solar batteries at the top, tools, repair parts, and spare floats on the others. Rea saw they were down to two spares, so she removed her phone, used the reminder app to make a note to order more, then slipped it back into her pocket. Grabbing one of the floats, Rea exited, relocked the door, and returned the way she'd come.

By the time she arrived back at the river, Patches had reappeared. He was now lying in the shade, panting from chasing who knew what. Bits of wet mud were matted in the fur on his feet and legs. Rea would have to clean him up a bit before letting him into the house when she got home. She broke into a smile. It was funny. He avoided the tub when it came to bath time, but had no issues playing in the river. It must be a guy thing, Rea mused.

The water was running at a steady clip this morning. The sun reflected off the ripples and waves, created by the hidden topography of the river bed as it rushed past. The whooshing, gurgling, plops gave voice to its passage through the world.

Not wanting to get her boots wet, Rea sat down in a dry spot and pulled them off along with her socks. Rising, she rolled up the pant legs of her jeans until they were level with the bottom of her knees. Maybe she should order some waders to keep in the sheds for just these types of occasions. She'd talk to Matty about it and see what he thought.

They'd chosen this stretch of the river to deploy the slurpy because the river split, flowing past a rocky spit of land in the center. It allowed them to sink a metal pole at the tip of the island. Then about fifty yards away, to Rea's right, an identical one was embedded in the bank. A braided wire cable with pullies was secured to both poles, and dead center was a bright yellow nylon rope that dropped into the water. This setup allowed them to haul the slurpy in and out of the river while keeping it from being swept away if it broke loose from the hose.

In a few steps, she'd reached the bank wadding in, following the hose. Rea sank deep into the muddy bottom, and it oozed up, cocooning her feet, as the icy water chilled her legs. The river was fed by the spring snowmelt from the mountains to the west that flowed eastward until it joined with the North Platte in Nebraska.

Within about ten feet of the bank, the water level reached the bottom of Rea's jeans, so she stopped, spreading her feet apart to stabilize her stance. Clipping the float to her belt loop, she slipped on her gloves, then reached up and pulled on the wire, bringing the slurpy toward her. When the nylon rope was within reach, she tugged on it until the white semi-curved top became visible with the hose connected to its side.

It was a simple yet ingenious device. Made of lightweight fiberglass, it had a hook on top where the rope and float attached. An inlet tube protruded out of the bottom, surrounded by a rigid filter basket with 1.5 mm nylon mesh netting around the outside. It kept debris from being sucked into the line, but not silt.

Rea pulled it up out of the water, and the hose vibrated for several seconds before stopping. As designed, the pump had kicked off when intake pressure dropped, keeping the motor from running when there was no water entering the line. The mesh was a little muddy on the bottom, but it would get washed out once it was back in the river. She detached the leader line from the missing float then hooked on the new one. Holding the slurpy above the water, she reversed the direction of the pulley until it was back in its proper position, where it bobbed rhythmically near the surface.

Even though she was done, Rea stood there for a minute, enjoying the sight, sound, and feel of the pulsing heartbeat of the river. Without it running through her land, Rea wouldn't have settled here. She'd wanted to make sure she had water for irrigation from as many sources as possible. With the seasonal rains, cisterns, and wells, she had her bases covered, but this asset guaranteed it.

When Rea caught movement out of the corner of her eye and turned her head. There, on the shore, about twenty feet away, Rea saw what she thought was a wolf—except it was a shimmering white, and its eyes were icy blue.

The animal tilted its head from side to side as if sizing her up. This made Rea a little nervous, but it made no move toward her, and she relaxed slightly. She was held immobile by the piercing look in those intelligent eyes. With a lift of its head, the animal pulled back its lips, baring sharp, gleaming canine teeth. Instead of looking aggressive, it seemed to be smiling at her, but Rea was careful not to move, lest she startle it. Especially when she was knee-deep in water and couldn't rapidly retreat.

Snapping to her senses, Rea wondered why Patches or Dolly hadn't alerted her to the presence of an unknown animal in the area. All had remained quiet except for the murmuring of the water—not a growl, bark, or whinny of alarm was raised.

Slowly, Rea turned her head to the left to check on both of them. Dolly was still grazing peacefully where she'd left her, and Patches was asleep in the shade. Relieved they were both alright, she glanced back toward the wolf and was startled to see it was gone.

Rea shivered as goosebumps erupted along her skin, but she wasn't sure if it was from the cold river water or the mysterious encounter. The whole episode seemed surreal to her now. Was it a wolf or someone's hybrid dog roaming the area? The latter was the more likely scenario. After all, wolves weren't a part of the fauna in this area. But there was something about its size and sheer majesty that convinced Rea it had been a wolf, although it didn't look like the ones she'd seen depicted in books or movies.

Why hadn't Patches or Dolly reacted to it, and where had it disappeared to?

Rea didn't understand, but shook off her confusion then waded back to the shore. She went to inspect the ground where the animal had stood on the bank and was confounded to see there were no paw prints in the soft mud.

"What the frick is going on?" Rea asked aloud.

Hearing her voice woke Patches, and came over to see what she was doing. He nuzzled her hand, then sniffed the ground, before looking back at her. "Smell anything, little man?" But he only sat at her side, panting.

Pinching the bridge of her nose, she squinted and checked the area one more time, but nothing had changed. "I think your mom is seeing things," Rea said to him, frowning. "It might be best for us to head home now so I can get some more coffee or maybe a G&T. If I am going to be seeing things, it should be because I've had one too many."

Laughing at herself over the whole incident, Rea stripped the gloves off her hands then shoved them back in her pocket before picking up her socks and boots. She gingerly advanced over the rocky section of the bank to rinse off her feet, then rolled down her damp pant legs. Making her way back to her boots, Rea sat down in the grass, allowing time for her feet to dry before putting them back on. Heaving herself up off the ground, Rea returned to Dolly, untethered her, mounted, then headed for the barn with Patches leading the way.

Chapter Five
Camping Out

It was early afternoon by the time Selina reached her camping spot at the mouth of a small canyon off Route 64, north of the much larger Canyon de Chelly. Shifting into four-wheel drive, she left the road and crawled along an unmarked trail, carefully navigating her way over the uneven ground. She didn't need to break an axle, which could happen if she hit a dip wrong in the rocky terrain. With her butt anchored by the seat belt, Selina's torso swayed and flopped around the cab like a rag doll—holding tightly to the steering wheel—as her tires churned up small bits of rock that pinged against the undercarriage, and whipped dirt into the air.

Selina drove toward a triangular pile of huge boulders, planning to use them to obscure her truck from view. Rangers patrolled the area regularly to keep the tourists from doing precisely what she was. But unlike the tourists, Selina wouldn't be trespassing. She had her tribal ID and could prove she had the right to be there. But Selina preferred to avoid them if possible.

She drove up behind a towering trio of stones then parked at an angle, the nose of her truck pointing toward the canyon mouth with the bed almost touching the rock. Selina left enough room to load and unload her camping stuff, but placing it here would also provide a windbreak if needed.

Stepping out of the truck, she twisted and stretched from side to side, loosening the muscles in her back as her gaze swept over the desolate landscape. The memory of the first time she'd ever come here washed over Selina. She'd been riding the motorcycle that now sat in the bed of her truck. Turning, she reached over the side, gently running her hand over the smooth leather seat in a petting motion. *Oh, how her grandfather had loved this bike.* He'd left it to Selina in his will because he knew she'd prized it as much as he had. She'd inherited more than the cycle from her Pop Pop. He'd gifted her his tall, lean figure and the light blue eyes that were the envy of many in Selina's family. The only other person to share this trait with her had been her mother, who'd passed on the gene—they also matched the eyes of her spirit guide—whose visitation this morning had sent Selina here.

The only time the wolf had shown her its woman face had been in this canyon. Selina had ridden the bike here that day and sat contemplating her attraction to one of the tribal girls. As she poured her thoughts out to the empty landscape, it had appeared. Turning its head, the wolf's canid features morphed into those of a woman. From the side, an angular nose, high cheekbones, and long hair braided with feathers were discernible. A feminine voice filled Selina's head, conveying that she was a "two-spirit" and let her know her feelings were true. Then it turned back, showing its wolf face again, before shimmering out of sight. That's why when Selina had seen the same thing this morning, she knew this was where it was directing her to go.

She walked to the rear of her truck, lowering the tailgate. To avoid running into anyone she knew, Selina had stopped in Chinle for supplies, instead of Holbrook. Removing the ice chest, she bent over and popped open the lid. Pulling out a cold bottle of water, she opened it, took a gulp, swishing it around her mouth before spitting it out onto the dry ground, taking the taste of the dusty road with it. As Selina drank down the last of the water, she looked for the best place to pitch her tent. She placed the empty bottle in a green nylon recycle bag she always kept on hand, doing her part to keep them out of the landfills, then got busy unpacking her gear.

Selina wished she could unload her bike and take a ride down the canyon, but it wasn't a practical idea. She would have to remove everything from the truck to free the ramps, and Selina needed to get the camp set up before dark. If she decided to stay a few days, she might do it later.

After a bit of struggling, Selina managed to get the stakes of the dome tent secured in the hard, rocky ground. She pulled out an air bed, with its foot pump, and put it inside, along with her sleeping bag for later. Selina had a camp stove for cooking and a lantern for light but wanted to have a fire tonight instead. So, she got out her canvas carryall, and a hatchet then started down the gentle slope into the mouth of the canyon to search for wood.

Her ten-minute hike had warmed Selina enough that she started to sweat, so she stopped in a shady spot and set the tote on the ground. Unzipping her hoodie, Selina took it off, cinched it to her waist, then removed a bandanna out of her pocket, wiping the perspiration from her face. She wished she would have thought to bring a bottle of water with her. Oh, well, hindsight was always twenty-twenty. Selina blew out an exasperated breath, then twirled the bandanna between her hands, looped it around her neck, and tied it there.

Picking up the carryall again, Selina navigated over to one of the jumbles of dead cedar limbs piled here and there in small bunches—after losing their tenacious hold on the rock-ribbed earth—during some gully washer. This was a dry canyon but could flash flood in a hurry, even during moderate rains.

Selina laid the canvas out flat on the ground then started collecting pieces of wood. The shaggy bark of the cedar could be easily stripped away and made excellent tinder. She pulled out a long limb, and placing her booted foot in the center, she bent up on each end until it snapped in two, then added it to the growing pile.

When Selina had collected almost more than she could carry, she stopped and looked about—wanting a little green wood because it burned slower. Spotting a sapling clinging to the base of the canyon wall, she headed over to it, hatchet in hand.

Choosing a stubby limb, Selina chopped through it. A sharp, woodsy, sweet aroma exuded from the fresh cut, as sticky sap was transferred to the blade. She stripped off the leafy branches first, then hacked the rest into smaller sections, and put them with her dead wood. The carryall was now very heavy, and Selina's muscles bunched under the weight of it. Reversing direction, she trudged back to her camp, switching hands the whole way. With a sigh of relief, Selina dropped her burden at the far side of one of the boulders where some melon-sized rocks were scattered about. She always used them to build a ring for a fire pit.

A loud growling, followed by a ripply feeling in her gut, reminded Selina she hadn't eaten since breakfast. It was too late in the afternoon for lunch and too early for dinner, so she decided to scrounge up a snack.

Most of the groceries stocked at the convenience store she'd stopped at, were along the lines of junk food, that tourists seemed to be the fondest of. They hadn't had stew or chili, but she was able to get some all-beef hot dogs, buns, and chips. Selina had been surprised to find a good selection of yogurt in the refrigerated case, so she'd picked up a four-pack of those also. But best of all, right at the register, was a big container with homemade jerky inside. Selina couldn't resist buying some. Now she was glad she had.

Pulling her camp chair from the back of her truck, Selina unfolded it, placing it in the shade cast by the large boulders facing the canyon. She grabbed a stick of jerky and stuck it in her shirt pocket, along with a spoon she removed from her camp kit. Opening the cooler next, Selina took out another bottle of water and a container of lemon yogurt. She thought the tart-sweet taste would pair nicely with the peppery flavor of the jerky. Laughing at herself over her culinary choices, Selina flopped into her chair. It felt good to sit again since her little sojourn to find firewood.

She put the bottled water in the cupholder then pulled back the foil top on the yogurt. Pulling the spoon from her pocket, Selina dug into the creamy mixture. It wasn't long before she was scraping the sides and bottom to get the last dregs out. After putting the empty container into the plastic trash bag, she always kept attached to the chair, Selina took the jerky from her pocket and tore off a hunk with her teeth. The peppery coating from the beef stung her tongue, causing saliva to fill Selina's mouth, softening the dried meat as she chewed. She finished the jerky and drank more water, washing it all down.

With her belly satisfied for the moment, Selina stretched out her legs, rested her head on the back of the chair, crossed her feet at the ankles, and relaxed. The sun had started its descendant arc toward the western horizon, but the shadows cast by the boulders protected her from its glare as she gazed up into the sky. Selina caught sight of a red-tailed hawk riding the thermals as it circled the area looking for its next meal.

She was far enough away from the road that only the faintest sounds of traffic reached her ears, and Selina's body sank further into the chair. The weeks of stress that she'd barely acknowledged lost its grip on her, leaving Selina sleepy after her snack. Before she knew it, she dozed off.

In a dreamy state, she became aware she was spooned against a soft, warm body. Selina could tell from the rhythmic rise and fall of the voluptuous breast she held cupped in her hand, that the woman was sleeping. A plump bottom was snuggled into her crotch, and one of her legs was thrown over a set of fleshy thighs. There was no need to move, Selina felt loved, and at peace like she was exactly where she was meant to be.

It was dark, and all Selina could make out was the woman's silhouette. She inhaled the musky scent of sandalwood clinging to the woman's skin, where Selina's nose was buried in the crook of her neck. A white-hot flame of arousal coursed through her body, igniting her soul, creating an overwhelming need to make love to the woman beside her.

Selina pulled back enough to gently kiss her way down a smooth, well-rounded shoulder. She paused when she saw an infinity symbol tattooed on the otherwise unblemished skin. Her initials *ST* were in the center of the left loop with *RT* in the other, confirming to her this was the person she belonged to. Selina ached to see the face of the woman she loved. Her heart thumped heavily in her chest as her arousal climbed. Pulling gently on the warm shoulder beneath her hand…

Selina jerked and blinked rapidly, attempting to clear the fog from her brain, not sure what had awakened her. She squinted her eyes, adjusting to the bright glare of the sinking ball of flame that was quickly approaching the ground. Selina looked to the right, and before her eyes sat, her spirit guide in the guise of the wolf. A ghostly apparition with omnipotent knowledge shining out of its ice-blue eyes that were mirrors of her own. Selina realized the wolf had been communicating with her once again through a dream.

Speaking aloud, she addressed it. "Honored guide, I thank you for coming to me when my life is muddled. I appreciate being shown the woman I hope is meant for me, but I still don't know where to find her. I need something a little more concrete from you, so I will know which road to take."

While Selina watched its unchanging features, she heard a tone from her phone indicating she'd received an email. Reaching into the back pocket of her jeans, Selina slipped it out, held it at eye level, allowing her to keep the wolf in sight. She placed her thumb on the power button, leaving it there until the phone registered her print. The notification window popped up, and Selina's eyes slid from the grinning wolf to her cell phone screen. She opened her email app then started to read.

It was from a Réalta Tobin, in response to the resume she'd submitted to Agnatural Farms this morning. Ms. Tobin was inquiring when Selina would be available for a FaceTime phone interview. When she looked back up from the screen, her wolf guide was gone. Selina was more than a little miffed at the interruption but brushed it off because she wanted that job. So, she typed out a quick response letting Ms. Tobin know she was available now, then settled back and waited for the woman's call.

During the interim, Selina closed her eyes once again, committing every aspect of her sumptuous dream woman to memory. She'd always been attracted to the ladies with Rubenesque figures, finding them to be way more appealing than the half-starved, stick versions that society viewed as pinnacles of beauty. Selina's fingers itched to map out every plush curve of the body she'd held briefly in her arms during her spirit guided dream. For now, Selina would be patient and trust she was being led where she needed to go.

Chapter Six

Getting Back to Business

It was a good thing Dolly knew her way home because Rea let her mind drift back to the strange encounter at the river. If it was a wolf, where had it come from, and where had it gone? There had to be some explanation, other than she'd just imagined it. But if she hadn't, why were there no paw prints, and why hadn't Patches or Dolly reacted?

Rea couldn't shake the feeling when the wolf had locked its eyes on her, that in some fashion, she was being weighed and measured. Maybe it had only been trying to determine if she was a threat, but it hadn't felt that way. The whole episode had an otherworldly feel to it. Rea considered herself to be a freethinker and was decidedly irreligious, but she couldn't discount the possibility it might have been some kind of mystical visitation.

Rea was abruptly shaken out of her reverie at the pull of the reins in her hand—shocked to realize she was back at the barn—with Dolly shaking her head impatiently, waiting for Rea to get off. She looked for Patches, but he was nowhere to be seen. More than likely, he'd made his way to the house for another nap.

Dismounting, Rea led Dolly into the barn then unsaddled her. She went into the tack room, retrieved a bucket holding a soft towel, curry comb, brush, and a hoof pick. On the way back she grabbed a feed bag, filled it with oats, and strapped it on Dolly, so she could eat while Rea groomed her. The simple act of caring for the easygoing animal was soothing, allowing her mental clutter to dissipate, so she could focus back on work.

When Rea finished, she led Dolly outside and put her into the paddock where Jupe was waiting for her. He immediately sidled up beside Dolly, arched his head up over her neck, and laid his cheek along her mane. Rea's heart leaped with joy, knowing Jupe's wounded spirit had found solace with the gentle mare. She hoped when the time was right, the two would mate and give her a beautiful little colt.

Turning away, Rea pulled her radio from its holster and keyed the mic. "Flash this is Wonder Woman, come in please."

It was answered immediately. *"Hola, Wonder Woman. I see'd the sprinkler spraying big, so ju fixed it?"*

"Yes, the filter was full of dirt because the float was gone. I got a new one on it, and the filter changed out, so all is taken care of out there. Do you have any updates for me this morning?"

"Sí, sí. Mama say to come over to get some soup an fresh tortillas."

"What?" she teased in an aggrieved manner. "Does she think I can't feed myself?"

"Ju know, Mama. She tink ju have too much baloney in jur diet." His deep belly laugh resonated through the speaker.

"Okay, Matty. Mia already told me this morning about the Caldo, so I'll come for lunch, but after that, I have paperwork to do. I need to make a decision on a botanist to work with us. Have you got all the labor you need lined up to get the fields prepped?

That much needs to be done before we can plant anyway, so at least we will be that far along."

"*Si. All de temp men from las season say dey be here in de nex week. An some oll friends from Cali be coming. Dey say dey want to work for such a good boss. We will haf plenty and Mama, she is ready, to run the kitchen wagons with de other weemon. We all set.*"

"I guess I best get my part done then and decide on a botanist. I'll see you in a bit for lunch."

"*Not if I see ju furst.*" With another belly laugh, he signed off.

Rea adored Matty, and his wife, Mia. She'd met them over sixteen years ago when she was working for the nonprofit Migrant Resource Organization. They'd come to her for help to find a way to send their daughter, Leticia, the oldest of five, to college. Matty had been employed by one of the local growers to locate and supervise workers coming into the country during harvests. They were in the country legally, and Letty had been born in the US. That had made it easier for Rea to find her a scholarship and some grants. Letty had graduated over ten years ago with a nursing degree and was now living out in Oregon with her husband and two children.

Matty and Mia had been so grateful they'd continually brought Rea little things. A bag of home-grown tomatoes here, some homemade salsa there or different kinds of Mexican sweet bread that her ample hips didn't need. She and Sherry had been invited to all their important celebrations over the years—birthdays, graduations, and anniversaries. More importantly, they'd been there for Rea after Sherry died. She considered them to be family, especially when Mia treated her like a pig-headed child, who didn't know what was best for them.

When Rea began her quest two years ago to start her farm, she'd coaxed Matty and Mia to leave California and join her in Colorado with their last offspring, Carlos,—who'd only been a toddler when they'd first met—in tow. It was one of the best decisions Rea had ever made.

Matty's vast network of contacts, which included farmworkers, building contractors, and general laborers, had been essential. They'd started by constructing five large greenhouses, heated by solar and wind power. Next up, they'd built the bunkhouse—as Rea referred to it. A housing complex made up of single rooms and two-bedroom suites, that doubled as a mini-hotel in the offseason. She'd also shelled out the funds to renovate and or build new homes for the families of the workers Rea employed year-round. Then, last but not least, was the all-important completion of a warehouse system for shipping and a botany testing lab.

The one employment rule Rea strictly followed was that all her workers had to be here legally—having either a green card or an H-2A visa. She wouldn't hire undocumented workers, and she didn't want to do business with anyone that did either. While Rea sympathized with their plight, she wasn't going to break the law. There were already too many people and companies out there exploiting the illegal workers. Those entities paid them next to nothing, finding it cheaper to pay the fine if caught. In doing so, they drove down the wages of the legal migrants until they could barely live on what they were paid for their back-breaking labor.

The country really needed to revamp the immigration system because they were doing a terrible job of it. Rea didn't know what the solution was, but until then, she was willing to help legally secure visas or green cards, for friends and family members of her employees. The people Matty had brought on worked harder than anyone had a right to expect because they said she treated them better than anybody ever had before.

Rea didn't believe she'd done anything all that special. She paid minimum wage to the seasonal workers and provided decent basic housing to them. There were a few additional perks thrown in like the lunches served from the food trucks. But she only furnished the ingredients and the vehicles; the women family members did all the work, cooking and serving the food to the hungry workers. Over the past two years, they'd built a community together that felt like family. It was something they all could take pride in—and she did—satisfied with the life she'd created for all of them. What more could she ask for?

Reaching the equipment shed attached to the garage holding her ATV, Rea flipped up the cover then keyed in the code. The smaller door creaked open slowly as it traveled up the metal rails until it stopped. *Huh, I guess I need to oil those.* She snagged a can of WD-40 off the shelf, squirted it on all the rollers, and inspected them, looking for rust. It was one of the types of things to watch for on the farm—something quickly and easily taken care of—saving money in the long run, if caught early.

Rea put the can back, then checked the gas tank on the quad. It was almost full, so she was good to go. She hopped onto the seat and fired up the Black Beast as she called her ATV. It had the necessary horsepower to pull an accessory trailer, and besides, it was fun to drive. Rea gunned the engine as she cleared the door then made a sharp turn, throwing bits of loose gravel up to ping against the metal siding.

The breeze whipped past her head, and the roar of the engine beat against Rea's eardrums since she'd chosen to keep wearing her ball cap instead of a helmet. To Rea, it wasn't any more dangerous than riding a horse if she was careful, which she always was.

In no time flat Rea arrived at a cute little cottage, with its proverbial white picket fence. A profusion of flower beds accentuated the lines of the home—a counterpoint to the shade trees and shrubs scattered about the yard. Mia was outside, whistling a tune as she filled the bird feeders. She and Matty had transformed the old clapboard house into a charming home. It had been on one of the parcels of land Rea purchased and had transported here. It had been a little run down, like hers, but worth saving. Moving it had only cost her eight thousand with another thirty for all the needed plumbing and electrical upgrades.

Rea had already deeded it to them along with ten acres, and it was the first home they'd ever owned. As a part of Matty's employment contract, she would grant him an additional five acres annually, as a bonus. The only stipulation being if they ever decided to sell, Agnatural would purchase it back, at the fair market rate.

Mia looked up when she stopped at the gate and waved. Rea killed the engine, got off, and walked to where Mia stood waiting for her. As soon as she was within touching distance, Mia grabbed Rea, pulling her into a fierce hug then immediately started admonishing her.

"Cariña, where ju helmat? Iss ju so hard-headed, ju no need one?"

Rea lived for these hugs and Mia's scoldings. It was something she could easily imagine her own mother would have done. She laughed and nodded her head in agreement.

"Yes, Mama, I have a hard head, so I can go without a helmet. You ordered me to come over for some soup this morning, so my head is not so hard that I didn't follow your command."

"Good ting ju lissen to me. Come inside." Mia waved her hand as she waddled toward the door.

Rea obediently followed behind her, climbing up the new steps to the old porch. All of which had a fresh coat of dark blue paint that matched the trim on the house. A board squeaked beneath her booted foot, as Rea made her way to the screen door being held open by Mia. The spicy smell of the Caldo warming on the stove had escaped the confines of the kitchen and floated through the air. The heavenly scent made her stomach growl loudly.

"Si, I hear it." Moving her hands to her hips, Mia gave Rea the evil eye. "Ju eat dis morning?"

"Yes, Mama. I ate something," she said sheepishly.

"What ju eat, Cariña?"

Knowing she was in for it, Rea replied, "Some toast."

"Dats no good and ju know it." Mia shook her index finger at Rea emphatically. "An I no want to hear ju tink ju too fat. Ju pretty an, how ju say,"— her hands moved in an hourglass configuration—"curvy. Any woman be lucky to get ju."

"Now, Mama, you know I'm not looking for a woman. I've had the love of my life, and I honestly can't see myself with anyone else."

"I know, Cariña. Is juss no good to be alone, an I donn count dat dog, even if he a good one."

The shorter woman stepped into Rea's personal space, reached up, grabbed her by the chin, and tilted her head down. A fierce light shown in Mia's dark, chocolate, brown eyes. "Ju lissen to me! Ju too jung to be alone for de ress of jur life. Juss donn close jur eyes or jur heart if love come along."

Letting go of her chin, Mia wrapped Rea up in her two strong arms, squeezing her like a boa constrictor. She felt the love and concern curl around her just as tightly. Rea rested her head on Mia's shoulder, her throat tightening with emotion.

"I know, Mama. I hear you."

Letting go, Rea stepped back and tried to ease the tension conjured by their conversation by teasing Mia. "Besides, I know what happens when Matty doesn't listen to you. I've seen the scorch marks on his ass."

"An donn ju forget it, Chica! Come, sit down at de table wile I feed dat wolf in jur stomack."

Hearing that, Rea once again thought of her unsettling encounter by the river. Hopefully, during their meal, she'd have a chance to let Matty know there might be...something in the area to watch out for.

With perfect timing, he entered the room and greeted them. "Hola mis hermosas damas. An wat have ju been up to?"

"None of jur bizznes, mister nosy man. Us weemen haf our secrets. Ju both go an clean jur hands, den sit jur butts down."

After washing up at the kitchen sink, Rea took a seat at the table, watching as Mia bustled around pulling large bowls from a cabinet, then dishing up big ladles of soup into each. Next, Mia turned a stove burner on low, beneath a flat, round, cast iron griddle, and heated some tortillas before placing them into a warmer.

Matty made it back just as Mia finished and brought everything over to the table, then slid into her chair. Rea stayed perfectly still while both Matty and Mia dropped their heads, offering up a mumbled prayer. Being agnostic, she didn't participate in their ritual but respected their beliefs. A moment later, their hands moved in a trinitarian, signaling the end of their benediction, and they started eating.

The Caldo was excellent, as usual. Rea, who wasn't much of a cook, was thankful Mia was willing to feed her a home-cooked meal several times a week. They chatted casually as they enjoyed the soup, and Mia caught her up on all the gossip. At the end of the meal, Rea decided to bring up her wolf sighting, but not how unusual it had been.

"Hey, Matty. I thought I better let you know, there may be a wolf around. I thought I saw one this morning along the river."

Startled, he blurted out questions and statements in rapid succession. "Wat? Ju juss tellin me dis now? Dey no been seen here before. I donn tink they be in dis area, in de mountains, but no here. Ju sure? Wat it look like, could be a dog maybe? Where ju see it, xactly? I go look for de tracks."

Holding up her hand, she stopped his rant long enough to answer. "Yes, it might have been some kind of wolf or a hybrid mix. So, no. I'm not sure. I just wanted you to know is all."

Rea didn't want to admit exactly what she'd experienced, so she tried to choose her words carefully. "Well…I inspected the ground where I saw it on the bank and there weren't any prints. It was white with blue eyes, but it didn't exactly have the look of a dog, but I'm not ready to say it was a wolf either. There was no growling, and it didn't make a move toward me. It just sat there watching me. I looked away for a second and when I turned back, it was gone."

Mia looked at Rea alarmed, then dramatically crossed herself before muttering, "Ay Dios mio."

"Now look, you two. It was a rather weird incident, but I'm sure there is some reasonable explanation. I wanted you to know, so you could be on the lookout for it. But that's all. Don't get worked up about it."

Matty's forehead wrinkled in distress, and Mia had a stranglehold on her rosary. Rea wished she'd kept her mouth shut. Deciding it was best to skedaddle, she pushed back from the table, rubbed her belly, and said, "Thanks for lunch, Mia, but I need to get back to my house. I have paperwork to catch up on."

All of them got up from the table, and the trio made their way outside. After saying goodbye, Rea mounted her ATV then glanced back over her shoulder to where her friends stood arm and arm. Rea hated the look of worry she saw etched on their faces, and even sorrier to know she'd been the cause. Waiving, she turned away, started the engine, and hurried home.

When Rea drove around the corner of her garage, she was greeted by excited barks. It seemed Patches had finally woken up from his nap. She parked the quad in the shed, shut the door, and went toward the house.

"Hey Patches, you are not coming inside till I wash off your dirty legs." Rea pointed to her left and said, "Go!" Patches hung his head and moved onto a small concrete slab just to the side of the porch where a hose sat wound up on a reel, as directed. He stood still while Rea rinsed his legs, then scrambled up the porch steps and stopped. She grabbed the towel off the hook, hanging by the door, that she kept there for just these occasions and dried Patches off as he squirmed impatiently.

"Okay, little man, I'm done."

Rea opened the door, and Patches preceded her into the mudroom. She paused, unclipped her radio and put it back into the charging station, then divested herself of her jacket and ballcap. When Rea arrived in the kitchen, she wasn't surprised to see that Patches had stopped at the counter where she kept his biscuit canister. Rea glanced down at him as she lifted the lid and pulled out one of his treats. Patches' eyes followed her movements intently but waited patiently for her to complete their ritual.

"Is this what you want, boy?" He barked in answer. "How much do you want it?" His front feet left the floor, and Patches waved them up and down in a begging gesture. "Good boy. Here you go." He snagged it from Rea's hand and trotted off to enjoy his treat elsewhere.

Rea stopped at the fridge and snagged a bottled water for herself. After the day she'd had so far, Rea would have preferred a glass of wine, but with the never-ending pile of paperwork waiting for her, she needed to get to work.

It was early evening by the time Rea got through most of her to-do list. The one glaring item she'd yet to address was hiring a botanist. She logged into the company email account to see if there were any new candidates, and bingo, there was one.

Rea opened the cover letter first, quickly scanning it. By the end, she was chuckling to herself, intrigued by the woman who wrote it. She moved on to the resume next and was even more impressed, as Rea read through all the details of the jobs the woman had held. Her educational credentials were impeccable—

master's degree in botany and a minor in agronomy—which, by far, made her the most qualified applicant.

To top it off, the woman had attended Texas A&M. Rea and Sherry's alma mater. Based on the dates listed, they would have been in their last semester at the university when the woman was a freshman. Rea wondered if they had ever met. It had been a particularly busy time for them both, so she doubted it.

Rea had a good feeling about this Selina Thorson, so she shot off an email requesting a FaceTime interview. She didn't expect an immediate response, so she got busy ordering the floats. When her email notification sounded, Rea opened it and was surprised to find it was from Selina, saying she was available right away.

She'd never been comfortable interviewing people, so Rea took a minute to get situated, put on her best professional face, then initiated the call from her computer.

Chapter Seven

First Contact

Thankfully, even though Selina was in the middle of the reservation, she had enough bars on her phone to have decent cell service. There weren't many towers out here, but there was one in Chinle, and the land was flat enough for signals to travel further out.

"Horse With No Name" rang out, signaling an incoming call from an unknown number. Straightening up in the chair, Selina tugged down on her long-sleeved thermal tee, becoming aware of how unprofessional she would appear to her caller. It was too late for her to worry about it now, and if the woman was that uptight, Selina wouldn't want to work for her anyway. She cradled the phone in her left hand, resting it comfortably on her thigh then tapped the answer key.

Selina was surprised at her first view of the stocky woman appearing on her phone screen. She was also dressed in casual attire, with the long sleeves of her blue chambray work shirt rolled up above her elbows. Her arm was casually resting on a wooden surface, probably a desk, while her hand fiddled with a mouse. Based on the angle and the view, Selina guessed she was calling from a computer with a webcam versus her phone.

The woman looked to be somewhere in her mid-forties. Strands of silver were starting to infiltrate the short, fluffy waves of dark red hair that topped the crown of her head, but couldn't be seen in the shorn sides. The face smiling back at her had crinkles of crow's feet radiating out, framing an incredible set of hazel eyes. A smattering of freckles dotted her nose then migrated across her plump cheeks. Soft, but still visible laugh lines formed around her mouth as she spoke.

"Hi, Ms. Thorson. I'm Réalta Tobin, but I generally go by Rea. I'm glad you were available to take my call right away."

"And I'm happy to be speaking with you as well, Ms. Tobin," Selina returned professionally.

"I was amused by your cover letter," Rea said, her smile getting broader. "I can say not many applicants would be willing to list their ability to develop a strain of pot that could both energize a person and not give them the munchies, as one of their crowning achievements."

The throaty laugh that followed, along with the laid-back personality emanating from the woman warmed Selina all over, changing the timbre of the interview entirely. She'd gambled, but Selina had guessed right in writing it that way—it had snagged her this interview, after all.

"Well, all of the best paying and most challenging botanical careers in the last fifteen years have been in the field of growing cannabis, whether for medical or recreational use." Selina allowed a tiny grin to crease her face. "So yeah, I felt I could brag about it."

Rea leaned back in the chair, her brows drawing together. "Seriously, what impressed me most are your dual degrees, so you definitely have the qualifications I'm looking for. I've spent the last several years setting up the infrastructure, and getting my land ready for full-scale organic farming." Rea placed her hand on the wood surface of the desktop, palm down, and started tapping out a staccato beat with her fingers. "But I want a fully holistic approach for growing crops on my farm based on the soil, weather, water resources, and any other factors which will allow me to grow the best organic produce possible."

After a moment's pause, her fingers ceased their drumming. Sliding her arm off the desk, she rested it on the arm of the chair. "Tell me why you think you would be the ideal candidate for this position."

Selina was also really impressed by Rea. The vast majority of growers were only concerned with increasing crop yields any way they could, not caring how destructive the use of GMO seeds, pesticides, and certain types of fertilizers were to people or the environment. Their use impacted the health of those consuming the food, and the workers in the fields. Over the long term, the harmful chemicals leached into the land and water tables, as well. This position would be more than a job, it would be the kind of work Selina could put her heart and soul into.

"Ms. Tobin, this would be my dream job," she said honestly. "I was brought up in a culture that believes in balance. If you care for the land and the animals, never taking more than you need, they will, in turn, care for you." Selina's voice took on an edge. "The rise in corporate farms, with their constant need to produce more and more food per acre, with the gleeful help of greedy chemical companies, has increased land contamination, causing harm to all living things. To me, it's a crime against humanity.

Their only credo is profits, and they don't care that they are destroying the planet at the same time," she ended angrily.

Selina mentally cursed herself. She hadn't meant to get so carried away—it was one of her personal sore spots—but didn't want to sink her interview by appearing like a hot-headed radical. It wouldn't score her any brownie points, so she reigned herself back in.

"Your approach is something I can get behind a million percent,"—she said earnestly—"and I would love an opportunity to work for you," Selina practically begged.

"If I decide to offer you the position, how soon would you be able to start?"

Selina felt her hopes rise. "I'm available right away. I'm currently camping near my family home in Holbrook, Arizona, so I could be there within a day."

"Well…I will need to check your references before I can make a final decision." A slow smile crept over Rea's lips. "But if those come back the way I think they will, you've got yourself a job. I'll contact you again via email as soon as possible. Do you have any questions for me before I let you go?"

Selina racked her brain, trying to think of anything she could say to keep Rea talking to her, but it was as if her mind had seized up. *Come on, Selina, snap out of it. Say something, anything, but don't sound like an idiot.* "I'm gay. I hope that won't be an issue." Selina immediately felt heat suffusing her face.

Lost & Found

A raspy chuckle escaped Rea's throat, and her lips curled up until a set of dimples appeared. Then her expression suddenly changed. Rea leaned forward, getting closer to the webcam, elbows on the desk, and fingers steepled. She had a look in her eyes, Selina couldn't quite interpret, then startled her by speaking directly to her heritage.

"I have no problem with who you want to share your blankets with, as long as it doesn't interfere with your work."

Seconds slid by as they looked at each other as if trying to find the answer to a question that hadn't been asked.

Finally, Rea broke the stalemate. "One way or another, I'll contact you in the next day or two with my decision." Without taking a breath, she continued, "I'll let you go, have a pleasant evening."

And the screen went blank before Selina could even respond.

*****

Rea's chair rocked slightly, as her back thumped against it, inhaling the first full breath she'd taken since Selina had answered her call. The name seemed to fit her like a glove. *Sellinna,* long and sensual sounding—Rea savored the name.

The woman was beautiful. A thick braid of black hair had been draped over one shoulder—the tip seeming to caress the small mounds outlined beneath her gray thermal t-shirt. Her sun-kissed, bronzed skin, angular face, and high cheekbones, bespoke of a Native American heritage, which Selina had confirmed during the call. Rea had noted her narrow nose was slightly crooked at the bridge, evidence of a previous break. Dark, arched brows sat atop her deep-set eyes. When Rea had read the last name Thorson on the resume, a vision of a tall blond, Nordic bombshell with blue eyes had come to mind. Those brilliant shimmering blue eyes were the only thing Rea had guessed right on.

Rea sucked in a shocked breath when she realized they were the exact same ice blue color as the spectral wolf that had held her spellbound this morning at the river. Was it any wonder she was sitting there stunned? Rea also felt like she'd hit a winning trifecta—perfect candidate, beautiful woman, and to top it all off, a lesbian to boot. Was it some sort of sign?

A shiver rippled through her body, raising the hairs on her arms. Rea had mentioned her trouble finding the right botanist during her discourse with Sherry this morning. Then right after that, she'd seen the wolf at the river. Could the two be related, she wondered? Rea felt almost compelled to hire Selina without checking her references. Of course, she wasn't going to do it. Rea was too practical for that, as Sherry well knew. So even if it were a heavenly set up of some kind, she would proceed rationally.

Rea settled down, composed an email, attaching the employment verification, then sent it off to the previous employers listed on Selina's resume. Since she was finished for the day and felt a great need for a glass of wine, Rea shut down her computer then headed for the kitchen.

Grabbing a goblet from the etched glass-fronted cabinet, she went to the refrigerator to fill it. When Rea opened the door, she thought about food; it wouldn't be smart to drink on an empty stomach. She hadn't eaten tonight, and the soup she'd had for lunch seemed like a distant memory. But the bare shelves inside seemed to damn her. Rea desperately needed to do some grocery shopping as well as visiting the greenhouse to get salad fixings and fresh veggies.

Sherry had been the one who did the shopping and cooking, always making sure their meals were healthy but low cal, as Rea tended to pack on weight with her thyroid issue. Good thing she was getting so much physical exercise on the farm these days, or she'd be rolling in fat.

Sighing, Rea stuck her glass under the spout of her favorite boxed wine, and filled it to the brim with Chardonnay, then set it down on the counter. Next, she opened the freezer and looked for something she could pop into the microwave. It was an easy search as the only carton inside was one of those single-serving sized Stouffer's lasagna. She removed the tray from the box, put it on a paper plate, and set about nuking it.

Rea picked up her glass, sipping the wine as the microwave hummed along cooking her dinner. The black plastic container seemed to mesmerize her as she watched its orbit around the center of the glass turntable. The ding snapped Rea out of her mindless state and announced the completion of the cycle. Pulling out the plate, she set it on the counter, doing her best to avoid getting burned by the escaping steam as she peeled back the plastic film. Rea's stomach growled as the cheesy aroma scented the air.

She left it to cool and went to the pantry to retrieve a couple of packets of parmesan cheese from a box she'd bought off Amazon. Rea brought them back to the counter, doctored up the lasagna with them, then added a little garlic salt. Putting the food and wine on a lap tray, she carefully carried it into the living room, sniffing hungrily at the hot food as she went.

Rea set it down on her rustic coffee table, grabbed the remote, and turned on the TV. She didn't have cable, but she didn't need it, preferring to read most of the time. Rea had subscriptions to Hulu, Netflix, and Amazon Prime if she wanted to watch anything. Tonight, she chose the Pandora app on the screen, and the sound of soft rock filled the room.

Flopping onto her plush, camel-colored leather sofa, Rea placed the tray across her lap and settled in to enjoy her meal. It didn't take long to finish the lasagna, then she sat back, relaxing with her wine, contemplating the events of the day. When the dulcet tones of Aretha Franklin filled the room, singing "Natural Woman," Rea hummed along. The song carried her back in time to the most pivotal moment of her life.

Rea hadn't dated in high school. She was too busy trying to keep up with her studies and help out her mom, who was slowly losing her battle with breast cancer. Her father died when she was young, so it had been just the two of them. Rea had been a pudgy teen, and while the guys always ogled her plump breasts, apparently, even those weren't enough to entice them to ask her out. It hadn't registered with Rea then that she couldn't have cared less, because she hadn't found any of them attractive anyway. She'd noted the cute, shy girls, however, and went out of her way to befriend them.

Rea's epiphany came the minute Sherry had entered her life. It was her first year in college, and Sherry had been a senior. Rea had literally run her down in the library. She'd been there to study but lost track of time. In a huge hurry to get to class on time, she'd rounded a corner and plowed straight into Sherry, knocking her smaller frame to the ground. That was the start of a friendship that quickly altered into a romance.

Everything about Sherry had captured Rea's attention, and all the puzzle pieces of her life fell into place. She was a lesbian. It hadn't taken her long to jump that rainbow fence, landing right into Sherry's waiting arms. This song had been playing the first time they'd kissed, and the melody had resonated through Rea, with lyrics that perfectly described exactly how she felt.

She laid her head back on the sofa, closed her eyes, and sighed. Rea rarely allowed herself to dwell on Sherry's death or how empty it made her feel, and this was the second time today it had invaded her thoughts. Rea still couldn't imagine being with anyone else, but tonight, a melancholy feeling seemed to settle over her as she longed for the comfort of some human touch.

As the closing strains of the song were dying away, a vision of a pair of ethereal blue eyes flashed into Rea's mind. They pierced hers as if searching for something within her, but seemed to be offering Rea something as well. She could almost hear Sherry's voice saying, *"Here's your lesbian."* Opening her eyes, Rea sat erect, trying to shake off the feeling of being surrounded by her mystical presence.

Chapter Eight
Talisman

Selina sat stunned for minutes after the end of her interview, wondering why Rea had ended the call so abruptly. Was it because she'd blurted out she was gay? Rea had responded positively, but maybe it did have something to do with it. There was no telling at this point. Either she'd get the job or she wouldn't. It was out of her hands now.

Darkness was rapidly approaching, and the light from the brightest stars were winking on in the east. Silence had descended with the sun as even the minimal traffic on the road had dropped to almost zero. The growling monster in Selina's stomach had returned, which had her thinking about food once again. She planned to roast her weenies over a fire, instead of using her camp stove, because, to Selina, they just tasted better that way.

She heaved herself up out of her seat and went about gathering up the stones scattered about. Selina arranged them in a circle around a natural depression in the ground, near the back of the biggest boulder. It was a perfect location to hide the glow of a fire from sight of the road. She strategically placed pieces of dry and green wood down in a crisscross fashion, leaving space so the fire could breathe. Using the shaggy bark and smaller twigs as tinder, Selina had the fire started in no time. The rich aroma of wood smoke filled the air as the flames danced along the burning cedar, accompanied by pops and crackles. Orange sparks launched themselves skyward, from the igniting sap, but quickly died as they ran out of fuel.

The sky was clear, and the temperature was dropping, so Selina put her hoodie back on as she ambled over to her truck. She pulled out a plate, skewers, two buns, then retrieved the hot dogs from the ice chest. Selina rummaged around until she found her stash of mustard packets. Grabbing a beer along with a bag of chips, she carried it all back to the fire. Placing the beer in the cup holder on the chair, she used the seat as a mini table.

Selina squatted by the fire to cook her skewered hot dogs. They sizzled, as the flames kissed and caressed their skins. The scent of the cooking meat sent her stomach into a fit of hunger pangs. When they were slightly charred, Selina carried them back to her plate. Opening the mouths of the buns, she dressed them with mustard, then clamped them around the hot dogs and slid them off. Selina picked up her plate with a sigh, then settled down in the chair to enjoy her food.

Selina preferred simple meals to the haute cuisine a few of her former girlfriends insisted on. Similarly, those relationships had burned out as quickly as the sparks leaping from her fire. Those kinds of women tended to have attractive packages, but no real substance, and above all, Selina required substance. Her idea of real beauty was what was on the inside instead of what their outside visage looked like.

That got her thinking about Rea again. Subjectively, Selina found her to be quite attractive but was aware not everyone would think so. The cherubic face and the proportions of the body she'd been able to see were not generally found to be as appealing to others as they were to her. And those hazel eyes, captured by the lens of the webcam, had beckoned her to come closer. Selina remembered the searching look Rea had given her before she'd hung up and wondered if Rea was gay. She was someone Selina wouldn't mind crawling into the sack with.

True night had finally descended, but the moon had yet to rise. Although it wasn't even nine o'clock, her full stomach and her early morning visit to Bell Rock had Selina thinking about turning in for the night. She took a sip of her beer, intending to finish it before heading to bed when a bright object lit up the sky—streaking toward her, hissing and grumbling in the cold night air. Seconds later, the ground shivered as a loud thud echoed down the canyon.

Selina catapulted to her feet in shock, and the beer bottle dropped from her nerveless fingers. A geyser of foamy liquid shot up as it hit the ground, wetting her pant leg. Dazed, she stood gazing toward the canyon with her mouth agape. The sound of the glass bottle scraping the ground as it spun, snapped Selina out of her stupor. Rushing to the tent, she grabbed her lantern and set off to find the meteorite.

Selina carefully trod over the uneven ground of the canyon, with the lantern held high above her head. There was an unfamiliar odor in the air that got stronger as she approached a faint glow, about twenty yards away, leading her like a beacon to a small crater. The meteorite seemed to pulse, the incandescence at its heart, brightening then dimming as Selina knelt next to a small crater. It was partially covered by pulverized soil, acting like a blanket, keeping it hot.

Wanting to fish it out, Selina quickly returned to her truck to find something she might use. Digging in her toolbox, she came up with a pair of large channel locks and a long flat-tipped screwdriver. She shoved them into the back pocket of her jeans, then closed the lid. Next, Selina plucked two bottles of cold water out of her ice chest, putting them in her hoodie pockets, before hurrying back into the canyon.

Selina dropped to her hands and knees, carefully digging around the sides of the crater with the screwdriver until she could pry the blistering rock loose from the ground. She opened the jaws of the channel locks wide enough to clamp onto the meteorite and pulled it free. Holding onto it with one hand, Selina opened the cap on one of the bottles of cold water with her teeth then poured it over the exposed rock. Hissing steam flashed into the air as the water hit the hot stone, followed by a sharp crackling sound. After Selina emptied the second bottle over it, she lowered her hand to gauge its temperature. It was still too hot to touch, so she stuffed everything, but the plyers holding her prize, back into her pockets, retrieved the lantern and carried it back to her campsite.

When Selina arrived at her truck a few minutes later, she gingerly set the meteorite on the tailgate. She angled the lantern sideways, getting her first good look at the dark, pockmarked rock. Selina sucked in her breath, as the shape registered in her stunned brain. *It's a heart!* The two rounded tops were of slightly differing sizes separated by a V shape. The bottom was also more rounded than pointy, but there was no mistaking its overall configuration.

Amazed, Selina reached out, running her fingers along its rugged façade that had cooled enough to touch. She picked up the meteorite and it fit perfectly in her palm. She was surprised that it still held a gentle warmth. Turning it over, Selina noticed a minute crack in the hard surface, toward the bottom of the V, where a tiny vein of orange ran along the black stone. She suspected the fissure had formed when she'd poured the cold water on it.

Selina stood there astounded as the astronomical implication of the event sank in. Her Amá sání had firmly believed that meteors were heavenly messengers—it wasn't a Diné teaching—but her personal ideology. She'd told Selina that every significant change in her life had come about after she'd sighted a meteor, and advised Selina to always watch for them. She'd seen several in the early morning sky when she was at Bell Rock and now this one.

On trembling legs, she managed to walk back to her chair before slumping into it. In reverence, Selina clutched the meteorite in her fist, then held it against her left breast. Was this the answer to her prayer? Had this talisman been sent by her Amá sání to help her find her soul mate?

The howl of a lone wolf rent the air drawing Selina's gaze across the canyon. There distinguishable against the night sky was the glowing white specter of her spirit guide, giving voice to that promise.

*****

Rea shook herself out of her contemplative mood as she carried her tray back to the kitchen. She threw the empty container in the trash then set the fork she used in the sink. Rea still had one more chore to do before bed, so she went to the mudroom and put her boots back on. Rea leaned out of the hallway door, calling Patches to her. "Hey, boy, let's go put Dolly and Jupe to bed."

Patches came on the run and shot out the back door, the moment Rea opened it, to visit his favorite potty places before bedtime. With his nose low to the ground, sniffing in exploration, Patches disappeared from view. Rea grabbed her jacket on the way out, as the temperature had dropped significantly with the loss of the sun.

The evening skies were clear and calm, with not even a breath of wind to disturb the stillness. The chickens had already sought the safety of their coop for the night, roosting peacefully in their nesting boxes. Rea noticed several new stacks of trays, had been left on the outside shelf, so she knew the ladies had been by today to gather the eggs. It was probably time to let Rory loose from his bachelor pad, to visit the ladies so they could have some baby chicks. As they matured, they would be put into separate pens. Some young hens were needed to replace aging ones that were no longer laying; the rest, male and female, were fattened up for consumption. Rea only kept those hens that she needed and gave the rest away.

As Rea approached the paddock, she heard Dolly whicker a friendly greeting, but Jupe's acknowledgment was a brief fluttering of his lips as he blew out a breath. Maybe she should look into finding a horse whisperer to help him make peace with his past. Rea had heard miraculous stories about their successes with timid animals, and she might need to look into that soon if he didn't come around.

Inside the barn, Rea put fresh hay into their feeders, checked their water, then opened their outside doors. With some careful maneuvering, she got Jupe settled in first then turned her attention to Dolly. The mare immediately cozied up to Rea when she stepped in to close the outside paddock door. Dolly nudged her with gentle affection until Rea turned to stroke her silky neck.

With a last pat, she exited the stall and voiced her thoughts. "Night, sweet girl. I enjoyed our ride today. I'll be busy tomorrow but will make sure we have another nice one in a day or two. I need it as much as you do." Turning toward the other stall, Rea eyed Jupe. "Your day will come. I'm not going to give up on you."

Turning down the lights, Rea left, securing the barn doors behind her. She leisurely walked back toward her house, enjoying the peace and quiet. The moon hadn't risen yet, so the sky was inky black, making the stars shine all the brighter. Rea paused as a flair of light shot across the expanse, heading to the southeast, streaking toward the ground, then disappeared. She quickly tried to come up with a wish, but the only thing Rea wanted was to fill the aching void in her heart, left behind by Sherry's death. She didn't have much faith that her wish would be granted but hoped if anyone else had seen it, they'd have theirs fulfilled.

Rea was tired but strangely alert at the same time. Calling to Patches, he raced to the back porch and waited for her. Letting him in, she closed and locked the door. Snagging her wine glass off the coffee table, she finished the last few sips on her way to the kitchen. Placing the empty goblet in the sink, Rea shut off the lights and retired to her bedroom. Patches was already there, snuggled into his doggie bed.

Stripping off her socks, pants, and shirt, she threw them onto her bed. Next, Rea hooked her thumbs under her sports bra, and with a relieved moan escaping her lips, pulled it over her head. It was her favorite part of the day when she could free her girls from their lycra prison. Rea rubbed the creases below her heavy breasts, where the band of the bra had dug into her skin. She could never understand why women went under the knife for bigger boobs. The only reason Rea would even consider something as drastic as surgery would be to make hers smaller.

She gathered up the clothes and stuffed them into the hamper as she padded to the bathroom. Rea brushed her teeth before moving into the shower to wash away the effects of her long day. The hot water felt glorious on her tired muscles, draining away the tension she hadn't been aware of until Rea felt its release. She plucked the bottle of sandalwood and vanilla-scented soap from the shower caddy. Rea squirted a blob of it into her palm, rubbing her hands together then spread the foamy lather along her body. Working it over her breasts, she closed her eyes when a trickle of arousal flickered to life, reminding her that while her libido was mostly dormant, it wasn't dead.

Rea rinsed the soap away then detached the showerhead, with its long hose, free from its holder. Twisting the adjustment ring, until water pulsed out in a firm, steady rhythm, she sat down on the tile bench. Rea directed the spray against one breast while she cupped the other in her hand, manipulating the already firm nipple with her fingers. The answering tug in her groin had Rea spreading her bent knees apart.

Conjuring up Sherry's presence in the shower, she imagined them making love as they had many times before. She could almost see the sexy gleam dancing in Sherry's deep brown eyes as her hand slowly slid to the top of her thighs. Rea's fingers parted the lips of her untrimmed mound, pulling back on the fleshy hood exposing her clit throbbing in need. She closed her eyes, lowered the showerhead, bringing the pulsating stream into play. The face of her phantom lover shifted. The eyes looking into Rea's with love and desire were no longer brown, but blue. They burned with lustful hunger, and she felt herself responding. It wasn't long before Rea threw back her head, crying out as she trembled and shook.

With a lax arm, Rea reached up and turned off the water. She let go of the showerhead, where it dangled loosely by its hose, while she caught her breath. Oh, Rea had needed that release, after opening some emotional doors she'd felt were best left shut.

Her conscious mind drifted in peace, never recognizing the little eye color change that had transpired in the middle of it all.

Totally relaxed from her orgasm, Rea rose, her legs still a little shaky, and exited the shower. She managed to dry herself off, hung up her towel, and retreated from the bathroom. She turned out the lights and slipped under the covers of her king-sized bed. Rea didn't really need a big one like this anymore, but it was a deluxe pillow top set that she and Sherry had splurged on. It was just seven years old, and still very comfy, so Rea kept it. Snuggling under the down comforter, she wrapped her arm around her extra pillow and drifted off to sleep.

Chapter Nine
New Directions

The next morning, Rea was jerked awake by the feel of a warm, wet tongue stroking across her left arm hanging down off the side of the bed. Her face was partially buried in the pillow, so she turned her head enough to crack open both eyelids. Blinking, Rea focused on the diffused light filtering into her bedroom from the window. The licking continued, accompanied by an insistent crowing, urging her to get up.

Rea peeked at the glowing red numbers on the digital clock sitting on her nightstand. It read two minutes after six, and Patches was seated at the side of the bed with what she thought was a concerned look on his face. It finally dawned on her that she'd slept past her normal rising time. Groaning, Rea rolled onto her back, then slung her legs over the edge of the mattress and sat up.

"Wow, Patches. I haven't slept this late in forever. I guess you'll want to take a trip outside before breakfast." A bark answered her in the affirmative before he turned away, and left the bedroom, his nails clicking against the hardwood floor marking his progress. *He'll have to wait for a minute. Mama needs to pee and get dressed first.*

It didn't take Rea long. She felt more energized this morning than she had in quite some time. It must have been a result of the extra rest she'd gotten or possibly the shower activity Rea had indulged in the night before. Whatever the reason, there was a spring in her step as she strode through the house.

Patches was waiting for Rea at the back door, and she let him out first then went to her coffee maker. She pulled the filter basket out of her coffee maker, and loaded it up, before adding water to the reservoir. As soon as she closed the lid, dark caffeinated nectar streamed into the pot, its blissful aroma scenting the air. She pulled a mug out of the cabinet, adding a dash of hazelnut creamer to it and waited impatiently. Rea slid the pot off the warmer, and a last few drops fell, hissing onto the hot surface, as she hurriedly filled her mug.

No sooner had she taken her first sip when Rea heard the sound of whining coming from the back of the house. In her haste to make coffee, she'd forgotten to unlatch Patches' doggie door. Setting her mug on the counter with a sigh, Rea went and let him in.

"Hey, boy. Sorry about that. But couldn't you have given mama a few more minutes to enjoy her coffee? I guess my oversleeping has wrecked your schedule, too, and you're hungry."

Patches instantly went to his empty food bowl and dropped down on his haunches, his tail beating out an impatient tattoo against the floor. Rea gave him a quick pat on the head before grabbing his bowl. "Okay, little man. I got it. You need your breakfast right away, just like I need my coffee."

She filled his dish, then set it down, and Patches proceeded to chomp away on the crunchy morsels. Rea snagged her mug off the counter and headed into her office as he ate. As her computer booted up, she thought about what she needed to do today.

Rea was convinced Selina was the right person for the post and was sure the employment verifications would bear this out. Selina's outlook about land care and crop management aligned perfectly with hers. Since Rea's plan had included having a full-time botanist onsite, she'd had a complete lab constructed in her warehouse complex. A big part of their duties would be to sample batches of the produce coming in from her farm, and the other growers in the co-op, to make sure of their organic quality. Rea had spent enough years with Sherry to be familiar with the type of equipment needed, so the lab was set up and ready to go.

Rea's original strategy was to house the botanist, at least temporarily, with the other workers, unless they had a family, then she would have put them in one of the vacant houses. If she hired Selina, she didn't want to do that. She knew, as a lesbian herself, she would find living in a complex with a bunch of men less than appealing, and Rea wanted Selina to be comfortable. But she couldn't justify using a house that she was saving for a family, for a single person.

Running alternatives through her mind, Rea decided Selina might not mind staying in her RV. It was nicely appointed, roomy, yet cozy. Rea should know because she'd lived in it for almost a year, while her house was being renovated. It was conveniently located next to the garage under a huge patio with all the necessary utility hookups. A part of Rea was anticipating having company close by and hoped that Selina would feel the same way. Of course, she could be getting ahead of herself because Rea still needed to get those verifications back first.

*****

Selina came awake slowly, feeling truly tranquil for the first time in years. She had a stranglehold on her extra pillow, clutching it to her body as she would a lover.

Lover? Her foggy thoughts finally cleared, and as Selina lay there, she thought back on the events of the previous day.

The implications of the meteorite and the subsequent appearance of her spirit guide had left Selina feeling a little overwhelmed. Even though she'd asked her Amá sání to intercede for her, she hadn't expected to receive such an elemental answer.

Selina had always been of two minds regarding her spirituality. There was her practical, scientific side that wanted to explain away anything mystical as an illusion created by her subconscious mind, which then pitted itself against her esoteric side that believed in the unfathomable powers of the universe. Last night the esoteric side had won.

Rising, Selina had gone to her truck and rummaged through her things until she found an old handmade deerskin pouch in one of her boxes. It had been given to her as a gift—during her Kinaalda party, which marked her entry into womanhood—at thirteen. Her family no longer practiced the original elaborate ritual, but they'd still celebrated the event. The pouch held what Selina considered to be her treasures—a nineteen twenty buffalo nickel from her Pop Pop, an ancient bone awl that was passed down to her from her Amá sání, and a silver bracelet that had belonged to her mother. Selina had untied the thong and added the meteorite to it, believing she was joining her past to her future.

Selina had been too excited and keyed up to sleep, so she'd searched her pack until she found her other leather pouch. This one contained a small pipe made from deer antler, and several clear plastic pill bottles, filled with cannabis. Selina had read the labels, picked one of her best, then put the others back inside. She popped the lid off, tweezered a small fragrant bud between her fingers, and packed it into the bowl.

Knowing she would get thirsty, she'd grabbed a beer from the cooler before returning to her chair. The fire had burned down low, but the full moon had finally risen, adding a mellow glow to the landscape. Selina had squeezed her fingers into the coin pocket of her jeans, fished out her zippo, and fired up her pipe.

When she'd inhaled, Selina's throat had contracted, trying to keep the smoke in her lungs. The custom bud was smoother than the weed she'd smoked in her teens, but it hadn't stopped her body from reflexively trying to expel it. She'd chased the first toke with a sip of her beer to soothe the slight irritation in her throat. After a second hit, she'd carefully placed the pipe in the crevice of her thighs.

It hadn't taken long for Selina to feel the potent effects of the THC filtering through her system. As her body had relaxed, so had her mind. In this hazy state, she'd accepted with certainty that her prayer had been answered in a very real and tangible way. Her thoughts had drifted toward Rea and what she considered to be the perfect job. She'd found them both to be tremendously attractive.

Réalta Tobin, *RT!* The thought had slammed into her when she'd recalled the dream woman from earlier in the afternoon. She wondered if it was a coincidence that Rea's initials were RT, or if she was the one Selina had been searching for all her life? Only time would tell, but the first step would be for her to get the position.

After draining the last of her beer, Selina had felt the weight of the long day wash over her. The fire had burned down, but for safety sake, she'd doused it before changing into sweats and crawling into bed. Sleep had come immediately but her rest was disturbed by snatches of vivid dreams that kept rousing her. The one where she watched a woman pleasuring herself in a shower had felt so real, that Selina had awakened with a throbbing need that she'd promptly taken care of, in a groggy state, before drifting back to sleep.

The dawn's light hadn't penetrated the tent yet, so Selina closed her eyes, trying to call back her vision of the fantasy woman, but unfortunately, she'd been lost in the dream world. Selina let go of the pillow, rolled onto her back, and reached over her head, stretching her body out under the blanket to ease her stiff muscles. The air mattress was okay but it wasn't the same as sleeping in a real bed.

An urgent need to pee, had Selina slipping on her shoes and leaving the tent. She liberated a few napkins from her camp supplies, then tramped over to the other side of her truck, about ten feet away, and relieved herself. The next order of business was to fire up her stove and make some coffee.

As it brewed, Selina grabbed a comb from her travel bag and ran it through her hair to remove the tangles. With nimble fingers, she sectioned her hair into three parts and braided it, as she had thousands of times before. Next, Selina pulled out a bottle of water, toothbrush, and paste, then finished up her morning ablutions by brushing her teeth.

The smell of the fresh coffee surrounded her, replacing the faint odor of wood smoke that still lingered in the air. Selina removed her travel mug from the cup holder in the cab of her truck and unscrewed the top. Adding several packets of sugar to it, Selina filled it with the steaming brew. With coffee in hand, she grabbed a protein bar, then made her way over to the camp chair and sat down. She sighed in enjoyment as the first sip hit her taste buds.

Even though the sky was just beginning to lighten, the faint sounds of traffic could already be heard in the distance, reminding Selina she wasn't the only one up and moving this morning. She spotted what she guessed was the same red-tailed hawk she'd seen yesterday soaring above her, riding a thermal. Only this time, it was probably searching for its breakfast. Selina ate hers between sips of coffee and contemplated her day.

*****

Rea spent the first hour this morning doing paperwork in her office, before heading to the barn to take care of the horses.

When she'd gotten back to her office, Rea found an email alert waiting for her. Bingo, it was an employment verification with a hearty recommendation containing the details of Selina's employment dates and salary. Rea hoped to have at least one more before she sent out an employment offer but felt confident enough to get started on her plan.

Rea grabbed her phone and keys then left the house, ready to hit the grocery store to stock her fridge plus the one in the RV. She took a minute to telephone Matty as she drove into town. Fortunately, he must have had a good signal because he answered on the first ring.

"Hola, Wonder Woman. What can I do for ju dis morning?"

"Good morning, Flash. I'm pretty sure I found us the perfect botanist, but being female, I think it best to house her in the RV. It needs to be aired out and dusted. Can you have one of the ladies take care of that today, then let me know who it was, so I can cut them a check for the work?"

"Sure, ting. I bet Mama will do it, an she no let you pay her. I call her. It sound like ju is driving, where ju go?"

"I'm heading into town to get some groceries. Do you need anything?"

"Sí, ju can save me a trip an bring Mama some seed for her birds. Den we all be even."

"No problem, Matty. I should be back in about an hour or so, and if Mia is at the RV, I'll give her the seed. If not, I can drop it off to her later."

"Bueno. Adiós Wonder Woman."

"Adiós, Flash."

Rea hung up, and five minutes later, she arrived at the store. Grabbing a cart, she cruised the aisles loading it up with her usual stuff, but adding other things to stock the RV with—bread, milk, butter, orange juice, coffee, along with condiments, and some canned goods. When she hit the liquor section, Rea thought back to her FaceTime interview with Selina. She recalled there'd been a beer bottle in the cupholder. Rea browsed the selections until she spotted the label she remembered seeing and added a six-pack of Shiner Bock to her cart.

Unfortunately, before she could get to the checkout, Hank cornered her. He was a nice enough man, but oh how he loved to hear the sound of his own voice. Usually, he followed Rea along the aisles with nonstop commentary as she tried to shop. Hank was also one of the primary links in the gossip train that ran through their town.

"Hey, Rea, good to see you. How is everything at the farm?"

"Things are coming along good, Hank. If the weather cooperates, we should be able to start our planting by the end of April or the first week of May."

"Any new businesses or people coming to town?"

"No new businesses yet, but I may have found a botanist."

"You don't say! That's wonderful news. I know you have been fretting about getting your farm into full production this year. You sure have a knack for building things up. Folks here sure appreciate everything you've done for us. Lord, there was hardly anything to Moirai before you got here. And when my son pulled his usual dumbass klutz routine recently, it was sure nice to be able to take him to the clinic here for those stitches, instead of having to hightail it to Greely for a visit to the doc-n-the-box."

"Thanks, Hank."

Rea didn't add anything to the conversation, because if she did, she'd be standing there for another ten minutes—so she wheeled her way toward June at the checkout—as he chattered on without a response from her.

"Hank, shut up already, and go stock something," his wife directed. "Sorry, Rea." She promptly rang everything up, then bagged it without another word.

After paying up and getting everything into her SUV, Rea made a quick stop at the feed store to get a twenty-pound bag of birdseed for Mia, then headed back to her house. On her way past the Harvey's place, Rea saw a trail of dust being kicked up by a tractor as it plowed furrows in the dirt. It looked like they were prepping their fields for planting, and she could hardly wait to get her workers started too.

A few minutes later, Rea left the road and turned into her private drive. As she approached the garage, she saw Mia moving around inside the RV through the windows. Once she got parked, Rea unfolded the blue canvas wagon she kept propped against the wall and loaded it up with the groceries.

Patches appeared at her side, sniffing the bags. "Hello there, little man. Keep your nose outta those bags, there's nothing in there for you."

Patches trained his expectant eyes on Rea, waiting to follow her to the house, but instead, she headed the other way. The RV door and windows were open, probably allowing the cool breeze to circulate through the interior. As Rea approached, she could hear Mia cheerfully humming inside. She took out the birdseed and sat it on a small table next to her barbeque pit, then hauled two grocery sacks inside. Even with everything open, a fresh lemony scent clashed with the more stringent odor of Pine-Sol, proving that Mia had been hard at work.

"Morning," Rea called out as she set the bags down on the counter. "Thanks for coming over to tidy up, Mia. I put your birdseed on the table outside. Matty said you needed some."

Mia waved a rag at Rea as she popped her head out of the bathroom. "Gracias Cariña. Dis woan take me long. It preety clean in here. Mateo say ju fine us a bottenis. He also say, it a woman. Is dat why ju wanna put her here?"

"Yes, I thought it would be better than housing her in the bunkhouse," she responded as she opened the fridge. "I'm going to unload this stuff, then get to my office and see if the last of those employment verifications came in."

"Bueno. I feenish soon. Ju come to dinner an tell us about her."

'Okay, Mia, I will."

It didn't take long to place all the items she'd purchased for the RV into the cabinets and fridge, then Rea headed back to her house with Patches following behind her. Once she'd gotten her own groceries put away, she grabbed a banana before retreating to her office. Moving the mouse brought her computer screen out of its sleep mode, and there on the screen was an email from Selina's last employer. Again, they gave her excellent marks, and that was enough for Rea to know she'd found her botanist.

She happily composed a message, attached an employment offer, and excitedly sent it off to Selina. The woman must have been waiting for her email because Rea received an acceptance within minutes. Selina confirmed she could be in Moirai the next day, apparently just as anxious as Rea was to get started—adding to her sense of certainty that things were heading in the right direction.

*****

Selina had spent a leisurely couple of hours at her spot watching the world around her go from monochrome to prismatic. She felt her own life was about to undergo the same type of change and was getting antsy to get it started. Selina had planned to stay at the canyon for a few days, but something else was pushing her to head out.

What she needed was a nice long shower and some decent food. That left her with a decision to make. Selina could check into a hotel in Chinle or head to the ranch, where she would face intense inquiries from her family. If her Amá sání and her Pop Pop were still alive, there would be no questions—but a grilling from her aunts, uncles, and cousins was another matter. Selina knew her family meant well, but their overly enthusiastic presence, especially when she hadn't been home in more than a year, was more than she thought she could tolerate.

Lost & Found

Selina had always been something of a loner. During her teens, she hadn't belonged to any clubs at school, not even 4-H, which all of her cousins were in. After school, she'd come home, saddle her mare, Sandy, a big chestnut roan, and would ride off to her favorite spot at the stream that ran through the corner of the ranch. In college, she had a single room in the dorm instead of a double, needing her own private space. Selina had rarely attended parties and spent most of her free time studying. In the intervening years, under duress from a girlfriend, she unhappily let them drag her to a few. They labeled her a party pooper and used it as a reason to ditch her. Even in her professional life, Selina preferred to work for individuals or small companies, where she was left mostly on her own. This was one of the reasons she wanted the new job so much, and it didn't hurt that she was intrigued by the woman behind it.

Selina didn't expect to hear back from Rea right away but hoped she would in the next day or so. Maybe instead of staying in Chinle, she should drive back to Flagstaff and check into a motel there again. Her intuition was telling Selina that's where she needed to go, and her logical side actually agreed. It would be a much better location to jump on the road to head to Colorado if she should get that job.

Selina finished the last of her coffee, then cleaned up, taking special care to remove all signs of her fire. She bagged up a few minuscule chunks of blackened wood and as much of the ash as she could before scattering the rocks again. Using the water from the melted ice in her cooler, Selina washed away the last of the sooty remains. Once she got everything situated in the back of her truck, she traveled back to the highway.

Checking the time on her truck's console, Selina figured she'd arrive in Flagstaff just in time for lunch. As she drove past the road leading to the ranch, she felt a twinge of guilt again for not stopping. Selina justified her actions by telling herself they'd never know she'd been in the area. If she got the post in Colorado, she'd need to head there straight away—if not, she could return in a few days, and they'd be none the wiser.

When Selina arrived in the city, she decided to stop at an Arby's for food, before heading to a hotel. She'd barely gotten back into her truck when the email notification pinged her phone. Crossing the fingers on her left hand, she reached up and removed the phone from its holder on the dash. Selina sucked in a deep breath when she saw it was from Rea. She cupped the phone tightly in her hand, then swiped into her email. A minute later, a big grin split her face as her fingers flew across the screen. Placing the phone back in its holder, Selina put her truck in gear and maneuvered out of the parking lot.

As she paused at the exit, a mechanical voice from her phone instructed her, *"Turn left onto Butler Avenue,"* the first step that would take Selina's life in a new direction.

Chapter Ten

First Impressions

Selina had driven all day, stopping only to gas up and have a quick dinner in Grand Junction. As the miles streamed by, she felt like she was being carried toward some fateful destination. Arriving in Greely around midnight, Selina checked into a Roadside Inn and sank into oblivion for some much-needed sleep. Rea had provided her cell number in her previous email, so after Selina had woken up and showered, she'd text her ETA. Rea had promptly messaged back with an address to meet at. Selina had taken extra care with her appearance this morning, dressing in more professional clothing, for this first all-important meeting. She'd even added a touch cologne for good measure.

Selina checked out, after a quick stop to help herself to coffee and a pastry from the hotel's continental breakfast bar, before leaving for Moirai. She was surprisingly nervous as she entered the outskirts of town but also a little shocked. Selina had googled the address, and the street view images on Maps didn't look anything like what she was seeing now. It had shown a sleepy little farm community with typical family homes, barns, and outbuildings, along with a lone gas station/repair shop combo, and a small country store. What Selina found instead was a bustling town. She drove past a large feed and seed, a decent-sized grocery store, and a strip center with various shops. There was even a hotel that hadn't shown up on Google called The Pioneer.

The trusty voice of her phone navigator broke through Selina's musings and announced that she would need to turn right in five hundred feet. Her final destination was easy to spot, as a huge commercial complex with a ten-foot-high chain-link fence came into view. The funnel-shaped entry was about a hundred feet across at the front, then narrowed to around forty-five feet with a wide median running down the center. At the end of the long driveway stood an empty guard shack, that was situated far enough away from the motorized gate, for a tractor-trailer to stop and check-in. There was also a keypad intercom unit located on a short pole a few feet behind the shack.

Selina stopped there, but instead of calling for entry, she took a moment to peruse the compound. She could see various vehicles parked in front of a long warehouse. The complex was obviously new and she spotted solar panels lining the roof. There were also solar panels mounted on posts at the top of each gate—that she guessed were powering the openers. To the far left close to the road was another building with its own entry, that looked like an automotive shop with large bay doors and a few commercial vehicles parked outside.

Inside the fence to the right, was a brick office structure with two large trees shading the front. Selina saw a blue SUV parked there with someone leaning against the side. She couldn't make out any details about the person from this distance, but something told her this was Rea. Selina sent off a quick text letting Rea know she was at the gate and saw the person pull out their phone. Yes, this was her.

A second later, Selina's phone pinged with a text—*0626 is the entry code. I'm at the building on the right*—she punched the numbers into the keypad, opening the gate, allowing her entry. Pulling forward, Selina's tires thunked over the metal track before turning to make her way toward the building, where Rea stood waiting.

*****

Rea leaned against the outside of her SUV, eagerly anticipating Selina's arrival. She'd been keyed up ever since receiving the woman's email yesterday, accepting the job. It was totally out of character for Rea to be so jittery about meeting someone, and she'd chalked it up to being on the precipice of having her farm go into full production.

She'd even awakened earlier than usual. There had been no oversleeping like the day before. Rea had put the extra time to good use in her home office, sending off her weekly bookkeeping records and the payroll hours early. Her accountant, Tomás, Matty, and Mia's oldest son, who still lived in California, would be amazed. He usually had to send her an email reminder every Friday.

After finishing her paperwork, Rea had raided the chicken coup for some fresh eggs. She'd cleaned them up, adding some to her fridge, then taking the rest to the RV. When Rea had arrived at the barn this morning, her nervous energy had disturbed Jupe, and he wouldn't let her into his stall. Ultimately, she'd had to go into the paddock to open his outside door. He hadn't come out until he spotted Dolly waiting for him. Rea had spent the next hour cleaning out the stalls, dumping the debris into the composter, then putting down clean wood shavings and fresh straw.

By the time she'd finished, Rea had been dirty and sweaty but much calmer, having worked out some of her angst. Patches had been running around Rea all morning with his own pent up energy making her wonder if he also felt like a big change was coming too.

She'd just finished when she got a text message from Selina. They'd set a time, and Rea had given her the address of the lab. It was a less personal spot to meet for the first time, and when they finished their tour, it would be close to lunch. So, Rea figured she could treat Selina to a good meal at the Hometown Café, before returning to the farm. Then Selina would have the rest of the afternoon to get settled into the RV. Since it was Friday, Rea would have either Saturday or Sunday to take Selina on a tour of her farm before she started work on Monday.

After she'd taken a shower to wash off the smell of the stable, Rea stood gazing at the clothes crammed into her closet, agonizing over what to wear. There was a section filled with slacks, silky shirts, and blazers—business attire, that had been an integral part of her old life. Rea couldn't even fit into most of them anymore, but she hadn't thought to let go of them.

Perhaps it was time to gather them up and take them to one of the women's shelters, so someone in need could get some use out of them. The rest of the closet was filled with jeans, tees, work shirts, and sets of comfy sweats. Rea hadn't had any reason to dress up for the last several years, so now she was stuck. Frustrated with herself, Rea yanked on her nicest pair of jeans, put on a button-down shirt, shoved her feet into a pair of boots, and left the farm.

Her anticipation increased the closer it got to ten. Rea was watching the road when she noticed an unfamiliar deep red pickup with a motorcycle stowed in the bed slowly pass by. She perked up as the back-right blinker came on, and she saw it pull into the driveway before stopping at the gate. Rea observed the truck as it sat there idling. It looked like an F-150 super cab long bed that was packed to the gills with boxes. It sat there for a few minutes longer, then she heard a ping from her phone. It was Selina at the gate, asking for entry. Rea sent her the code and her location at the lab, although she'd bet Selina had already spotted her as she'd waited in the drive. As the truck came through the gate, Rea raised her arm and waved her hand madly in the air. Thinking she probably looked like a loon, she dropped it to her side. For some reason, Rea couldn't name; she felt like something momentous was about to happen.

*****

Selina slowly pulled into the parking spot next to the SUV. In front of her on the shady sidewalk, Rea stood waiting. She got a good look at the redhead as she stepped down from her truck. To Selina's eyes, Rea was immensely attractive with a body style she preferred. She was dressed casually in jeans and a silky looking, forest green button-down shirt that complemented her hazel eyes. A welcoming smile crinkled the lines around them, as her lush lips curled upward into a smile, causing a set of deep dimples to dent her cheeks.

Oh yes, Rea was her kind of woman, Selina thought, as she stopped a foot away. She was working hard to keep from drooling all over the hand, reaching out to greet her before she'd even heard the sultry voice say, "Hello Selina, it's my great pleasure to welcome you to Moirai."

Selina dazedly reached out, taking the other woman's hand, amazed at how perfectly it fit into hers. No rings adorned Rea's fingers, and her unpainted nails were trimmed short. Selina held it for a moment longer than might have been appropriate, then found her voice. "It's a pleasure to be here as well, Ms. Tobin."

"Please call me Rea. I'm not very formal with any of my workers. Most of the men tend to call me Miss, except for my main manager, Matty, who calls me Wonder Woman," she said, chuckling. "I'm to blame for that, though, because I called him Flash first. It's mostly a joke between us. You'll meet him later. Right now, I thought I would get you started by taking you on a tour of your new lab."

"A tour would be great," Selina said as she followed behind Rea, enjoying the sway of her ample hips.

When they arrived at the entry, Rea turned to the left, where an elaborate security panel was embedded in the brick wall. She placed her right thumb on a scanner then looked into a lens about an inch in diameter that was covered by the glass screen. Selina heard the lock on the metal door click. Rea turned back to her, and said as she opened it, "I'll get you programmed in today before we leave. The only people coded to enter the building right now are Matty and me." Rea pointed to an intercom outside the door. "Visitors call from here, so you can buzz them in."

When they stepped inside, Selina was pleased to see several potted plants were placed here and there, giving the space a homey feel. There were two chairs in the small lobby with a few nature landscapes on one wall. There was no carpet, tile, or vinyl. Instead, the floors were a soothing swirl of blue-green colored concrete.

Selina's focus returned to Rea when she said, "Matty has been coming in every week to take care of the plants, rotating them out with the others we keep in the growing room. Now that you will be coming in regularly, I guess you can take over that duty for him."

"Yes, I can definitely take charge of that."

Rea lifted her hand toward the open door on her left. "This will be your office. As you can see, there's an iMac on the desk loaded with all the basic programs. You'll also have an iPad that's been synced with it so you can transfer data easily. The building is wired for satellite internet with a wireless router, providing an excellent signal inside."

Selina stepped inside the large office, taking a brief look around. It was windowless, but natural light was filtering into the room from a skylight in the ceiling. The desk had a matching set of oak bookcases behind it, with the leafy runners from an ivy plant strung out along the top. There were more landscapes hanging on the walls, and a comfy ergonomic chair sat next to the desk. Selina smiled, then nodded at Rea. "This is a very nice office and well-appointed. I also prefer having a Mac to work on, and having an iPad is a definite plus."

"I agree, they are easier to use and maintain."

Next, Rea turned toward an open door on the right of the entry and walked to it. "This is the break room."

Selina followed and looked through the doorway. This room was much smaller but had a fridge, microwave, coffee maker, and sink. A bistro table with two chairs sat off in a corner next to a potted palm tree.

"And this,"—Rea pointed at the other door—"is the bathroom. The next stop will be the lab."

Selina was led down a short hallway to where two doors stood opposite each other. Unlike the solid metal door on the left, the one on the right had a glass window. Rea paused at this one, punched in a code on the keypad, opened the door, and ushered her inside.

Stepping through the door, Selina stopped dead in her tracks, blown away by the spacious interior that seemed to be filled with a plethora of the best lab equipment money could buy. Selina had assumed, incorrectly, that the setup here would be along the same lines of what she'd worked with in her last job—but this lab would please even the maddest of mad scientist. Dazzled, Selina walked around the space, occasionally stopping to run her fingers over a machine, lovingly.

"I think everything you need to do your testing should be here, but we can order anything I missed," Rea said, giving her a searching look.

Selina realized she hadn't said anything since her Mac comment. Her face flamed hotly as a blush lit her cheeks. She couldn't imagine what Rea thought of her at this point. Hopefully, she wasn't regretting hiring someone who didn't appear to be able to even carry on a basic conversation.

Selina was just so awestruck by everything but managed to spit out, "No, no, everything looks fine."

"Okay, ...let's head to the growing room next."

Rea led her to another door at the back, on the left wall. There was no keypad or lock on this one, and when it opened, Selina stepped inside, again freezing in place, agape at what she saw. This room was swamped with sunlight from a much higher peaked ceiling full of glass panels that she guessed were designed to open and close as needed. Misters ran down the length of the room over rolling metal bench tables, but there were also supplemental grow lights extending over them. On one wall was a row of philodendrons, ficus, and small palms trees, like the ones in the lobby. At the back were carts stacked with bags of soil. Next to that were shelves with different sized trays and containers waiting for her to fill them with seedlings. Like everything else Selina had seen, it was top-notch.

Her revolving gaze finally landed on Rea, standing off to the side, waiting patiently while she appraised everything. Though her language skills had undoubtedly taken a hiatus during the tour, Selina managed to utter, in a somewhat stilted tone. "This is an exceptionally professional setup," before her voice fled once again.

"Uhm…I'm glad it meets with your approval," Rea answered rather haltingly. "Of course, just like with the lab, if there's anything you need that's not here, it can be ordered."

Rea arched a brow, and her eyes probed Selina's before dropping them to her phone. "It's after eleven, how would you feel about having an early lunch at our local café before we head to the farm?"

Selina was famished, so she nodded eagerly. "That would be nice." Maybe over lunch, she'd find a way to string more than a few words together at a time. Selina felt like she was making a terrible first impression, but the combination of the beautiful woman conducting the tour, and this phenomenal facility had robbed her of her usual poise.

Rea led the way out but stopped in another room, just a bit larger than a walk-in closet. She explained to Selina it housed the security system, router, and other control panels for the building's mechanical equipment. Rea had Selina key in a personal access code for the doors first. Then she stared into a goggle-like apparatus that mapped her irises, before finally registering her thumbprint for the outside scanner. Selina could understand the need for heightened security—the lab was chocked full of some very pricey equipment.

When they exited the building, Rea stopped underneath a tree and pointed at the warehouse facility. "That's our collection and distribution center. All our produce ships out of there along with the other growers I've made agreements with. Their crops will also need to be sample tested like ours are as well. I won't support any growers who are using unsafe pesticides or fertilizers, by allowing them to use our facilities. Those people can find another way to get their crops to market," she stated adamantly.

Selina's opinion of Rea went up several more notches, and she spontaneously spouted out, "I love the way you think."

A shy smile bloomed on Rea's face, and her chin dipped a little. Looking up at Selina through her long lashes, she said, "Why, thank you. That was a very nice compliment." Rea shuffled her feet nervously before turning toward their vehicles. "Are you ready to follow me?"

Oh boy, was she. "Yes, lead the way."

Selina wondered as she got back into her truck what had prompted Rea's jitters a few moments before. Between the two of them, she thought she had a better reason to be anxious, because, after all, she was on Rea's home turf. Oh well, hopefully, things would smooth out over lunch. Rea backed out first, then Selina slotted in behind her for the drive to the café.

*****

From the moment Selina had stepped out of her truck, Rea had been fascinated by the statuesque woman. She judged her to be around five-ten, lean, but with an athletic build. Her blue-black hair was loose today, hanging straight down the middle of her back, almost to her derriere. She was dressed in a nice pair of khaki pants, with a silky looking light blue blouse tucked into them. A hand-tooled leather belt accentuated her small waist, drawing Rea's eyes to the feminine flair of her hips.

Rea had managed to find her voice holding out her hand to greet Selina. She'd noted the turquoise bracelet adorning one wrist with a matching ring on her right hand. A hand that was soft, with long supple fingers, and well-trimmed nails. There had been something vaguely familiar about her, making Rea wonder if they hadn't met at some point in college after all.

Selina hadn't said much during the tour of the building. Her comments had been short and polite, but the silvery tone of her voice had struck a chord inside Rea. She hadn't been able to read anything in the impassive face that seemed to have only a cursory interest in the equipment. Rea had put a lot of effort in setting up the lab, but if it had been Sherry standing there, she wouldn't have been able to contain her excitement.

They'd finally finished the tour and taken care of setting up Selina's access, then exited the building to head to lunch. Rea had pointed to the warehouse, explaining how it was operated, and when she'd finished, Selina's face finally showed its first bit of animation. Her blue eyes had brightened with approval and complimented Rea by saying that she loved the way she thought.

For some reason, Selina's positive praise had warmed her, and she'd colored a little in embarrassment. The woman was captivating and physically alluring. Rea worried that Selina might have detected her frank appraisal of her beauty. Based on their limited conversation inside the lab, she got the impression Selina wanted to keep their interactions more professional. Well, Rea could do that. She was just glad that she'd have a few minutes on the drive over to the café to settle herself down.

Chapter Eleven

Insights

Selina had been following Rea for a couple of miles when she pulled into a parking lot in front of a quaint structure. It was built to resemble a large, two-story house with a wide porch at the entry. Just above that was a sign with a chalkboard motif with the name Hometown Café painted on it. Selina could tell the building was new, like many of the others she'd seen. It seemed to her that Rea's little enterprise was having a real impact on the area, and the town was growing.

When they stepped inside, Selina saw there were a dozen or so customers in the place, some sharing a meal, but others sitting on their own. All of a sudden, it went dead silent, except for the sounds emanating from the kitchen, as every eye in the place turned toward them. Selina felt self-conscious, and her posture stiffened under their scrutiny.

"Rea," a voice called out. Selina saw a matronly woman with a rolling gait, her hair in a tight bun, heading their way. Her gunmetal gray eyes narrowed, as her head swiveled around the room, landing on one person after another, till they all refocused on their meals and conversations.

The woman wrapped Rea up in a brief but fierce hug. "How have you been, sugar, and who is your new friend?" she said, turning a critical eye toward Selina. She felt like she was being sized up under that steely gaze.

With a hand out pointing toward her, Rea answered. "This is Selina Thorson, my newest employee, and a botanist. With her expert help, we should be able to gear up to full production this season."

"Then, welcome to Moirai, Selina. I'm Emma, the chief cook and bottle washer for all these galloots that come in here to scarf up my food. Everything is homemade, mostly from my granny's recipes, so set yourselves down, and I'll get you a menu," she said, somewhat brusquely. Then she marched back into the kitchen before Selina could even respond.

Rea led her away from the entrance, and several people said hello as they passed. Rea returned their greetings but didn't stop to chat. She picked a table off in a corner far enough away to allow them some privacy, and Selina was relieved to be out of their direct line of sight.

Rea broke the tension. "Sorry about that. In a small town like this, anyone they've never seen before garners a lot of attention. You should see how they reacted to me when I hit town. You'd have thought they were experiencing an alien invasion," she explained, a sincere smile lighting up her face.

"It's fine, Rea. It's not the first time I've been stared at before, and it probably won't be the last. But it's been a while."

Nothing more was said as Emma approached their table with a single laminated sheet in her hand that she gave to Selina. She hadn't provided one to Rea, which spoke of a real familiarity with the place. Emma put down two sets of flatware, rolled up in a white linen napkin, and a full cup of coffee in front of Rea, with two of those little tubs of creamer on the saucer, then she turned to Selina. "Look the menu over and see if there is anything you find appetizing. The special of the day is Chicken and Dumplings. You want coffee, tea, or water?"

"I'll have water to start with, thank you," Selina replied, sheepishly. Without another word, Emma whirled and marched away. The woman sure did have a direct communication style, Selina thought.

She looked across at Rea and saw her lips trying to pull out of a grimace or maybe a grin before she said, "Don't mind her, Emma's a little crusty around the edges until she gets to know you. She and her wife are good people. They used to run a food truck in downtown Semi Valley, and my office building was one of their stops."

Wow, an old lesbian couple in town—that boded well. Selina was curious. "How did they end up here?"

"The majority of our seasonal workers are single men. I wanted to make sure they had at least one substantial meal each day. I thought food trucks might be the answer, but needed advice before moving forward, so I called them up. We got to talking about all my plans and what I was putting together out here. I happened to mention there wasn't even a restaurant in town, and voila, they packed up and moved here."

Selina suspected there was more to the story, but before she could ask, they were interrupted by the approach of an older woman with beautiful coffee-colored skin. Her head was covered with a cascade of tiny braids with colorful beads woven into the ends, that clicked together as she moved. She was carrying a glass of ice water and wearing an apron like Emma's. But unlike Emma, this woman had a toothy grin on her face.

She stopped at the table, set down the water, then held out her hand to Selina. "Hi, I'm Durene, but you can call me Reenie, everyone else does. My Emma told me you are going to be working with our Rea." Though her English was perfect, Selina heard the lilt and cadence of a Jamaican accent. She took the proffered hand, grateful that Reenie was more friendly than her wife.

"It's nice to meet you. Yes, I was lucky enough to land a job with her."

She gave Selina another smile, then turned and trained her big, brown eyes on Rea. "Hello to you as well. What can I get you ladies for lunch?"

Oh shit. Selina hadn't even looked at the menu yet, but then remembered the chicken and dumplings. "I'll have the special."

"Make that two, Reenie. You know I'd never miss out on Emma's dumplings. But can you bring us an extra hunk or two of cornbread and lots of your special butter," she coaxed in a wheedling voice of a child trying to persuade a parent to let her stay up an hour past bedtime.

"Sure thing, Rea. I'll be back in a jiffy. Do you need more coffee?" After Rea shook her head no, she turned to Selina. "Can I get you anything to drink besides water…sweet tea, or maybe a soda?"

"I'd love a big glass of cold milk with my meal if you have it."

Rea perked up. "Oh, that sounds good, Selina. Can I have a glass too, Reenie?"

"Absolutely. Milk is good for the bones." Her braids clicked together as she turned away and zipped off toward the kitchen.

"You're in for a treat, Selina. They are awesome cooks, but their cornbread and whipped honey butter are to die for. I try to limit my visits to once or twice a week, or I'd pack on even more unwanted pounds."

Was that a dig about her own weight, Selina wondered?

Their conversation was cut short when Reenie appeared carrying a large tray. She set it down on one of those fold-out stands and started unloading it. Two giant steaming bowls of dumplings were set down, then smaller ones with fresh green peas. Next came a basket with four large squares of cornbread and a dish full of light golden colored butter. "I'll be right back with your milk, dig in."

Everything smelled enticing. Selina unrolled her napkin, setting the flatware to the side then placed it in her lap. Picking up the spoon, she took her first bite of the creamy dish in front of her. She might have moaned a little, it was that good. A few minutes later, a glass of milk slid into view along with an empty saucer-sized plate. Selina looked up, and Reenie was staring down at her bowl, which was already half empty.

"You like?" Reenie's beaming smile was dazzling. "My Emma's a good cook, which is how she won my heart."

"It's excellent. Best, I ever tasted. Give her my compliments," Selina replied sincerely.

"Will do. Enjoy ladies, and just wave me over if you need anything else," she offered in parting then sashayed away.

All talking ceased as they both concentrated on consuming the sumptuous meal before them. By the time they'd finished off the last two squares of cornbread slathered in sweet butter, Selina felt ready to pop. Rea was right, this was one of the best meals she'd had in a long time.

The place had filled up quite a bit since they'd sat down, and Selina took a moment to look around, noticing for the first time its down-home atmosphere. Red checkered curtains were drawn back from the windows, sporting slatted wood blinds. The flower prints hanging on the walls added even more touches of color. There was quite a mix of patrons in the place, and she spied a young Hispanic waitress weaving her way between tables with a tray of food.

Rea had caught her interested gaze. "That's Carmen. She's the wife of one of my managers. She's helping out here till I start running the food trucks. She and four of the other women take turns serving here for extra money. Most have extended family in Mexico, so they send a lot of the money they earn back there. Almost all of my employees are Hispanic, and they are either legal immigrants or have documented work visas. The seasonal ones are all migrant workers that usually return home after harvest time."

Rea gave her a detailed explanation of how they were paid and housed, which accounted for the hotel she'd seen. It was one more thing setting Rea apart from any other commercial grower she'd ever heard of. Selina was willing to bet there wasn't another operation like this in the whole country.

She felt something more was driving Rea's endeavors. Making money didn't seem to be her main priority, and Selina wondered what it was. The cash outlay for the lab and warehouse alone would take at least a decade or more to recoup if everything went perfectly. Weather, crop yields, product demand, and fluctuating market prices could make or break any farm.

The giant corporate ones made out better, but the family farms were dying out fast because they were finding it increasingly hard to compete. There were definitely easier ways to make a living that also made bigger profits too. To Selina, farming was a labor of love, not to mention dedication. There was so much more to this woman than met the eye, she thought, and what was before her eyes was already remarkable.

"I guess we should head home now, so you can get unpacked. I planned on putting you in my RV there. It's going to be further away from the lab, but I thought you would prefer a more private space, instead of being housed at the hotel with the men. If not, I can take you over there and have them assign you one of the suites with a kitchenette."

Selina was surprised and pleased at Rea's consideration. She hadn't given much thought to where she'd be living, even though her contract said housing would be provided. Yes, she'd much prefer living near Rea.

"That would be wonderful, and I accept the hospitality of your offer to live in the RV."

"You're more than welcome. Let's go, then."

They'd just risen and pushed their chairs back under the table when Emma exited the kitchen. She headed directly for them, carrying a small take out container, then stopped, handing it over to Rea.

"Can you drop this off to Mia? It's some cobbler. She sent me six quarts of blueberries yesterday with a note that said they came out of the greenhouse. Mia's a sneaky sort, though. She always sends stuff in with Matty or one of the ladies, and none of them will take my money—so she'll have to put up with me sending food back to her." With a huff, she turned then went back into the kitchen.

Selina walked toward the register, reaching toward her pocket for her wallet when Rea put a hand on her arm.

"They won't let me pay, and since you are with me, they won't take your money either. We send them things like fresh produce, eggs, and fruit, so it's a little like a barter situation. We both get something good, and neither of us is out anything but a little of our labor."

Selina thought it was the best type of system, where everyone helped each other out.

Standing outside their vehicles, Rea directed her, "If you'll follow me, I'm only six miles away, so we'll be there in about ten minutes."

Selina got into her truck and happily trailed Rea out of town.

*****

Rea thought lunch had gone much better. Selina seemed to relax after her initial stiffness upon entering the café. She understood how disconcerting it was to be thrust into an unfamiliar environment. The small-town stare down and the greeting from Emma hadn't helped either, but Reenie's open, friendly manner had made up for it.

Rea had carried on most of the conversation during lunch, much like she had during the tour of the lab, but Selina had perked up and even asked a few questions. Perhaps she was just a quieter person, much like Sherry had been, measuring her words out like ingredients in a recipe. Rea had always been the outgoing one, meeting and conversing with people easily, whereas Sherry tended to sit back and observe their interactions. Maybe it was a botanist thing. One trait Rea did share with her, however, was a healthy appetite, but Selina's body didn't show it.

Rea turned off the county road and onto a wide gravel drive running between two rock pillars. They were topped by a long rectangular sign that's top gradually rose in a parabolic curve with the sun sitting dead center, shining down on verdant green fields. The name Agnatural Farms in raised letters gleamed white against the deep green. It was her company logo and had been designed by one of her friends. Good thing too, because Rea had zero artistic ability.

She pulled up to the garage at the back of her house, and using her remote, opened both doors. Rea drove into the right side, leaving the left for Selina, but noted she stopped outside the door. It dawned on her; it was because the motorcycle wouldn't clear the door and would have to be unloaded first. Exiting her SUV, Rea made her way over to Selina, who was standing at the back of her truck, gazing around. She'd give a lot to know what Selina's first impression was of her farm. When those intense blue eyes swung toward her, elation seemed to paint their gleaming surface. Rea hoped so, as she was awfully proud of her home.

"I've got a ramp in the shed that you can use to unload your motorcycle. We utilize them to move our ATVs when we take them in for maintenance, and there's also room inside to store your bike. I'll give you a remote that will open all three doors." Rea pointed to the left. "As you can see, the RV is there. I'll get you a key for it, but right now it's unlocked. It's stocked with all the basics to get you started, but if you should need anything right away that's not there, come ask me. I might not have it, but if I do, it's yours. I'm going to leave you to unload and get settled in. Oh, and I will also need to bring my dog out in a bit, so I can introduce you two. He can be a little standoffish at first, but he's a good sort and smart as a whip."

"Thanks, Rea. I have a ramp buried underneath my junk, but I'll need to unload some of this stuff first to get my bike down. I'll take you up on your offer to store it in your ATV shed, however, and I'd also love to meet your fur baby." Selina beamed. "I'm pretty good with animals, so I'm sure we will get along fine."

"Okay, I'll leave you to it and be back in a while."

Rea pivoted, striding toward her house when the thunk of the tailgate being dropped brought her head around. She gazed back at the woman who would be close at hand and could perhaps become more than an employee. She could use a friend who shared her vision for the farm, but also someone she knew understood her lifestyle.

Chapter Twelve

Settling In

Selina enjoyed the drive to Rea's farm, watching the fields flashing by her window in various stages of production. Some were already planted, and green shoots could be seen erupting through the mounds of soil in straight rows, while others were fallow awaiting their chosen seed. Finally, as they turned down a narrow county road, the fields she passed were undisturbed, biding their time until the steel teeth of a tractor came to rip open their skins. Selina thought these must be Rea's fields, and they were waiting for her to shape them.

Rea's SUV slowed, turning left onto a gravel road with an eye-catching sign arching over the entry. Selina recognized that is was a replica of the company logo she'd seen on the letterhead of her employment contract. It seemed much more vibrant now with the clear blue sky as a backdrop.

The road split, and they veered to the right, where Selina could barely make out the shape of a house through some trees. Off to the side of the left fork sat a diminutive house with a white picket fence, and on the land in between, stood a massive greenhouse that looked to be around eight thousand square feet. She observed a narrow row of solar panels running down the center of its arched roof with a wind turbine at one end.

Selina slowed her truck as Rea's house came into view, it wasn't what she was expecting. She would have guessed that someone as wealthy as Rea would live in something more modern and upscale—but the home before her was reminiscent of the ones that graced old historic New England farmsteads. Like those turn of the century homes, this one had their typical clapboard siding and wraparound porches that were accented with brackets and spandrels. The house itself was a pale, yellow, butter color, but the porch floors and the trims were painted hunter green like the metal roof. Barely visible from the driveway, a red brick chimney jutted up above the bottom of the roofline on the right side of the structure. Several large pecan trees shaded the yard, and two rows of hedge roses ran along both sides of the front porch steps. They weren't blooming yet but would add nice touches of color when they did. It had grace and beauty, much like its owner did, and Selina wondered if Rea was sharing it with a significant other.

As she rounded to the rear corner of the house, about fifty yards away, Selina saw a huge two-car garage. Sprouting out like wings on the left was a large carport, with an RV parked underneath, and to the right was an attached building with a smaller overhead door. Rea slowed as both garage doors opened, and she pulled into the right side. Selina was happy to see the left one was vacant, apparently awaiting her use. If Rea were married or had someone living with her, that wouldn't be the case. She stopped outside the door so she could unload her bike first. It would never make it under the door.

Selina stepped out onto the running board of her truck, taking a moment to look around before stepping down to the ground. There was a lot to take in, and she was eager to explore, but it would have to wait till later. Rea approached her with a welcoming smile, offering her the use of a ramp and space in the shed to store her bike. She declined one but accepted the other, glad her precious cycle wouldn't be exposed to the weather. Rea also explained about the supplies, keys, and her dog, which she would introduce her to later. Selina was happy at the thought of living around a dog again. She hadn't had a pet of her own in years. Her last few girlfriends hadn't been animal people—which should have been a big clue that they weren't right for her. Rea left her alone to start unpacking, and Selina couldn't help but admire the arresting figure as she made her way to her house.

Dropping the tailgate, she removed the first box and carried it toward the RV, where it sat on a large concrete pad, with a patio cover extending out past the front by a good twenty feet. There was a short, round, cast iron, slate topped table with a fire pit at its center, filled with sticks of wood. Three outdoor chairs surrounded it, creating an inviting spot to lounge around on a chilly night. A stainless-steel propane grill, with a three-foot square butcher block table, was placed next to it. Selina was delighted. She could easily picture herself sitting out here, enjoying a beer, while she cooked up a meal.

To the right, Selina saw that two wide wooden steps were placed at the door of the RV for easy entry and egress. She rested the box on her hip, and using her free hand, pulled open the door and went inside. Selina's first impression of the space was one of luxury. Instead of carpeting, the floors were a rich, honey oak that matched the cabinets in the modest-sized kitchen. The counters were granite with a white porcelain drop sink sitting directly under a small window that looked out onto the patio. There was a double burner ceramic cooktop range, and a microwave sat on a shelf between two cabinets at eye level.

Selina gaze zeroed in on the Bunn coffee maker in the corner with a can of Maxwell House French Roast sitting beside it and smiled. After all, to her, morning coffee was a vital necessity. She glanced to the right where she saw a slim refrigerator, about two feet wide and a little over five feet tall, was tucked into its own alcove. Selina put down the box on the counter and opened the fridge door, finding it stocked with the basics, but was ecstatic to find a six-pack of Shiner Bock on one shelf. She'd have to bend down and kiss Rea's feet for this.

She entered a short hallway with four doors. Three were opposite each other, and one was at the very end. She investigated the one on the left first. It was a petite bathroom but had a full-sized tub shower combo. A mirrored medicine cabinet was mounted over a pedestal sink that sat next to the commode. The walls were painted a lovely turquoise blue with white trim. Selina stopped momentarily to admire several tropical beach prints that adorned one wall and wondered if they were from places Rea had visited.

Of the two doors on the right, one held a stackable washer and dryer, a bonus in most RV's, and the other was to a tiny linen closet. The final door opened into the compact bedroom. It had a queen-sized platform bed with drawers on both sides. It sat below a window bracketed by oak built-ins. The blinds were closed, but

Selina guessed it would look out onto the back of Rea's property when opened. There was a set of accordion doors to a closet on one wall, and opposite that, was an alcove with a dresser. A flat-screen TV was mounted above it, and when tilted down, would be easily viewable from the bed.

She returned through the kitchen, running her hand over the dinette tabletop with its cushioned bench seats, as she made her way over to a cozy seating area. A comfy looking light gray loveseat with matching chair was situated in the corner, and another TV mounted on a movable arm was positioned flat against the wall, capping off the inviting space. Selina bet the couch would also make into another bed, but since she didn't plan to have any guests, she wasn't concerned about that.

Selina exited the RV, making her way back to her truck. Within ten minutes, she'd moved all her personal items inside, leaving only her camping gear and her bike left to unload.

*****

Entering through the back door, Patches darted toward Rea, his rump vibrating as his tail waved in greeting. She'd locked down his doggie door before leaving this morning, to keep him from flying out when she got home with Selina and could control their initial introduction.

Rea leaned down, stroking his head, and said, "Hey, little man. There's someone I want to introduce you to. I've got a feeling you two will hit it off, but let's give her fifteen or twenty minutes to get some of her things unloaded, okay? Besides, I need to use the restroom and check my email anyway."

In answer, he jumped up, putting his front paws against her, trying to push her back toward the door. Laughing at his antics, Rea snapped her fingers, signaling him down. "No. You'll just have to be patient."

Rea walked into the kitchen with Patches following behind her. Stopping, she eyed him, then opened the paw-printed canister, pulled out a treat, and handed it to him. "Here, this should appease you while I take care of things...*I'll be back,*" Rea said, in her best Arnold Schwarzenegger impersonation. She laughed as he snatched it from her hand then turned into the laundry room, probably to enjoy it inside his kennel or hide it to snack on later.

Within fifteen minutes, Rea had finished up with things in her office and wandered back into the kitchen. She looked through the window over the sink and could see Selina was backing the cycle off her truck.

"Okay, Patches, let's go, but remember no growling, give the woman a chance." Rea stopped in the mudroom on her way out and picked up the RV key and remote that she'd left next to the radio base station earlier.

Opening the door, Patches shot past Rea with a yip and made a beeline toward Selina. She hurried after her canine companion but stopped short, stunned by what was transpiring before her eyes. Selina was crouched next to her bike, one knee on the ground with her hand out, and Patches was sniffing it. He never got within ten feet of anyone new, but there he was within arm's reach of the woman. His tail wagged as if signaling Rea to come over.

Somewhat in awe, she approached the two. Patches was next to Selina's bent knee, allowing her to rub along his head, ears, and cheeks. He had never done that with a total stranger before. It always took repeated visits by someone to even keep him from snarling at them. The only others he showed any affection for were Matty and Mia. To have him immediately take to Selina was shocking.

Well, well, well, Selina had said she was good with animals, but this was more than good, it was astounding. Rea wondered what kind of special magic this woman possessed because Selina had already charmed her dog, and she was starting to feel a little captivated herself.

*****

Pulling out her ramp, Selina secured it to the tailgate then gently rolled her cycle out of the bed. She'd just lowered the kickstand when the sound of a yip greeted her ears and knew she was about to meet Rea's dog. Selina knelt down next to the bike, holding onto the seat with one hand and put the other out in greeting.

A knee-high, multi-colored dog of indeterminate background, approached Selina with his ears slightly flattened, but he slowly moved toward her. In her gentlest voice, she enticed him over, "Hey there, little dude, I'm glad to meet a sweet pup like you." Selina slowly reached forward, presenting her hand for him to sniff, which he cautiously did. His ears perked up, so she turned her palm over to pet and fondle him. "I know your mom was worried you wouldn't like me, but I felt certain we would get along,"—her voice dropped to a whisper—"because we seem to have similar taste in women. I think your mom is pretty sweet and very sexy. A good combo, wouldn't you say?" His lips pulled back, in what Selina interpreted as his doggie grin, then licked her hand, presumably in agreement.

She looked up and caught sight of Rea standing stone still, giving them both a most perplexed look. With a final pat on Patches' head, Selina rose slowly, and this seemed to break Rea free of her trance.

"I guess you two have already made friends, but I should at least introduce you. Selina, this is Patches, my fur baby, as you called him. And Patches, this is our new botanist, Selina." Rea smiled at them both. "I can see I had nothing to worry about with you two, but he's never let a stranger anywhere near him before. Saying you're good with animals seems like an understatement if you can make friends with my dog this fast."

"I grew up on my grandparents' ranch with all kinds of critters, and it seems to come naturally to me. My grandmother always joked that I'd used up all my patience on them, and didn't have any leftover for people—so it was a trade-off of sorts," Selina confessed.

"You should feel right at home here, then." Rea pointed to the right. "As you can see over that way, I have a huge fenced-in area with a coop for my chickens, and over behind the garage, is a barn where I keep my horses."

Horses! Oh my god, she has horses! Selina's excitement bubbled to the surface, and she had to ask, "Would you allow me the opportunity to ride occasionally? I sure have missed it. The only opportunities I've gotten to get on the back of a horse have been during my visits home, and the last time was almost two years ago. Before I left for college, I'd spend at least an hour or so every day in the saddle, when school was in session, and even longer during the summers."

"I actually have two. I ride my mare, Dolly, several times a week, but Jupiter,"—a sad look crossed her face—"the stallion I adopted is still settling in. He came to me through a rescue organization. He arrived emaciated, with definite signs of abuse and neglect. In the last six months, he's healed physically, but so far, I haven't been able to get him to trust me enough to start working with him. I'd be willing to share my riding time with Dolly, though."

"I'd love that, thanks," Selina said gratefully.

Rea handed her a door key. "This one, of course, is for the RV." Then she handed Selina a keychain fob. "And this three-button remote will open both garage doors and the one for the shed. If you don't have it with you, the keypads on the doors all open with 0626, along with any of the combo locks here."

Selina remembered it also opened the gate at the warehouse and wondered about the significance of the numbers. She decided to dig for a little information. "Is that your birthday or maybe someone close to you?"

"No, but I thought you might recognize it." Rea's voice wavered. She drew in a deep breath, then continued. "It was the date D.O.M.A. was declared unconstitutional, and I'd finally been allowed to legally marry my partner."

Selina was glad Rea's back was turned to her, so she wouldn't see her fist-pumping in the air. *She's a lesbian! Thank the stars.* This was now officially the best job she'd ever gotten.

She sobered quickly, though. Where was the wife? Selina glanced at the left hand that was gently swaying back and forth as Rea walked. She couldn't see any evidence that Rea had worn a ring—no finger dent, and the skin was all uniform in color. Was she divorced? Selina had registered Rea's somber tone as she'd spoken about her marriage, and seen the defeated slump of her shoulders as well. A little voice inside—that often spoke to her—was telling Selina that Rea's wife was no longer among the living.

*****

Rea's body felt heavy, and she swallowed hard, trying to force down the lump rising in her throat, as she answered Selina's question about the code. Yes, she had lost Sherry, but they'd had almost twenty-five years together, and the world had changed enough during that time that they'd finally won the right to wed. That had been one of the highpoints in a lifetime filled with love and happy memories. She wasn't so self-centered that she didn't realize she'd been lucky to find someone as special as Sherry—not everyone did.

Rea turned her back to Selina and said, "Follow me so we can get your bike put up."

As she led the way, Rea digested the little snippet Selina divulged about her life and the fact she'd grown up on her grandparents' ranch. There was probably some tragedy in Selina's past that was tied to that. Usually, when a child was raised by extended family members, there was a heartbreaking reason behind it. Rea decided that whatever the circumstances had been, Selina had grown past it, as her features had come to life when she talked about her home.

When she'd heard about her horses, the smile gracing Selina's face had widened, showing perfect white teeth, and there'd been an answering sparkle in her eyes. Rea was more than willing to share her rides with Dolly if it would make this woman happy.

"If you'll hit the bottom button on the remote, it will open this shed door," she instructed. "When we get your bike stored, I'll take you back to the barn so you can meet my favorite lady and her skittish counterpart."

"No sooner said than done, Rea."

As Selina rolled the bike past her, she noted it was an older model. Rea didn't know anything about motorcycles, but anyone with eyes could see it was unique and expertly maintained. There had to be a story behind this treasure and Rea wanted to find out what it was, so she prompted, "That's a nice motorcycle, but it looks like an antique."

"Chief?" Selina stroked the leather seat affectionately. "I wouldn't call him an antique, but he's a classic Chief Indian motorcycle, hence the name. My grandfather bought him new in 1946, after the war. Neither my Grandfather or my Great-Uncle Dóntso would talk about that time much. Pop Pop was tasked with protecting Uncle Don, who was a Navajo Code Talker, so they were right in the thick of things. But he did tell me once that a motorcycle like this one saved both their lives."

Rea noticed Selina's eyes took on an unfocused look. "One of my earliest memories was of him, slowly driving me around the yard as I clung to his back like a monkey. In later years, after I'd gone to live with them, he not only taught me to ride but how to fix and maintain it too. No one else was ever allowed to ride him except me. My grandparents had three daughters but no sons. So, I guess because I loved this hunk of metal as much as he did, he left Chief to me."

Rea knew from the way Selina's voice had deepened it was more than just a hunk of metal to her; it was a link to family. Selina parked it toward the back, then looked about, her eyes halting as they passed over Rea's ATV. "That's a Yamaha Grizzly, right?"

"Yes, it is. I bought six of them over a year ago. One for Matty and one for each of my three other managers, then this one for me. We also keep a spare which is at the shop right now being serviced. They make it easy to get around on the farm and are more fuel-efficient than going everywhere in trucks. I've been thinking of replacing them with electric UTVs to reduce our carbon footprint even more."

"I admire that. I noticed you are also using solar and wind power here. That is notably progressive and forward-thinking." Selina's tone and expression conveyed honest approval.

"I'd like to be able to take all the credit, but the truth is most of these ideas came from my wife. She was dismayed at the continued use of fossil fuels when there were better alternatives available, especially with the adverse effects it was having on climate change. She said it wasn't a perfect solution because of battery recycling and disposal, but hoped in the future there would be even better substitutes found."

"Oh, so your wife is an environmentalist, then?"

"The correct wording would be—was an environmentalist—she passed away. But she had first-hand experience that the most damaging things being done to the planet, were being driven by greed." Rea felt the old anger at her wife's death bubble up inside her.

"My sincere condolences for your loss," Selina said, and the look in her eyes conveyed true sadness. "Then my hat's off to your wife. It sounds like she was one hell of a woman. Was she by any chance Native American?"

"No, but she did have one thing in common with you; she was a botanist. So, any environmental repercussions affecting the earth's plant life concerned her, and she wanted to do everything she could to minimize it. It was part of her dream for this place, and she left me to carry it out," Rea said with a sigh. The light brush of fingertips along her arm had Rea glancing up, and she searched the blue ones looking back at her with such sympathy.

"Again, it sounds like she was an amazing woman."

"Thank you." Rea turned away exiting the shed quickly. The solicitous touch and comfort she'd felt from Selina's gesture had unsettled her. Rea hadn't meant to offer up so much personal information to a virtual stranger, but there was something about Selina that drew her in. It must have been how Patches felt too. She was highly interested to see how Jupe would react. With that in mind, she turned back to Selina and said, "Let's head to the barn."

Chapter Thirteen

Making Friends

As Selina followed behind Rea, she was processing what she'd just learned about her new employer. She'd guessed correctly, and Rea's wife was dead. Selina's momentary elation at finding out Rea was a lesbian, was tempered by the empathy she felt for her over the loss of her wife. As Rea continued to talk, the discernable grief in her voice had morphed into anger then a barely suppressed rage. Selina hadn't missed the watery look in her eyes from unshed tears that spoke of a hurt that hadn't healed. Though curious to know more, there had been no way for her to ask—they didn't know each other well enough.

All those thoughts were chased out of her brain as they approached the barn. Selina could tell the structure was old but had been skillfully maintained. She guesstimated the paddock was around two acres and had a windmill near in the middle. About six feet away sat a galvanized stock tank on a steel stand that kept it off the ground. It was enclosed with a relatively new three-rail wood fence that started at the front corners of the barn and had a gate on each side. The barn itself was painted a reddish-brown with a green metal roof like the house, and the ever-present solar panels were in evidence.

But what took Selina's breath away was the sight of the two horses standing toward the back of the paddock, with their heads up, ears cocked forward watching from a distance as they approached. Rea opened the gate so they could go through then closed it. A piercing whistle made Selina's head whip around to find Rea removing her thumb and forefinger from her mouth. That must have been the signal they'd been waiting for. In a matter of seconds, a big, red quarter horse started trotting their way, followed more slowly by a stallion sporting a beautiful blanket of spots across his rump.

"Oh, Rea, you have an Appaloosa! They are fine animals. Some people say they are a little high-strung, but really, they are just more discerning and cautious till they get to know you," Selina said, as the stallion slowly approached them.

He stopped about ten yards away, blowing out a nervous breath as he bobbed his head up and down. She looked him straight in the eye as she moved forward slowly. When Selina got closer, she lowered her voice and crooned soothingly, "Yá'át'ééh Jupiter. What a fine beastie you are." He restlessly shifted his weight from side to side, then stilled. "Shik'is, you have nothing to fear here," and Selina reached forward to gently lay a hand on his neck.

*****

Rea stood off to the side, draped across Dolly's back, watching a miracle take place in front of her eyes. She wasn't close enough to hear everything Selina was saying but had caught a few unfamiliar words that she guessed were more than likely Diné. But whether it was the words or the woman speaking them, Jupe was actually letting Selina touch him. He hadn't voluntarily permitted anyone that close to him before. His rescuers had to sedate him for transport, and so did the vet every time she visited.

Making friends with Patches right off the bat was one thing, but her interactions with Jupe went way beyond that. This woman had an extraordinary gift.

In a slightly louder voice, Selina beckoned her. "Hey Rea, come on over and give this good boy a few pats. I think he is ready to be a little more friendly."

Rea left Dolly's side, gingerly making her way over to Selina, who at his head and continued her calming caresses. Jupe stood steady, and Rea placed a tentative hand on his neck, stroking him gently. Amazed, she turned her admiring eyes on Selina. They stood close enough together that she could feel Selina's body heat and caught a hint of some spicy fragrance that she wore. There was a controlled energy about Selina that she'd somehow shared with Jupe. They both seemed to epitomize an untamed spirit that called out to the other and, strangely enough, engendered something in her as well.

Rea decided Dolly must have wanted to get in on the petting action when she nudged Selina in the back. She kept one hand on Jupe's neck to keep him steady then turned to Dolly. "Hey there, beautiful girl, you want some loving too, do you? Your mom sure has good taste in horseflesh. You two make a fine pair, and when the time comes, I bet you two will produce an awesome foal."

They stood in companionable silence for a few minutes more before Selina turned to gaze into Rea's eyes and said, "Give me a little time to show Jupiter he's safe here, and I think he will let me ride him. Then when he gets used to it, I bet he will let you ride him too."

"Of that, I have no doubt, Selina," Rea said emphatically. "You managed in ten minutes what no one else could in the last six months. You truly have a special touch, and I'm ecstatic to see Jupe is letting you get close. I think he gets lonely, especially when I take Dolly for a ride without him, and just like with people, he needs the closeness."

Rea saw Selina's eyes deepen in understanding. "You're right, everyone needs it. Animals seemed to be the best though, at giving love and comfort, without expecting anything in return, except to be given the same thing." A shadow of sadness passed over her features but disappeared just as quickly as it had appeared.

To break the seriousness of the moment, Rea asked, "We have several hours till it gets dark, how about I take you for a drive to show you some of my farm?"

"Sounds like a good plan to me. If you wouldn't mind detouring by the store after the tour so I can pick up a few things, I'd be grateful. I think I would like to try out the grill I saw on the patio."

"Absolutely. Let's go."

*****

With a last few pats, they bid farewell to the horses, left the paddock, and walked back to the garage. Selina had forgotten about her camping gear in the back of her truck that she hadn't unloaded. "Hey, Rea. Do you have someplace I can put this stuff? It's just my tent, stove, and other camping gear, so it doesn't need to be stored anyplace special."

"Sure, there is a storage closet in the back of the shed with plenty of room for it. Let me help you put it away before we leave."

They got it all moved in a few minutes, and Selina put her truck inside the garage, while Rea backed out her SUV. She sat behind the wheel, smiling at Selina as she made her way to the passenger side of the Toyota Highlander. Selina took note it was the hybrid edition. Again, Rea had chosen a more expensive option to cut her carbon footprint a little. That had her looking back at her gas guzzler truck, making her realize that Rea was living a more balanced life than she'd been. Selina had also noted when they were returning from the barn that on the backside of the garage roof, there were rows of solar panels installed there. She bet herself that there were also some on Rea's house as well, but she hadn't seen them on way drive-in.

As they drove up the road, Rea pointed to the right. "That's one of our five greenhouses. They provide enough produce for our needs and the surplus we sell to the local store or gift to our neighbors. On the other side is Matty and Mia's house but I'll introduce you to them later. If we tried to stop now, Mia wouldn't let us go, then we'd never get to tour anything," she said with a beaming smile. "She thinks it's her mission to oversee my life and feed me till I pop."

As they drove in and out of the different parcels of land, Selina tried to keep track of the acreage. The farm was a lot bigger than she'd imagined. The sections were identifiable by the blue posts outlining the boundaries. She was also gratified to find hive boxes placed at every field location.

"How much land do you own, Rea?"

"Between all the parcels, I have twenty-eight hundred and forty-two acres, which includes the warehouse, hotel, and other structures. For straight cultivation, it's around the twenty-seven hundred mark. I have a large orchard I haven't shown you yet, which sits near my house."

Selina let out a low whistle. "Wow, I could tell it was large, but I didn't realize it was this big. I also applaud you for having bee habitats along your fields and your overall holistic approach to everything. What do you do with all the honey?"

"Matty put out his feelers and found a beekeeper willing to relocate with his family. He takes care of all my hives, plus most of the others around here. He gives me five percent of his profits and all the free honey I need for my families. The honey in the butter we had at lunch today was from our bees. I also provided the boxes to the other farms in my organic co-op."

This woman kept getting more and more impressive in Selina's estimation. For the first time since leaving home at eighteen, she felt she'd found a place she would never want to leave.

*****

Pulling into the parking lot of the grocery store, Rea killed the engine. Selina had been quiet the last five minutes of the drive, and Rea wondered what she was thinking about. She was gratified by Selina's appreciation of her farm and felt confident they were both on the same page regarding her approach to it. Rea felt lucky to have found the perfect person to help her realize her dream.

Before they got out of her car, Rea thought she'd better warn Selina about Hank. "Hey, before we go inside, if you see a tall, rawboned man with a greengrocers' apron on, don't let him engage you in conversation; otherwise, we'll be here all evening. He and his wife, June, own the store. She's as quiet as he is talkative. I think he also runs the info hotline in town—which to me, is funny because most people think it's women that gossip the most."

"I will be the proverbial wooden Indian and grunt at him." Selina's tinkling laughter followed the statement, inviting her own.

They entered the store, and Selina grabbed a cart right next to the produce section. When she paused to peruse the contents of the bins, Rea stopped her before she could pick anything out.

"Selina, depending on what you are looking for, we have most of these things in the greenhouse at home, and they'd be even fresher."

"Oh. I was thinking about grilling up a steak, and roasting an ear of corn, with a baked potato, and possibly a side salad as well."

"Sounds yummy. We have all that growing in our greenhouse except for the steak, of course. So put the cart up unless you want a bunch of other things, and we can hit it on the way home."

"Would you like to join me for supper? I grill up a mean steak, but if you prefer, I can make some chicken too." Selina asked demurely.

"If you're willing to feed me, I'll eat anything you make. I'm not much of a cook myself, so I live off nuked frozen dinners, sandwiches, and soup. I've already admitted that I eat at the café a lot, and Mia also takes it upon herself to make sure I come to lunch or dinner several times a week."

"She sounds like a wonderful person to have around, then. I'm especially good at crockpot meals, but I don't have one here. Maybe it's something I should order on Amazon."

"No need to. I have one but never use it. You can borrow it as long as you like, and if you feel like sharing your eats, I'm your girl," Rea said, then blushed at the accidental double entendre. She hadn't been anyone's girl in a long time, and there certainly hadn't been any of that kind of eating either.

The heat in her face increased when Selina's voice dropped several registers, and her eyes darkened. "I'll have to keep that in mind," she offered with a sexy grin, and Rea felt she might melt right there on the spot.

Before she could become totally unglued, she turned, picked up one of the handheld baskets, and gave it to Selina. Rea pointed toward the back. "The meat counter is this way."

Rea waited as Selina chose two packaged rib-eyes and two chicken breasts from the refrigerated case. When they passed the dairy section, Selina added a pint of sour cream and a four-ounce bag of shredded cheddar cheese to her basket. As they turned the corner to head for the checkout, they ran right into Hank. *Oh, boy, here we go!* Which had Rea shaking her head over their bad luck.

"Rea! This must be Selina with you. I'm Hank. I heard she got into town this morning. Emma said you ate at her place and also you were quite the looker. Reenie, on the other hand, said the men in town shouldn't get too excited about it, because she was sure you're a lesbian like our Rea here. I declare our town is getting to be an LGBT destination, with Bud and Bert's bee business coming to town. Then with the arrival of Doc and her partner, we've gotten even more diverse. What do you think of our community, Selina? Are you getting settled in, alright? I know you'll love it here."

"Great…yes…and I think so," was Selina's minimal response.

The whole time Rea was edging them closer to the checkout. One glaring look from June shut down any further discourse from Hank, and he slunk away like a whipped dog without another word. As usual, June was all business, ringing up the groceries with a minimum of chatter, and sent them on their way.

"Wow, you weren't kidding about him. Hank reminds me of Donkey from *Shrek*. He never shut up and answered his own questions most of the time."

Rea couldn't help the hearty chuckle that escaped her as they got in her SUV. "That's the most accurate comparison you could find. He even brays when he laughs."

Rea started her car then looked at the time. "It's almost four, so I guess I'd better call Matty to see where he's at. He may be on the farm someplace and not at home. But I'd like to introduce you to him and Mia at the same time, if possible."

Rea thumbed the hand's free button on her steering wheel and called Matty, but it went straight to voicemail. Next, she tried the house, and as usual, Mia answered. *"Hola, Cariña."*

"Hi, Mia. I'm calling to see if Flash is home, he didn't answer his cell."

"No, he over to the greenhouse. He has his radio."

"Yes, but I don't have mine, I'm in the car. I wanted to introduce you both to Selina. We need to stop at the greenhouse anyway, so he can meet her there, and I'll bring her by to meet you later."

"No, I go meet ju dere. I need tings to, so I see ju in a meanit."

"Okay, Mia, I'll be there in ten," Rea said as she pulled out of the lot and headed home.

*****

Since the phone call went through the car speakers, Selina had heard the whole thing. She could tell by the greeting and the friendly banter that Mia was more than fond of Rea, and it went both ways. She was looking forward to meeting them.

Rea broke into her thoughts. "That reminds me I need to get you a radio and charging base. The cell signals here aren't always reliable. I'm hoping when the town grows a little bigger, one of the phone companies might construct a tower here. The nearest one to us right now is in Fort Morgan, and it just a bit too far away for dependable service."

"I noticed that when I was trying to check my email earlier. I had one bar that flickered on and off, but never connected."

"I'll give you the Wi-Fi password that you can use to connect to the internet. The TVs in the RV are already synced for Netflix and Amazon Prime video services that I subscribe to if you want to watch anything on those."

Selina smiled. "I don't watch a lot of TV, but I enjoy an occasional movie. Oh, and one of the Netflix series—Grace and Frankie. Lily Tomlin is a hoot, and her wife, Jane Wagner, is a gifted writer. Have you seen the show?"

"No, I've heard about it but haven't gotten around to checking it out yet. I generally read at night instead. I have quite a collection of DVDs but have to admit, I haven't viewed many of them in the last few years."

Selina believed you could tell something about a person by what they watched, and asked, "So what type of movies are in your collection?"

Selina watched a warm, pink glow bloom on Rea's cheeks as she stumbled through her answer. "Oh,…um…sci-fi, romcoms, and some old classic movies. How about you?" Selina was sure Rea was hiding something but decided to let it go for now and see if she could get a peek at her DVDs at some later date.

"I love sci-fi. I've watched all the Star Wars movies. I'm a confirmed Trekkie, so I've seen those movies too, and watched all the different series on TV. I was more than half in love with Counselor Deanna Troi, and I thought she was way too good for a playboy like Riker. And don't even get me started on Voyager, with the forceful, but oh so sexy, Captain Janeway, and the cool, unemotional beauty of Seven of Nine. I also still have a big-time crush on Gates McFadden." But didn't voice it was because she had a thing for redheads.

"Then we have that in common, but you left out Princess Leia. She was beautiful but also pretty kick-ass with a blaster."

*****

Rea was thankful that Selina had lapsed into silence for the rest of their drive home. When she'd asked about her movies, Rea's thoughts immediately went to her extensive collection of lesbian films. Most of which included some very passionate sex scenes, bordering on erotica. She and Sherry would watch them from time to time to jump-start their libidos. Rea wasn't about to admit that to Selina, though. It seemed much better to admit to being a sci-fi nerd instead, and Rea was gratified to learn they shared this interest. Maybe they could have a few movie nights in the future. It was much more fun to enjoy them with a fellow fan than watching them alone.

It was funny, but Rea had felt less lonely today than she had in a long time. She attributed it to Selina's arrival in Moirai, and it wasn't because of the amount of time they'd been together either. Rea could spend the whole day surrounded by people and still feel alone. But not with Selina. With her, Rea had felt an instant rapport. Selina had made an impact on more than just her, but Patches, Dolly, and Jupe as well. They all seemed to have fallen quite happily under her special form of enchantment.

Chapter Fourteen
Meeting the Family

Rea pulled up next to a gravel path running in front of the greenhouse, bisecting the two roads, and they got out. Fifty yards away, Selina saw a short, roly-poly Hispanic woman with shoulder-length, wavy, gray hair standing near the structure. She had a basket hanging off her left arm, and a flowered apron tied around her middle. Her right hand rested on an ample hip, and she was tapping the toe of one tennis shoe impatiently on the ground. Selina got the impression this was a no-nonsense woman that didn't suffer fools gladly, and in the next moment, it was confirmed.

"Dere ju are! How come ju no bring her by furse ting? I spected ju for lunch. Now ju come to dinner," she demanded.

"Selina. The woman here treating me like an errant child is Mia Otero, and Mama Mia, this is our new botanist, Selina Thorson," Rea said as she tried to keep a straight face.

"Buenas tardes, Mia. Es un placer conocerte."

"Hablas español bien, eso será útil," Mia offered with a beaming smile and eagerly shook Selina's hand. "Is good to meet ju too. But we speak inglés, so Rea understan us. She no good to speak Spanish, but know some to lissen. But I no speak very good ether."

"Well, now I've been shamed twice in quick succession," Rea said and hunched her shoulders. "I'm sorry I didn't bring Selina by for lunch, Mia, but I was showing her the lab, so we dropped by the café for a bite. Oh, and we can't come to dinner. Selina bought some steaks and is planning to grill tonight. We are actually going to pick some stuff from the greenhouse to go with them too. Oh here,"—Rea handed Mia the container—"Emma sent you some berry cobbler."

Mia took it, gently placing it atop the tomatoes and bell peppers that partially filled the basket she was holding. "Oh, I know ju eat at de café, Carmen tell me she see ju dere."

"And the grapevine is alive and spreading fast. First, the store and now here. We can't get away from it. You're big news Selina," Rea said with an exasperated sigh.

"Don't worry about it, Rea. I lived in a small town in Texas before going to live with my grandparents in another one in Arizona, so I know the drill. As my grandmother always said, 'If you don't want people knowing what your underwear looks like, don't be hanging your drawers on the line.' Sage advice that I've always followed," Selina related with a grin.

In response, Mia's deep brown eyes danced with delight as she pulled Selina into her stout body with her free arm and said, "Ju did good, Cariña. I like dis one." She let Selina go then shooed them away. "Ju go meet Mateo. Tomorrow is Saturday. Ju come to lunch, or brekfas if ju like some sweetbread or tacos, Selina. Weeth or weethout dis one," she said, pointing at Rea, before turning and heading toward the little white house.

"Whether you know it or not, Selina, you've received the Mama Mia seal of approval. She doesn't offer her sweetbreads to just anybody."

"I can see why you tagged her with that nickname. She managed to give me a big mama bear hug with one arm, and it took me totally by surprise. I'm not used to anyone hugging me outside of my family, and even they are more restrained with them," Selina commented with a touch of longing in her voice.

Rea was staring over Selina's shoulder, where a moment before Mia had stood her gaze unfocused, lips puckered slightly. An almost imperceptible nod followed, and she said, "Yeah…she is a hugger, alright."

Selina could tell by the look in Rea's eyes and her statement that there was a story behind it, but their acquaintance was too new to ask about it. In the future, Selina hoped she'd know Rea well enough to ask.

Rea diverted her attention by saying, "Let's go in and find Matty. I promise he is much more subdued than Mia is."

Stepping inside, Selina smiled at Rea as she cataloged the room. It was impressive, to say the least. The greenhouse had to be around fifty feet wide and a hundred and fifty feet long. It had polycarbonate walls with louvered windows on the sides and movable panels on the top for ventilation. Selina inhaled, relishing the familiar odor of damp soil, and flowering plants that filled the space. Two rows of corn, heavy with ripe ears, ran down the long center aisle. Tubs of tomatoes, bell peppers, okra, and squash were growing on wire cages, adding a riot of color against the glassy backdrop. There were deep bed boxes for root vegetables and more shallow ones sporting leafy greens. Selina had seen duplicates of this greenhouse during her tour with Rea, so she had some idea of what those might contain.

Selina noticed a man standing near the top of a ten-foot ladder pruning a tree, and from the shape of the leaves, she knew it was an avocado. It didn't look like it was mature enough yet to bear fruit, but this confirmed to her that Rea planned for the long term. Selina turned back to Rea and felt the focus of her intense gaze. Rea's riveting hazel eyes reflected the patina of the plants flourishing around her.

"So, what do you think?"

"I think you've got a great setup here and a nice variety of flora. Are the other greenhouses growing the same things?"

"Mostly, but the planting rotation is different, so we always have certain things available like the corn."

"That's markedly smart management of your assets, Rea."

As they walked down the aisle, Selina could hear the distinct sound of buzzing and noted a hive box was half encapsulated in the west wall. It was another smart move on Rea's part, as the bees provided the necessary pollination for the plants. The structure would also keep the bees warm in winter, afford them with a constant source of food, and as a bonus, they'd always have fresh honey.

Continuing their journey, Rea led her to the tall ladder where the man was busily snipping on some of the branches. As they approached, he stopped and smiled down at them.

Rea waved a hand at him. "Afternoon Matty. This is our new botanist, Selina Thorson, and this,"—Rea said, turning to

Selina— "as you already know, is Matty or Flash, as he is better known."

He set his clippers aside and slowly climbed down to the ground. After wiping his hand on his pants, he offered it to her. "It is good to meet ju, Selina."

Selina took it in hers and felt the calloused palm slide against her own, a testament to years of manual labor. "And you, also. I'm highly impressed by everything I've seen of the farm this afternoon, but this greenhouse takes the cake. I can see you are very skilled in growing things, and I look forward to working with you," she said respectfully as she shook it.

"Gracias. Ju need anyting, ju let me know." With that said, he simply climbed back up the ladder.

Selina felt a hand grip her arm as Rea rose on her tiptoes, leaned in close, and whispered, "He will talk a little more once he gets to know you, but Mia more than makes up for it." The husky timbre of the words struck Selina like a tuning fork, vibrating through her, bringing to mind secrets whispered in the dark.

Letting go, Rea stepped back and said, "We'll see you later, Flash. We're just going to browse the plants and pick a few things for dinner," breaking Selina out of her fanciful musing.

"Sí, Wonder Woman." He chuckled. "What ju going do wit it den."

Rea huffed, as she walked away. "Shut it, smart ass, it's for Selina. She's grilling tonight." He didn't answer, but his laugh followed them as they walked away.

Rea grabbed a wicker basket, like the one Mia had carried, from a stack next to a large, commercial, stainless-steel sink, and handed it to Selina. "Have at it. We can wash it here before we leave."

She wandered up and down the aisles, harvesting a variety of salad items, some fresh herbs, corn, and potatoes. Off in a corner was a small shelf unit covered in clear plastic. Its shadowed walls were dotted with perspiration. Selina unzipped the front and found a variety of mushrooms. She removed a couple of handfuls of the white buttons she thought would go nicely with the steaks. With the greenhouse and chicken coop within walking distance of the RV, Selina realized all she would need to eat well was a little meat from time to time. Having homegrown veggies, this close, had her excited by the thought of cooking whatever she wanted for a change. Bran had been way too picky about her food and didn't always appreciate what Selina made. It had her wondering about Rea's culinary likes and dislikes.

"What are your favorite types of foods, Rea?"

"Anything that doesn't come in black plastic frozen trays. I'll eat almost anything, but I'm not fond of any type of shellfish like shrimp or lobster. It wasn't something we ate when I was growing up, so I never developed a taste for it." Rea rolled her eyes. "I've had people tell me it must not have been cooked right or it wasn't fresh enough, but it's something about the textures I don't like. To me, it was like chewing erasers."

"I understand. We lived a long way from any coast, and the local store didn't sell it either. I'm also not a fan of sushi or any of those other supposed raw delicacies people rave about like oysters, clams, and octopus. We did have fresh trout, bass, and catfish we caught in the river, so I do cook those when I can catch them."

"Now those I will eat if fried, grilled, or broiled. You can do some fishing down at the river anytime you want. You will need to get a license, just in case you catch anything. We don't want to go breaking the law even though you probably wouldn't get caught. The game wardens hardly ever come here. They mostly cruise around Jackson Lake or the reservoirs."

Selina stopped at the sink and washed off the vegetables in the basin. As she placed them back in the basket, she was thinking about meal prep and realized she hadn't thought to check the cabinets for foil before they'd left for the store. Selina had also forgotten to get any salad dressing, as well. She'd been too distracted by flirting with Rea during their shopping expedition, so it hadn't entered her mind. Selina planned to check that as soon as she returned to the RV, and then make a quick trip back into town if needed.

Leaving the greenhouse, Rea drove them back home and parked in the garage. The moment they got out of the SUV, a furry blur shot toward them. Both women laughed as Patches raced around them in a dizzying circle, interspersed with happy yips.

Selina watched in amusement, barely containing her laughter, as Rea attempted to calm him. "Okay, little man, I know you're excited, but if you want some loving, you'll have to slow down."

Bending over, Rea took Patches' face between both of her hands and gave him the attention he demanded.

Retrieving the basket and grocery bag from the SUV, Selina slung them over one arm then closed the car door. She approached the duo and with her free hand, added to the love fest, stroking Patches along his back a few times before scratching his rump. He promptly wiggled his rear back and forth in pleasure.

"Okay, Patches, I think that's enough for now. Go on, we have things to do, and you have places to sniff. Get to it!" He looked up at them imploringly, with puppy dog eyes. "No, that's enough." Reluctantly he moved away but then took off in a sprint around the corner of the garage a second later.

"I'm going inside the house for a bit and let you get to whatever you need to do," Rea said. "I will text you the password for the Wi-Fi when I get to my office, I can never remember it off the top of my head. Then when you want me to come over, you can text me back. If you don't have any bars on your phone, you will need to get out from under the patio, the roof tends to impede the cell signal."

"Sounds like a plan. I didn't take time to look through the cabinets, so I may need a few things to get dinner ready." Not willing to admit the real reason for her distraction, she said, "Oh, and while we were trying to avoid Hank, I forgot to get any salad dressing."

"If I haven't got what you need, I guarantee you Mia does. I can always run over there and get it. But I do have dressing since

I eat a lot of salads. I've got ranch, blue cheese, and Italian in my fridge."

"Ranch will be good for me. Ah…I'll let you know about anything else, though."

"Just ask. Whatever I've got is yours."

Selina couldn't help the flush of desire that raced through her system with the fantasies a statement that conjured.

They stood awkwardly for a moment. "Well, I guess I should let you go do your thing, and I'll go do mine, then we'll meet up later," Rea said.

"Good plan," Selina offered hastily in parting. She needed to get away so she could cool off before she embarrassed herself.

Selina entered the RV and sat everything on the counter. She took stock of the contents of the cabinets as she put her goodies away, and located foil, so she wouldn't need that. What Selina was missing, though, was some Worcestershire sauce to make her marinade for the steaks.

Selina pulled out her cell to shoot Rea a quick text and frowned when she discovered she had no bars. She went outside, holding up her phone. As soon as she cleared the patio cover, a message notification popped up. It was a text from Rea with the Wi-Fi password. Selina took a moment to copy and paste it into the phone settings, before sending one back, asking about the sauce.

She watched the bubbles ripple across the screen, quickly followed by a woot sound with the message—*come on over*. Shoving her cell in her pocket, Selina made her way over to the main house. The angle of the sunlight streaming into the shady overhang of the porch silhouetted Rea's alluring figure as she held open the screen door, drawing her gaze. As Selina climbed the wooden steps, she had an overwhelming feeling of being welcomed home.

Chapter Fifteen
A Glimpse Inside

Rea stood in the mudroom holding open the screen door and watched as Selina made her way across the back yard. The sun shimmered along her blue-black hair, flowing freely down her back, in contrast to the warm glow of her light bronze skin. Selina's long legs and her natural, graceful movements reminded Rea of an Akhal-Teke horse, she'd seen once in a video. She'd thought they were one of the most beautiful, majestic creatures on earth, and now she was looking at its human equivalent.

Get a hold of yourself, Rea. She's an employee and not for you! Rea chastised herself, but her breath hitched anyway, as Selina stepped onto the porch—retreating a step—anxious all of a sudden about letting her inside.

*****

Selina grabbed the screen door and looked into Rea's flustered face. The briefest flash of desire had lit her eyes before she turned and scurried out a door on the opposite side. Rea's quick withdrawal had Selina curious about what had unsettled her.

A distinctive click of her boot heel as she entered the room had her looking down. A multicolored slate floor, with its random sized tiles, lent character and functionality to the mudroom. A wooden cubby hole bench was snugged in tight next to the inner door, with several pairs of shoes and boots tucked inside. On the right wall were bracketed longleaf pine shelves holding a myriad of items, and a table with radio equipment was to the immediate left. Located caddy-corner to that was a closet door with a pegged coat rack where a jean jacket and two ball caps hung.

The spring tension from the door pushed against her back, urging her forward into a short but wide, open-ended hallway. Gleaming longleaf pine adorned the floor. By the uneven widths of the planks, Selina surmised they were original to the house but had been meticulously refinished and sealed to protect the wood.

Off to the right, Rea was standing in what she guessed was the kitchen, from the view of the shiny surface of a stainless-steel refrigerator behind her. In a few steps, she was able to take in the rest of the space. Sleek, white cabinets abutted a dishwasher and a stove microwave combo unit, while old-styled, pine, glass-fronted cabinets lined the walls, holding an assortment of dishes. Dark red-brown veins of color ran through the creamy marble counters, accentuated by biscuit hued walls—easing the transition between the two discordant themes, blending the old with the new. A deep basined white porcelain sink sat below a window facing west—the setting sun adding an orange glow to the space.

The aroma of fresh coffee wafted through the air from the Bunn, situated next to a wide-mouthed toaster and some ceramic canisters—the only items in the kitchen that looked like they got much use. To the left was a wide peninsular bar top with three stools tucked underneath, adding a visible demarcation to the open great room. A rustic dining table with four high-backed chairs sat atop a circular, earth-toned, rag rug, and a matching china hutch had its back against the short wall it shared with the hallway.

The red brick fireplace was the focal point of the living area, with built-in bookshelves on either side. Another large rag rug, this one oval, adorned the floors, with a brown leather sofa and chairs grouped around it. A distressed wood coffee table sat in the center. Matching end tables graced one end of the cushioned sofa, and the other sat between two easy chairs. Tiffany table and floor lamps added touches of color as the light shone through their variegated shades. The only thing intruding on the utter silence of the house was the ticking of a stately grandfather clock situated between two windows facing south.

Selina turned back to see Rea was standing next to what appeared to be an old door on rails with a brass pull attached, seemingly studying her as intently as she had studied Rea's home. Selina couldn't decipher the look but hoped Rea hadn't thought she was snooping.

To break the quiet stalemate, she offered, "Ah…your home is lovely, from what I can see of it." She pointed at the door and added with a lift of her eyebrow, "Is that the pantry?"

In answer, Rea tugged on the pull and slid the door to the left. "Yes, it is. Help yourself."

*****

From the moment Selina had entered her domain, Rea had felt an almost foreign energy filling up every corner. She'd stood by the pantry door anxiously watching as Selina surveyed her home. For reasons she didn't want to acknowledge, Selina's opinion was important to her. She hadn't been able to read anything in

Selina's face or body language but felt her uttered compliment had been sincere.

While Selina rummaged in her pantry, Rea grabbed a mug, filled it with coffee, added cream, then leaned against the counter with it cradled in her hands. She crossed one foot over the other on the floor—a staged pose meant to convey relaxation—she was anything but.

Why hadn't she just taken the Worcestershire to Selina instead of inviting her over, she wondered? To date, Matty and Mia were the two people she'd allowed inside her personal domain, but they were family to Rea. Selina, on the other hand, while not quite a stranger, couldn't be labeled as anything more than an acquaintance at this juncture.

The farmhouse was the first place that was totally hers. Rea had sold off or donated everything, but some personal keepsakes from her home in California. Those things had reflected the blended taste of a couple that had compromised on decor. This space, though, was intimately hers and embodied who she was today without Sherry—comfortable, but a little austere, with a lack of knickknacks anywhere. It was a bit of a lonely place, waiting to be filled up with mementos of a life Rea hadn't been fully living—something she promised Sherry she'd do, but as of yet, failed to.

Now she'd given Selina a glimpse inside her private world, leaving her feeling slightly exposed. Maybe sharing dinner with her wasn't such a great idea, but how could Rea wiggle out of it now?

She was snapped out of her musing by the sound of Selina's voice. "I found it." Followed by her reappearance with a bottle in her hand.

"Great. Glad I actually had some, since I don't cook much," Rea responded. "I was thinking…with the long day you've had, maybe I should stay home and let you spend your first evening here, relaxing. You know…instead of cooking for two."

"No, please come. It's exactly the same amount of work, and I would appreciate the company," Selina replied sincerely.

Rea couldn't think of any excuse that wouldn't seem off-putting, so she agreed, "Okay, but can I bring anything?"

"Just yourself. Oh, and anything you prefer to drink that's not stocked in the fridge at the RV. I meant to thank you for the beer, it's my favorite brand too."

Rea wasn't about to admit how closely she'd watched Selina during the interview. She preferred wine herself, but prevaricated by saying, "I enjoy a good, cold beer every once in a while, so I figured if you weren't a drinker they wouldn't go to waste."

"Then we're all set," Selina stated as she headed back outside, with Rea following behind.

The sun was low enough on the western horizon to cast long shadows across the yard. It would be dark within the hour, and Rea still had a few things to do, so she asked, "What time do you want me to come over? I have got a few emails to answer, then I'll need to go bed down Dolly and Jupe for the night."

Selina lit up at the mention of the horses. "I need to make my marinade for the meat, and I'd like to give them at least an hour to soak before I start grilling. Can you answer your emails and let me meet you at the barn to help out with them? Then we get finished, I'll start the grill, and you can relax on the patio while I cook."

Rea was torn by the request. It was something she hadn't shared with anyone else since she was young. Sherry had been afraid of horses, so they'd never even ridden together. And neither Matty nor Mia had any interest in them, so it had become a solitary pursuit. The thought of letting Selina help with it was slightly unnerving, like when Rea had allowed Selina into her home.

"Ah…okay…I'll see you at the barn in about twenty minutes. You'll also want to change out of your nice khakis too," Rea offered unnecessarily. Like Selina didn't know what to wear to handle horses, proving just how flustered she was feeling all of a sudden.

Giving her a thumbs up, Selina said, "Great. I'll be there." Then she turned and hoofed it back to the RV.

"Yeah, great," Rea replied under her breath and decided to have a quick glass of wine instead of working on emails. Five minutes ago, Rea had felt normal, but there was something about Selina that caused jitters to erupt inside her. Now she was feeling trepidatious and wouldn't be able to keep her mind on them anyway. So, it was off to the fridge to swill down a little liquid courage.

Interlude

Bright particles of light swam together until three figures formed out of the cosmic soup around them. The old woman spoke first, "How did their first meeting go?"

"Well, Selina is already hooked and ecstatic that Rea is a lesbian. She loves the farm and all the animals, as we knew she would," Nita said.

"How's Rea doing, Sherry?" Lily asked.

"She's equally enchanted by Selina, but she's nervous with the situation and still has her barriers up. It's going to take something more to punch through them, or she won't open up. We need to prod her a bit. Do you have any ideas?"

"Humm. My Lina isn't one to share her most intimate thoughts with others either, and it's crucial she do so at this time. I'll nudge another meteor their way to get them talking, and Nita, why don't you show them your wolf guise again." Lily was quiet for a moment while she contemplated more options.

"The timing is not quite right tonight, but soon Nita, I'll want you to appear to them when they are both together. That should be shocking enough to shake a few more things loose. Are you up for that?"

"Yes, I'll stay close and watch for the right opening, but Sherry, you need to keep up the subliminal push against Rea's emotional defenses."

"My influence with her usually comes into play when she's dreaming, so I will focus on that. But I will do my best to make my presence felt when Rea's awake as well."

"Okay, so Nita will make her impact felt on the physical plane, while you, Sherry, can work on Rea's subconscious. I'll use my energy to try and draw both halves of their souls together when I feel their emotions are aligning. Is there anything else?"

"I could use a little metaphysical boost if I'm going to be manifesting more," Nita stated.

"Well, let's share energy then," Lily said, lifting her shining arms out, and both women gravitated toward her. She brought them in for a group embrace, and waves of ethereal light danced around them like the aurora borealis.

When their forms separated again, Lily said, "Okay, let's get to it then," and they flickered out of sight.

Chapter Sixteen

More Than Meets The Eye

Selina quickly prepped the meat with her homemade marinade, changed clothes, and arrived at the corral in less than twenty minutes. Both Dolly and Jupe were lounging by the fence, so she let herself into the paddock. As she approached, Jupe came to attention, his ears twitching back and forth while he pawed the ground with his right front hoof. He was less nervous this time but still not at ease. Yá'át'ééh, Shik'is she crooned softly to him in Diné, and he settled.

Reaching out, she ran a gentle hand along his back as she praised him, "You've found a safe place to belong now, Jupe. Let go of your unease, there is nothing to be afraid of." Selina brought some of her weight against his back, stroking him along his flank and side. He shifted a little but didn't flinch, a good sign he was starting to trust her.

"I'm sure you'd enjoy exploring a little more of your new home. Maybe soon, you might think about letting me ride you." Selina really wanted to grab a hunk of mane and vault onto his back, but she knew that would be rushing things.

The creak of the gate brought Selina's head around, and she watched as Rea carefully made her way over to them—her tread slow and sure. It showed an innate understanding of how to approach a timid horse that only those who grew up around them seemed to acquire. Selina wondered what her history was, but based on their short acquaintance, she wisely chose not to pry into her background yet.

"Hi, Rea. Are you ready to bed these babies down for the night?"

"Yeah. I usually lead Dolly through Jupe's stall, and he follows behind her. So, I'll go first and open his door."

Selina kept an appreciative eye on the well-rounded tush swaying gently in front of her. As Rea led the way, Selina thought she was one good-looking filly. She grabbed Jupe's mane to urge him forward, then leaned in and whispered in his ear, "Hey man, let's follow those fine pieces of tail."

Just like everything else Selina had seen since arriving, the barn showed Rea's detailed touch. There were only four stalls, but they were very roomy with wood plank walls and open wrought iron rails on top. Each also had a Classic Equine Autofount unit, so there would always be fresh water available for the horses. Above Selina's head, spaced evenly about, were recessed lights glowing softly, making everything inside clearly visible. Fresh straw and wood shavings were spread on the ground of the stalls that had a feeder rack attached to the wall. At the front next to the door, was a bucket in a holder for supplemental feed.

Selina closed the outside door and made her way over to Jupe, running her hand along his back. She heard a rattling sound and looked over to see Rea coming out of Dolly's stall.

When Rea caught her eye, she said, "Hey, Selina. Can you grab his bucket, then I can show you where the feed is stored?"

Selina retrieved it and followed her over to what appeared to be an old wooden bin with a hinged aluminum top. When Rea opened it, Selina could see three cleverly concealed tubs inside with a protrusive lid attached to the metal one that sealed the containers when closed.

"I give them two scoops each of oats and grains in the mornings,"—Rea said, pointing at each of the tubs—"but at night, four of the sweet feed pellets." She waved her hand toward the closed door. "Inside the tack room, I also have a container with special treats that I usually give Dolly before a ride. Jupe won't take one from me, but I put one in his bucket from time to time, so he doesn't feel left out."

An indecisive look crossed Rea's face. "Would you like to help me groom them in the morning? Jupe could use a good one. He barely lets me brush him, and I can't get anywhere near his hooves."

"Sure thing. I'd love to, and I don't think Jupe will have a problem with it either."

"I just bet he won't," Rea said under her breath.

Selina smiled to herself when she heard that, wondering if Rea realized she'd spoken.

They were finished within minutes, but Rea stopped to point out the stairs to the hayloft, and the light control panel, switching it over to the night setting as they exited. While they were inside, night had fallen. The outside security lights on the house, barn, and garage had come on. There were just enough of them to softly illuminate the structures, but not intrude upon the nocturnal landscape.

The chilly kiss of the night air caressed Selina's cheeks, and she put her hands into the pockets of her hoodie to warm them. A fire would feel wonderful about now, she thought. Selina looked over to see that Rea had turned up the collar of her unbuttoned jacket, and her hands were shoved into the back pockets of her jeans. With her shoulders thrust back, her full breasts were even more prominent, as her shirt molded around them. Selina turned away quickly before Rea caught her amorous stare.

A hush had descended along with the sun, creating a peaceful but shared solitude. Selina appreciated a person who didn't find it necessary to fill the void with chatter, and could simply enjoy the quiet. The more she was around Rea, the more she admired her. Rea embodied all the attributes Selina found irresistible in a person; looks, intelligence, and compassion. That reminded Selina that she hadn't seen Patches since they'd gotten back from town. Though she was loath to break the silence, she asked, "Where is Patches?"

"Oh, he came in for his dinner right after you left for the RV. I told him I was going to bed down the horses, so he's probably still inside the house. When I don't come back, and you start grilling, he will come running in a hurry." Rea chuckled.

When they arrived at the patio, Selina offered, "Why don't you have a seat, and I'll get our meal started. I think if I light this firepit, it should be warm enough for us to sit out here while I cook."

"You go on inside, and I'll light the pit, it should be plenty warm enough when it gets going."

With that, Selina went inside the RV, leaving Rea on her own.

*****

Once Selina left her alone on the patio, Rea lit the kindling in the firepit, then she sat down and zoned out as she watched the hungry flames lick their way along the dry wood. Her previous angst about sharing the job of settling the horses for the night had disappeared, and Rea felt more relaxed with Selina now than she had earlier inside her kitchen. Selina's company had been a pleasant addition, that not only had Rea enjoyed, but the horses as well. She'd never seen Jupe act so docile before, and Selina had practically been laying across his back when Rea had arrived at the paddock. Selina exuded a peaceful aura that soothed anyone in her orbit.

Something cold and wet touched her hand, startling her out of her thoughts. Rea gazed down to find that Patches had made his entrance. "Hey there, boy. Did you miss me, or did you smell the food that isn't even cooking yet?" He pawed her arm, indicating he wanted her attention. "Okay, so you missed me, huh?" she said, stroking his head.

Selina came out of the door with a plate holding two potatoes wrapped in foil, two ears of corn, and a glass pan holding the meat. She set them down, started the grill, then placed the potatoes inside before closing the lid. Selina pulled out her phone, and Rea could see from her chair that she'd set a timer app on it, then went back inside. She could hear Selina moving around through the open door, and a few minutes later, she reappeared.

"We have about twenty minutes, then I'll put the chicken on. How do you like your steak?"

"I like mine medium-rare, Selina. Just sear it well on the outside, and leave its hot, red center intact."

"Wonderful. A woman after my own heart. That is something else we share in common, and it will make the timing on the cooking much easier," Selina said with a big grin. "I also see you were right about Patches showing up."

"Yes, he said he missed me by sticking his cold nose in my hand, which has now been nicely warmed by his body heat."

Selina sat down in the chair nearest the grill, holding her hands out toward the firepit, rubbing them together. "Mine could use a little warming too," she said and patted her leg. "Come over here, dude, and let me say hello. It will be worth rewashing my hands for."

He skimmed below the bridge of Rea's crossed legs, created by her booted foot resting on the edge of the low slate table, and over to Selina. She cradled the sides of his face in her hands and rubbed her thumbs along his cheeks in a circular motion before massaging his ears. He closed his eyes in apparent bliss, his head drooping in relaxation.

Rea sucked in a deep breath as she watched Selina fondle Patches' cheeks and ears, growing envious of the attention he was getting. Rea hadn't felt the touch of gentle fingers on her skin for so long. Just the thought of it sparked a flicker of desire, warming her blood.

Rea needed to shut down that train of thought, so she asked, "So, now that you have seen our set up, when do you think we could start the planting?"

"On Monday, I plan to take soil samples and run tests on them in the lab so I can make up a soil map. Once I have those results, I'll know if there are any adverse conditions, we need to address first. Also, the soil makeup will tell me what crops would do best in those fields."

"I think I can speed things up in that regard. I had the parcels professionally tested before the purchase, and I still have those records. There were no adverse contaminants, but you can retest if you want. The credentials of the company I used were excellent."

"I have no problem using data from an outside lab. To be honest, I'm a little rusty on soil testing anyway. It's been at least a decade since I've done any real agronomy work. None of the growers I worked for could afford the type of setup you have here. I have to tell you I was amazed by everything. In my experience, it's usually only the big farm corps who can fund a set-up like you've put together."

Rea heard the unasked question, but wasn't ready to talk about Sherry, and where the money had come from. "It's a long story, best left for another time. I'm also pretty hungry, and I don't want to cause you to ruin anything." Rea wrapped her arms tightly around her chest as if protecting herself from the memory.

"Yeah, I definitely don't want to…ruin anything."

Rea turned as the double-entendre hit home, and she saw a sexy grin being aimed at her. She couldn't think of a witty comeback, and wasn't good at flirting anyway, but was saved from responding by the chiming of the timer on Selina's phone.

Rea watched as Selina rose, went to the grill, where she added the corn and chicken before closing the lid again. She turned to Rea and said, "I'm going in now, so I can put our salad together. Those need to cook for about fifteen minutes before I put the steaks on. Oh, and we'll need the dressing. I forgot to ask you for it earlier when I got the Worcestershire sauce."

Rea bolted from her seat, happy for an excuse to make a brief escape. "I'll go get it. Be right back," she said and fled the patio.

*****

Selina sensed she'd stumbled into a sensitive area with her remark about the farming setup. It had definitely touched a tender spot. Rea had withdrawn as any shy animal would, and Selina realized she would have to proceed with more care. She quickly threw the salad together, then set the bowl on the table along with the butter, cheese, and sour cream.

Selina had just finished slicing the onion and mushrooms for grilling when she heard a soft knock. "Come on in," she said.

Rea stepped through the door, a bottle of Ranch dressing in one hand, and an open bottle of wine in the other. "Since you're grilling both chicken and steak, I brought over some Shiraz that I thought would pair well with both, if you'd like to have some with dinner."

Lost & Found

"Sounds good. You know your way around the kitchen, so why don't you get the glasses out while I go put on the steaks."

Selina went outside and lifted the lid of the grill. The smell of the roasting food filled the air, and her stomach growled in response. She turned everything then added the steaks. They immediately started sizzling when they hit the hot metal. Finally, Selina put down a tray she'd fashioned out of foil, with onions, and mushrooms inside, that she'd topped with a little leftover marinade, then closed the lid.

As she waited, Selina started humming "Hand in my Pocket" to herself. Swaying to the music that filled her head, she used one of her's to mimic a part of the lyrics. A loud snort brought her head around, and she saw Rea lounging in the doorway, looking down at her with a glass of wine in her hand, trying hard to hide her mirth.

"Okay, you caught me. Go ahead and laugh, but there is a method to my madness. It's a great way to time the cooking," she offered with a grin.

The laughter that Rea had worked to contain escape in a rush, deepening the dimples in her cheeks, and causing her breasts to jiggle. Selina tried hard not to let her mind go there, but she couldn't help but imagine those lush globes in her hands. She dropped her head, turned, and fidgeted with the meat tongs as heat rode up her neck. Selina hoped if Rea noticed her heightened color, it would be attributed to embarrassment, and not desire.

"I'm sorry for laughing, but I was waiting for you to do a little headbanging action to accompany your musical pantomime."

Rea's eyes sparkled with humor. "I think it's a very creative way to cook. However, I actually came out to see if you want a glass of wine or if you would prefer a beer instead."

Yeah, Selina thought, as she flipped over the meat, I need something to douse these flames. "Thanks, a beer would be nice right now."

Rea was back out in a minute and handed her a cold bottle. "I noticed one beer was already missing, so maybe I have some catching up to do?" she queried with a lifted brow.

Selina saw the slight tightening of her lips and wasn't sure if Rea was fighting back a smile or a frown. "Oh no, you're actually ahead of me. I use beer in my marinade, so one of them had to be sacrificed to the grill gods."

Seeing the merriment bloom on Rea's face, Selina knew her comment hadn't been meant seriously. Relieved, she took a swig and sighed as the brew slid down her suddenly parched throat. Those few seconds of uncertainty brought home to Selina, that although she felt an unusual level of comfort with Rea, they were still virtually strangers. She didn't usually let her guard down with people until she really got to know them—but with Rea—Selina didn't feel the need to hide herself away.

Chapter Seventeen

Revelations

Rea finished downing her second glass of wine since making her brief escape to the house and felt its soothing effects filtering through her system. Selina left her feeling unbalanced for some reason, and Rea had found herself on an emotional see-saw all day—up one moment then down the next. Catching Selina's little singing act and being a bit tipsy from the alcohol she'd used to calm herself, Rea had playfully asked about the missing beer. And while Selina's rejoinder was delivered with a joke at the end, the quick gulp from her beer and the sigh that followed spoke volumes to Rea. She'd somehow shifted her own anxiety over to Selina, so it was up to her to shift it back again.

"The food smells delicious, it must be the marinade you made. What's in it?"

"Oh, it's easy to make. Melted butter with Worcestershire sauce and some beer for flavoring, but it also acts as a tenderizer. If I'm not cooking with briquets or wood chips, I'll add a bit of Liquid Smoke to it. Of course, I didn't have any here, so I skipped it this time. Those ribeyes are such a tender cut of meat, I only used the marinade for flavoring. With something like flank steak, I would have let them soak most of the day. I'm also cooking some mushrooms and onions in it to top the steaks."

"That's a lot of food along with the salad, so you might have to roll me home. There's a collapsible wagon in the garage if needed, plus I may drink that whole bottle of wine tonight."

"Then, I will definitely limit my alcohol intake if I'm going to be the designated wagoneer. If not, you'll just have to sleep here," Selina answered flirtatiously.

The thought hit Rea like a sledgehammer and generated heat that immediately traveled south. The sudden spurt of arousal was followed by a picture conjured in her head of Selina lying naked across a bed. Rea turned away from the door, trying to shake the vision from her brain. She lifted her wine glass to her lips and was disconcerted to find it empty.

Through the open door, Selina asked with a raised voice, "Hey Rea, could you bring me those plates on the table?"

Thankful for the distraction, Rea carried them outside to Selina as she lifted the lid on the grill. Placing a cob of corn and a potato on each of the plates, she handed them back to Rea.

"If you'll put these on the table, I'll bring in the meat."

Rea retreated inside and scooted into the middle of one of the bench seats. Selina followed a moment later, a sizzling platter of meat in her hand. Little trickles of red leaked from the ribeyes, which were smothered in grilled onions and mushrooms. Selina slid a steak onto both their plates, then paused.

"Doesn't look like there's enough room for these breasts right now. I'll leave them here until we have room for them," Selina said as she set the platter down. "Let's dig in while it's hot."

Rea didn't need to be told twice. She hurriedly doctored up her potato with butter, and a small dab of sour cream then added a fist full of cheese. But what sent Rea's taste buds into orbit was her first bite of the tender, juicy steak. She hadn't eaten a lot of red meat over the last twenty years, as Sherry had preferred chicken or broiled fish for their main entrée. The flavor of the steak brought out Rea's hidden carnivore, and she ended up devouring the whole thing in short order. She left half her potato, and the ends of her corn untouched as her stomach rebelled with how full she'd stuffed it.

Rea leaned back against the bench seat, wishing there was some way to loosen her jeans. Next time she ate with Selina, she would wear a pair of sweats. The thought slipped through her mind without Rea questioning that there would be more shared meals. The excellent food and the three glasses of wine made her feel less antsy, so she was enjoying the novelty of having a companionable dinner with a beautiful woman.

Rea glanced up when she heard the clatter of Selina's cutlery hitting her plate—a sure sign her dinner date was done. Her breath caught, and Rea's eyes locked onto Selina's right hand as she raised glistening fingers to her mouth, sucking the butter off their tips. For the second time in the last hour, a flair of lust lit in her body, and Rea tried valiantly to stamp it out.

She was overly warm and felt the need for some cool night air. "Let me help you get the table cleared, then we can sit outside while we digest this fabulous supper."

"I'll take you up on that. I feel as full as a tick about to pop."

They both rose from the table, grabbing the plates and bowls, then sat them on the counter. Selina went out to the grill to bring in the pan she used for the steaks and the tongs. Rea stored the uneaten chicken breast in the fridge, then moved all the food scraps onto one plate.

She opened the cabinet door under the sink, and when Selina came into the kitchen, Rea pointed at three lidded garbage cans. "The white one is for compost items, green is for recyclables, and the black as you can deduce is for real trash. We have several large commercial composters in a separate building for food waste, straw, wood shavings, and horse dung. I'll show you them tomorrow along with the larger cans for trash and recyclables, which are picked up by a disposal service from Greely."

Working in unison, they got everything sorted, rinsed, and put into the compact dishwasher. Rea poured more wine into her glass, while Selina got another beer from the fridge, and they retreated outside.

Rea eased down into the chair next to the firepit, where small flames still danced merrily away. The temperature had dropped with the sun, but there was enough warmth coming from the fire to keep things comfortable.

Before Selina sat down, she asked Rea, "Do you mind if I kill the patio lights, so we can enjoy the night sky?"

"Not at all." Even though the thought of sitting in the near darkness, alone, with an attractive woman, sent a little shiver down Rea's spine. Patches had parked himself in one of the other chairs and had picked his head up when she sat down. So, as silly as it seemed to her, Rea felt like she had a chaperone.

Once the patio lights went out, Selina slouched down into the chair next to hers and sighed as she stretched her long legs out in front of her, crossing them at the ankles. The subdued crackle of the fire was the only sound reaching Rea's ears, and the gentle quiet enveloped her. A soft breeze flitted around her, drawing the smell of the wood smoke into the air. Her eyes followed its wispy trail until Rea was gazing into the clear night sky, laced with glittering stars that weren't masked by light pollution. It was pleasant, and the easy-going company made her feel less alone for a change.

When Rea saw a streak of light arcing across the sky, she pointed and said, "Quick. Make a wish."

"Oh, I don't need to," Selina confessed. "I made one a few nights ago, and I have a token that promises it will come true."

Intrigued, Rea asked, "What kind of token do you mean…if you don't mind my asking?"

"Give me a minute to go get something, then I'll tell you a little about it."

When she disappeared inside, Rea speculated on what Selina was going to show her, but was quickly distracted by the intrusion of a revenant presence near her. The sensation caused her heart to race and the hair on the back of her neck to rise. Rea searched the dark landscape then finally spotted the ghostly form of the white wolf about a hundred yards away—captured momentarily in a beam of light from the moon as it played hide and seek through the swaying branches of a tree—when the spot was next illuminated, the wolf was gone. This was the second time in as many days that the white specter had appeared, and she wasn't sure if she could believe her eyes. Rea felt caught out by the encounter and the notion there was something mystical at work.

*****

Selina hustled inside, feeling a strong desire to share at least a part of the story of her recent journey with Rea. She sat on the edge of the bed, opened her pouch, and pulled out the meteorite. Running her fingers over the bumpy surface of the heart-shaped rock, Selina contemplated precisely how much she should reveal. A flicker of movement outside the window caught Selina's attention. She stepped closer, peering through the glass, as her eyes probed the shadowed yard until she spotted her spirit guide. It flickered in and out of sight between heartbeats, but its appearance here, to her, was a sign confirming she was precisely where she was meant to be.

Everything Selina had been missing in her life seemed to reside here—the perfect job, the horses she'd missed so much, but most of all, the uncommonly beautiful woman, whose interests and life philosophies melded with her own. Selina believed that most of the day, Rea had only displayed her public face, allowing the merest snippets of her inner soul to surface, and she wanted to uncover more of it. Selina hoped that when Rea heard her mystic meteor tale, it might jar things loose.

She quietly made her way to the door and found Rea's still form, staring off into the darkness, almost as if she was in a trance. So as not to startle her, Selina withdrew a step. Spotting the wine bottle, she called out, "I'm going to grab another beer, do you need more wine?"

"I could use a little more, why don't you bring the bottle out with you."

Selina settled a beer and the wine bottle in the crook of her arm then went back outside. She put down both then dragged her chair closer to Rea, so she'd be able to see her face. Selina noted a slight tremor in Rea's hand as she poured the last of the wine into her glass, and contemplated its cause. She didn't think it was anything she'd said or done. Selina had been friendly, but like Rea, she'd guarded her personal side—it was about trust—she needed to give it to get it. So, she'd make the first move, lift the veil, and give Rea a peek beneath it.

Selina opened her fist and held out her hand. "Here, take a look," she said, offering her talisman to Rea. "This meteorite landed near my campsite the evening of our interview."

Rea reached over and gently took it from her. Selina focused on the agile fingers as they fondled the rock, discovering its contours with a sensitive touch.

She continued, "I went home to Arizona four days ago after my latest relationship, and job ended at the same time. In the Native American culture, when wisdom or guidance is needed, you seek out a respected elder. For me, that was always my Amá sání, which is Diné for grandmother, but she passed away a few years back. I made a pilgrimage to a place that has special meaning for me and had a little one-sided ceremonial talk with her. I was feeling lost and wished for her to guide my next steps in life. Meteors in many cultures are seen as lucky objects, omens, or signs of change. My grandmother told me they were heavenly messengers. I believe they are all of those things, and I think she sent it to me as a promise that I would get my wish."

As she'd spoken, Selina had kept her gaze locked onto Rea's hand. Watching her thumb run over the crack, as if to rub it away. She had purposefully kept from looking up, feeling exposed by sharing something so personal. Selina had never revealed aspects of her cultural beliefs with any of her girlfriends, but here she was, sharing them with Rea.

Selina tilted her head up to look into Rea's eyes as she confessed. "I think this meteorite is my talisman, and it's led me to where I am supposed to be." Seeing a look of shock deep in Rea's eyes, she quickly added, "And at least for the time being, that's here."

*****

From the moment Selina had handed Rea the meteorite, she felt something tingle across her awareness. As the story unfolded, she recalled the night vividly. Rea had seen a meteor streaking to earth too, and she'd made a wish. She wished she could find a way to fill the hole left in her heart by her wife's death. Rea had also had a one-sided conversation with Sherry that day, just like Selina had one with her grandmother, regarding divine intervention. Whereas Selina had requested hers, she'd dared Sherry to intervene, so that part wasn't exactly a wish.

Rea hadn't missed the overall shape of the rock or the minute crack she traced with her thumb, and it was perfectly symbolic of how she'd felt for the last three years. What was Selina's part in this cosmic equation? When those compelling blue eyes sought

Rea's and revealed her belief that some outside force was directing things, like a mirage, the evanescent features of a wolf superimposed itself over Selina's face, then was gone. Shock filtered through Rea's system. Blinking rapidly, she tried to dispel the feeling she'd been caught up in some bizarre fairy tale.

Wary eyes searched hers, making Rea realize how much personal information Selina had shared, and she felt compelled to reciprocate.

"I think I witnessed this falling," Rea said, looking at the rock in her hand. "It was around nine, and I was coming in from bedding down the horses when I saw a meteor streaking to earth in the southeast. I made a wish, but also expressed my hope that anyone else doing the same would be granted theirs too." Rea looked into Selina's eyes. "Hearing your story, I can't help but think you are right, and we're both being nudged in the same direction."

Rea felt drained and emotionally raw. She imagined Selina might be too and decided to bring their evening to a close. She handed the meteorite back to Selina, rose from the chair, then grabbed the empty wine bottle off the table.

Rea turned to Selina, who was still sitting in her chair and said, "I want to thank you for the delicious dinner. I haven't had a good steak like that in too long. The company was also appreciated, but I think it's time for me to hit the hay. As you know, morning comes early on a farm."

"Yes, it does. I also enjoyed the meal and the company. Please text me in the morning when you get ready to head to the barn, so I can help you with the horses."

Rea nodded. "I will. Goodnight then." She slapped her hand against her thigh and directed, "Come along Patches."

He hopped off the chair, stretched, then went over to Selina to offer his own goodnight, before following Rea to the house. Once inside the mudroom, her back smacked against the door, and she intoned, "Oh, Sherry, this is, *SO*, not good!"

Chapter Eighteen

The Morning After

After Rea left, Selina stayed on the patio, sipping the last of her beer, and staring into the fire, while contemplating the events of the evening. She was unabashedly attracted to Rea, but what's more, they seemed to fit together. Selina sensed Rea was drawn to her as well but was fighting it. She'd caught the sound of Rea's indrawn breath, and the flush on her cheeks, as she'd sucked the butter off her fingers at dinner.

Despite the fact Rea hadn't shared the particulars about her wife's death, the unmistakable signs of melancholy and anger still remained. Selina didn't know how long ago it was, but apparently, Rea was still grieving. Any loss was painful, but those with a tragic aspect took much longer to move beyond. Selina was sure of one thing, however—whatever the story was—Rea was suffering from a wounded heart.

Selina turned the meteorite over and over in her hand, as endless questions spun through her mind. What had Rea wished for, and were their fates now intertwined? Her hand tightened on her talisman. Selina thought she felt the throb of power hidden at its heart, echoing in the pulse of her fingers. She knew what she believed—the signs were all there—but only time would tell.

Feeling genuinely content for the first time in years, Selina smothered the last of the burning coals and went inside the RV. She luxuriated in a hot shower before sinking into the softness of the pillowtop bed. Selina turned onto her side and wrapped her arms around the extra pillow hugging it to herself as she would embrace a lover. Her last thought before being pulled into a dreamless sleep was that maybe soon, she might share a bed with Rea.

*****

In contrast only fifty yards away, Rea tossed and turned, finding it impossible to shut off her brain. Having consumed a whole bottle of wine by herself, she ought to have passed out by now. Instead, Rea lay in bed, her mind going over and over her interactions with Selina, from the moment she'd stepped out of her truck at the warehouse until Rea left the patio. Selina was undeniably a perfect fit for the job, and someone Rea shared many common interests with. Even Patches, Dolly and Jupe, had bonded with her quickly, and Rea had been thanking her lucky stars for finding her. But that thought had taken on a whole new connotation now. Whether it was a talisman, as Selina believed, or some other kind of cosmic tampering, Rea felt inexorably pulled toward her.

She finally fell into a restless sleep tormented by fitful dreams. Rea wasn't sure if it was the reverberating sound of Rory's crowing cascading through her throbbing skull or her wine-filled bladder that woke her. She rolled onto her back and pulled the pillow down over her head, hoping the change of position would ease her urgent need to pee for a few minutes while she unglued her brain. Her mouth was dry, so Rea ran her tongue over her teeth and the roof of her mouth as she swallowed, trying to generate some spit. She'd probably been snoring all night, as

Sherry said she tended to do when she had a tad too much to drink.

Sherry! Fragments of the dreams filtered through Rea's groggy brain and twined together. Sherry had been lecturing her on her promise, telling her she'd mourned long enough. In another, Rea was standing in the yard naked, while a wolf looked on with its light blue eyes boring into hers. Finally, the clearest was right before Rea woke. Selina had been holding out the heart-shaped rock, cupped in her hands, a look of desire on her face, offering it to her like a gift—and this last one had left her yearning.

That thought catapulted Rea out of bed. Chill bumps erupted over her naked skin as she left her warm cocoon for the bathroom. A hiss escaped her lips as her ass cheeks came into contact with the cold toilet seat, but was soon followed by a sigh of relief. Rea washed down some aspirin, before stepping into a steamy shower. The heat helped ease the ache in her head and soothed her tense muscles. By the time she'd dressed, let Patches out, then sat down at the bar with her first cup of coffee, Rea was ready to try and sort out her thoughts and feelings.

Dreams are the windows of the soul, or so the saying went, and hers seemed to be urging her to let someone new into her heart. Selina had said last night she thought she'd been guided here, but for what? The job or for Rea? She recalled the appearance of the wolf last night, then in her dream. Those blue eyes, like Selina's, had been drawing her in. But Rea had seen the wolf before she'd even gotten Selina's resume, so what was its part in this mystical play? There were so many questions, and Rea didn't have answers to any of them. What she needed to do was relax, go with the flow, and try not to over-analyze every little thing, like she tended to do.

With a grunt, Rea got to her feet and went to the coffee pot for a refill. As she gazed out the window, her eyes gravitated toward the RV. In the low light of dawn, she could just make out the form of Selina sitting on the patio with Patches at her side. That explained why he hadn't been back in for his breakfast yet. But Rea needed to eat soon to help soak up the last of the alcohol in her system.

One thing she could cook was breakfast tacos, and Rea had some homemade tortillas double wrapped in the freezer. Before she could overthink things, Rea scooped up her phone and sent a message to Selina, inviting her over for a morning meal. A minute later, she got a gif of a baby pig rubbing its belly, followed by—*When?*

Rea texted back—*thirty minutes*—and got a thumbs-up emoji. She started pulling things from the fridge as she hummed the tune, "Ironic" by Alanis Morissette.

*****

Selina had awakened before sunrise to the crowing of a rooster, something she hadn't experienced since the last time she'd been home. She'd set the thermostat to sixty-four before going to bed, so she was snuggled up under the soft cotton sheets and the warm down comforter. Selina's mind drifted in a comfortable haze, thinking about the day ahead.

Finally, she rolled over, sat up, put her feet on the floor, then raised both arms over her head and stretched. After loosening the kinks, Selina rose from the bed, dressed in layers, then hit the kitchen to make a half pot of coffee. She sniffed appreciatively, as the rich aroma of the French roast permeated the air. There was nothing finer in the morning than the smell of brewing coffee. Filling her insulated travel mug, Selina left the RV to enjoy the sunrise from the patio.

She'd only been outside for a few minutes when Patches appeared. "Well, hello there handsome, does this mean your mom's up?" He looked back to the house as if he expected Rea to be behind him, before ambling over. "I guess she will be along later then." Patches pawed her arm till she dropped her hand over the chair and started petting him.

Selina's phone pinged, interrupting their quiet interlude. She pulled it out of her pocket to find a message from Rea, inviting her to breakfast. Pleased at the invitation and feeling more than one kind of hunger, Selina found a funny gif to text back, also asking when. Another ding and she had her answer.

A smile formed at the corners of her lips as she glanced at Patches. "Your mom invited me to breakfast, and I can't wait to share her company again. I've got thirty minutes, want to hang out with me till then?" He cocked his head to the side with a look she interpreted to mean—What do you think? So, Selina shoved her phone back into her pocket and resumed stroking his soft fur.

She'd felt on top of the world this morning, and the thought of sharing breakfast with Rea had her thinking about possibilities.

Selina innately understood she would need to let Rea set the pace, just like with Jupe. She'd reach out to both of them but would have to let them come to her. It was all about trust. They needed to learn that she cared for them, and would treat them gently, handling their hearts with care. Selina hoped by spending as much time as possible with both of them, they would find out.

*****

Rea had thrown a half dozen foil-wrapped tortillas into the oven on low while she fixed the eggs. She couldn't help glancing out the window as she moved between the sink and stove, wondering what it would be like to be with Selina. Rea thought, not for the first time that Selina was one of the most beautiful women she'd ever seen. Her wife had also been exquisite, and Rea had been thrilled when Sherry had found her attractive. Would Selina even be interested in an older, pudgy woman like her? She could have any woman she turned those sexy, blue eyes on, and it was hard for Rea to imagine that Selina would turn them on her. She needed to put that thought away, or her insecurities would stop her, before seeing if there might even be anything between them.

Rea heard the knock on the back door just as she was setting the serving dish with the warmed tortillas on the breakfast bar. Taking a deep breath, she called out, "Come in," then returned to the stove to scoop the cooked taco mixture into a bowl.

The click of nails on the floor preceded the thud of boot heels announcing the arrival of both Patches and Selina. Not ready to face her yet, Rea directed, "Have a seat at the bar. You've got perfect timing. I'm just finishing up now."

"Thanks for inviting me, it smells delicious."

Steadying herself, Rea turned around. "It's just your basic scrambled eggs with potatoes, chorizo, and some chopped bell pepper. Mia's fresh tortillas and homemade salsa are what will make them delicious."

Rea focused on Patches as she set the bowl down. "I guess I should get your breakfast ready too, hey boy? Go ahead and dig in Selina, while I get Patches his food."

She filled his bowl with special grain-free organic morsels from the sealed tub in the pantry. Rea ordered it from a lesbian couple that set up shop in Santa Barbara. They sent her a fresh shipment every two weeks. Setting it down next to his water bowl, Patches scurried over and happily started crunching away.

Rea glanced over her shoulder in time to see Selina leaning over her plate, taking a huge bite out of an overstuffed tortilla. A glob of the salsa dripped onto her chin, and as soon as Selina swallowed, her tongue streaked out, trying to wipe it clean. Rea's throat went dry at the sight and made her realize she hadn't put out any drinks.

"Would you like coffee, milk, or maybe some orange juice, Selina?"

"I'd love a glass of milk, thank you. I try to have at least one glass a day. You know what they say—Milk does a body good."

It's certainly done yours good! Flustered, Rea opened the cabinet and took out two glasses. She filled both with milk, then carried them back to the bar top and put them down. Instead of sitting next to Selina, Rea opted to stand on the other side and eat her tacos standing up, feeling the need to keep some space between them.

A congenial silence descended on them as they devoured their tacos. At the sound of a sensual moan, Rea lifted her eyes from her plate and watched as Selina drained half her glass of milk in a series of long swallows.

Selina caught her gaze, smiling as she held up the glass. "This is first-rate milk, so rich and creamy. What brand is it?"

"Promised Land. It's my favorite. I got used to having it when I lived in College Station. For the longest time, it wasn't available in Semi Valley. But when it finally hit the market there, I started buying it again and haven't stopped since. I talked Hank and June into ordering it in for the store. Since I'm basically their landlord they humor me. I'm glad you like it."

"Oh, it is delicious, and I recall having it as a kid, too, when I lived in Llano. It came in glass bottles if I remember correctly, but I'm not sure." A note of sadness had crept into Selina's voice. "When I went to live with my grandparents, the only milk brand I think our market carried was Bordens."

Rea had wanted to ask about her grandparents before, and couldn't help but inquire about it this time, "Why did you go to live with them? If the question is too personal, you don't need to answer."

"It's not exactly a happy story, are you sure you want to hear it?"

"Only if it won't dredge up any unpleasant memories."

"I can't promise that, but here goes. My mother and little brother died when I was almost twelve. Her car was swept away during heavy rains. She was on her way to pick me up from school. I normally rode the bus, but Mom decided to come into town that afternoon to get me because of the storm. I got on the bus as usual, but it had to stop and turn around at the same creek because it was flooded, and the water was too high to drive through. When the driver took the few of us that were still on the bus back to school, they called my dad to let him know, and that's when he realized my mom hadn't made it into town. They had to wait until the rain let up to start the search. They located the car right away, but it took several more days to find them."

Rea tried to swallow the lump rising in her throat as Selina's tale unfolded, her heart aching over the tragic loss.

Selina's intonation traversed from sad to hollow. "Dad didn't take the loss well and started drinking heavily. When he was drunk, he would start ranting and raving about how their deaths were all my fault. If not for me, she wouldn't have gone out in the storm, taking my little brother with her."

Selina's head tilted to the left, and she seemed to focus inward. "I was never sure whether it was the loss of my mom or my little brother, Hunter, that bothered him the most. He doted on Hunter and merely tolerated me. He was a male chauvinist pig and treated my mom like a drudge."

Selina took a large gulp of milk as if to remove the bitter taste of her words before continuing. "We were both immensely grateful when my grandparents came and got me. He died a few years later, in a bar fight, down in San Antonio. They never said a bad word about him, but my aunt sure did. She said Mom was taken in by his superficial good looks. They'd met at a rodeo, that my dad was competing in, and eloped a week later before Mom discovered it only went skin-deep." Selina's tone was somber.

There wasn't much Rea could say to that but felt the need to connect with her. She reached across the counter and gently laid her hand over Selina's, which was pressing hard against the bar top, as if forcing the memories down, offering her comfort. The hand beneath hers gradually relaxed.

A sad little smile tugged at her lips, then Selina continued. "It was a long time ago, and while it was hard at first, I was lucky. My grandparents were great, and I felt more at home in Holbrook than I ever had in Llano. Back there, some of the kids would taunt me by singing 'Half Breed' whenever the teachers weren't around. But in Holbrook, most of the kids at my school had at least a little Native blood, so it was a whole new world for me."

Selina's eyes had lost their faraway look as she stared down at Rea's hand. She turned hers over and gave Rea's a gentle squeeze before pulling it back into her lap. Rea understood Selina's profound loss—even though hers was different—they might both benefit if she shared hers.

Chapter Nineteen

Tit for Tat

Selina hadn't meant to turn a pleasant breakfast into a discourse of her shitty childhood, but when Rea asked about her grandparents, the story flowed out, like a dam being breached. She'd been so lost in the memories she hadn't been aware Rea had reached out and made physical contact until she'd purged them. She acknowledged the quiet comfort before pulling back, waiting for the expected platitude.

"I lost the love of my life, my wife Sherry, a little over three years ago. I thought I understood loss because both my parents died before I'd turned nineteen. But they'd lived good full lives, and I came to terms with it by knowing they were together. Sherry's death was nothing like that. With her gone, I was totally alone again. She was my only family and my whole world. Yes, we had friends, and they reached out to me, but they couldn't touch my grief."

Rea stood up abruptly, grabbed both plates, and moved stiffly toward the sink, clearly agitated. She set them down with a loud clatter, and without turning around, asked, "I need a cup of coffee, how about you?"

"No, I'm good." Selina stayed quiet, understanding Rea might need a minute to gather herself together.

Rea returned, put a cup down in front of the empty barstool this time, and took a seat before turning toward Selina. "You asked about the money for the farm. It was a payoff for Sherry's death. She worked for a company called Excologen, and since they are big in the agricultural market, I'm sure you've heard of them."

She only nodded, afraid that even a word from her right now might interrupt Rea's revelations. As the story unfolded, Selina felt every bit of Rea's emotions as she revisited the grief and the anger she lived through, before finding contentment and purpose in life by working to fulfill her dead wife's wishes.

Rea broadcast every nuance of her poignant journey through the inflections of her voice, expressive hazel eyes, and animated face. With furrowed brows and eyes darkened in pain, the words trembling past Rea's lips painted an all too familiar story of the effects of corporate wealth taking precedence over human life. Golden flecks of ire had fired the green eyes in a face tightened by disgust, and the timbre of her voice increased, conveying the retribution she'd extracted. Finally, all of them lightened as she spoke of the need to make Sherry's dream into a reality. Her hope that if she could bring it all to fruition, she could somehow make Sherry's death count for something.

Selina now understood why the farm wasn't just a business to Rea. It was meant to be a tribute to someone she had loved deeply and lost. Yes, they both shared a deep and abiding grief, that, while in the past, was still keenly felt.

In empathy, Selina reached out, as Rea had done earlier. She placed her hand palm up on Rea's knee and waited for her to grip it before saying, "Your wife was a truly remarkable person, and I feel privileged to help you in any way I can."

The eyes that locked onto hers changed to a stormy gray-green color, and what she saw there tugged at Selina's soul. They were filled with a look she couldn't quite read but seemed to plead for an emotional anchor. Unconsciously Selina stood up and pulled Rea into a protective embrace offering solace, the only way she knew how. Rea accepted the gesture and molded her soft body into Selina's. She heard Rea's gentle sigh then felt a warm wetness stain her shirt. Selina didn't know what the tears meant, but she felt closer to Rea than she had with anyone else in a very long time.

*****

Reliving the last five years with Selina had been cathartic. It was the first time Rea had been able to share it all with someone other than Sherry, and that wasn't the same. Sherry was gone. A ghost couldn't look into her eyes, hear the hitch in her breathing, or touch her in comfort. Loneliness filled Rea until Selina reached out and offered her something more than understanding. She offered herself. A solid presence in Rea's life that she felt drawn to. The compassionate arms that wound around her felt so right. The tears she'd let slip free were as much from gratitude as a release from the tension the memories had wrought.

Cradled in Selina's quiet embrace, her thoughts returned to the dreams again. This is what they were telling her. To let go of the past and look toward a future, possibly with the woman holding her so tenderly. With her cheek pillowed against a rounded breast, and Selina's chin resting atop her head, she inhaled the spicy scent permeating the soft flannel shirt beneath her nose.

Though she was loath to move, she was starting to feel a little vulnerable by the intimacy of it all. With a last squeeze, Rea let go and pulled back. Selina's arms slowly loosened, but she moved one of her hands to Rea's shoulder, not allowing her to retreat too far.

Rea looked up into those mesmerizing, blue eyes filled with caring concern, and said, "Thank you. I'm okay now." She reached up across her body and patted Selina's hand. "Why don't we move on to something more pleasant, like enjoying some time with the horses this morning?"

A grin broke out on Selina's face, effectively changing the mood instantly, and she stepped back. "I'd love that. By the way, breakfast was delicious, so let me help you clean up the dishes."

Freed, Rea hustled around the bar top, taking the glasses and cups to the sink to join the plates. Selina followed, so they got everything rinsed and put in the dishwasher in no time.

In the mudroom, Patches paced back and forth as if put out by the short delay while Rea put on her boots. When she and Selina stepped out onto the porch, he shot off to explore as they headed for the barn.

The walk dissipated most of the tension that had built up during her emotionally charged morning. Maybe Rea should take Dolly for a ride since they hadn't been out for the past two days. Perhaps she should offer the opportunity to Selina instead. Rea knew it would brighten her day.

With Selina's longer stride, Rea followed a few steps behind, and openly admired the androgynous figure ahead of her. Selina's hair was expertly braided this morning and hung more than halfway down her back. Rea imagined loosening the strands that appeared silky soft and running her fingers through them. She quickly quashed the thought when Selina paused and looked back at her, waiting for Rea to catch up.

As soon as the barn doors opened, Dolly greeted them with a welcoming whinny, and surprisingly, Jupe had his head over the stall door. He generally stayed to the back whenever Rea came in. He'd really warmed up since Selina came, but then again, so had she.

Selina stopped at Jupe's stall, unlatched the gate, and went inside, while Rea continued on into the tack room. She grabbed an extra bucket and was filling it with cleaning tools when the flowing strains of what Rea guessed was Native American music filtered through the barn. She peeked out to see Selina and Jupe caught in a shaft of light from the morning sun, beaming in through the barn door. They seemed to glow as they stood cheek to cheek with Selina serenely stroking his neck. Jupe seemed utterly relaxed and content.

Selina stopped, then glanced her way, capturing Rea's gaze, before starting toward where she stood frozen in the doorway. Selina moved with cat-like grace and paused a hair's breadth away from Rea. The mellow warmth in Selina's blue eyes flowed over her and blended with the melodic tones of the flute playing in the background. Rea's heartbeat slowed, and her breathing eased, until Selina reached out, and touched her forearm, then slowly ran her fingers down to where Rea's gripped the bucket.

Heat suffused her muscles, and her bones liquefied, triggering the release of the handle from her nerveless digits. Selina caught it as it dropped. Giving Rea a knowing smile, she turned without a word and went back to Jupe.

Rea was at a loss to explain the impact the encounter had on her, but she felt its effects. In a daze, she gathered up her own bucket and returned to Dolly's stall. Rea worked the soft rubber curry comb along Dolly's flank but kept looking across the way, unsurprised to see Jupe's placid acceptance of his grooming. Selina definitely had a magic touch, and Rea felt just as spellbound.

*****

Selina lovingly cleaned every inch of Jupe's coat as she reflected on her interactions with Rea this morning. She felt like she'd breached an invisible door that Rea had locked herself behind, after the death of her wife. It hadn't kept Rea from caring for those around her, nor the animals she chose to rescue, but it limited their access to her in return. Selina knew from experience it was a means of self-preservation that she, herself, had used in the past.

On autopilot, she retrieved a pick from the bucket, and bent one of Jupe's knees between her legs, removing the debris from his unshod hoof, as she recalled the feel of Rea in her arms this morning. Something unspoken and healing had flowed between them as they shared their painful pasts with each other. The intimate exchange went a long way toward filling up the empty space inside her with comfort.

Selina had just finished with Jupe when the haunting refrains of her favorite song started playing. There was something in the way those pure tones flowed together that spoke to her soul, and brought her serenity. When Selina picked up the bucket, she noticed Jupe's head had drooped, and he'd locked his legs, preparing to nap. She smiled in satisfaction, knowing she'd also breached the trust barrier with him.

Selina exited the stall, and her phone fell silent as the playlist reached its end. Her gaze immediately fell on Rea, who was sitting on a stool with her back resting against the stall wall, with her eyes closed. A chuckle broke loose from Selina, causing Rea to jerk awake.

A light shade of pink blossomed on Rea's cherubic cheeks as she looked down sheepishly at the floor. When Selina's chuckle turned into a full-throated laugh, Rea looked up, and the flush deepened. A mutinous pout played about her lips as her eyes crinkled up.

"I wasn't asleep," Rea huffed. "I just had my eyes closed to better enjoy the music. It was lovely and so soothing. What was it?"

Selina didn't know why Rea was embarrassed about napping, but she allowed the diversion. "They're from an album—Closer to Far Away—by Douglas Spotted Eagle. Although he has no Native American blood and he adopted the name himself, I enjoy the arrangements he created. They are not true Native songs, but he managed to capture some of the spirit of our traditional music.

The last one that played is called 'Still Waters,' and it's my favorite."

"I would love to have a copy of those to listen to when I read in the evenings."

"I can lend you the CD, or you can rip them into your computer if it has a disk player."

Rea's lips pulled up into an exuberant smile bringing out the darling dimples at the base of her cheeks. "I'd love that, thank you. I was thinking…you might enjoy taking Dolly out this morning. She's due for a ride, and I can clean the barn while you're gone."

As much as Selina relished the thought of galloping away on Dolly, she didn't want to part ways from Rea yet. Jupe wasn't ready to carry a passenger, but she thought he would easily follow behind on a lead rope. It was something Selina felt she could use to perhaps coax Rea into riding with her.

"I was going to suggest a different outing. I think Jupe's eager to explore a bit but would require Dolly's company. I'll need to keep my attention on him, so…it would be best if we could ride double," she cajoled.

Selina watched closely, as surprise and indecision were plainly displayed on Rea's face. Her eyes moved left to right and back again like she was playing a game of Pong. Clearly, there was an internal argument going on, and she held her breath, waiting to see what the outcome would be.

*****

Rea was still slightly flustered from the whole napping thing, but the thought of riding double with Selina increased it. If she did, she would be in Selina's arms again for a second time this morning, and the thought brought on a tingle of desire. Rea wasn't sure if she was ready to let Selina any closer yet.

On the other hand, it would be good for Jupe to get out, and what Selina said made sense. Rea couldn't help but think Selina would have no trouble controlling both horses, so why did she suggest it? Was Selina actually attracted to her, too, Rea wondered?

Finding no answer to her internal questions, she fastened her gaze on Selina, who'd gone still. The pleading look in those eyes, deepening to a china blue, drew Rea in. Unable to deny them both something that would obviously bring them pleasure, she capitulated.

"Okay, we can take a short ride together, as long as we go at an easy pace. I don't want Dolly to have to carry the extra weight around for long. Come into the tack room, and we'll get them both ready. What type of halter do you want?"

"I'd prefer a hackamore versus a bridle if you have one."

"I have two of them, and the only bridle here was the one they used on Jupe when they brought him here. I only use a hackamore on Dolly, which is all a good rider and a well-trained horse needs," she stated emphatically.

"You're right. I can tell by your setup and your way with them, you're experienced. Did you grow up with horses?"

"No. I only got to work with them and ride during the summers at Girl Scout camp. I always wanted one, but it wasn't an option before I got this farm. I was a little rusty to start with, but Dolly was patient with me while I relearned things." Rea smiled at the memories.

"Oh, where did you go to camp?"

"In Angel Fire, New Mexico. Even though we lived in Colorado Springs, it was the best camp near us with a horse training program."

Selina's head jerked back, and her mouth formed a perfect 'O' then she said excitedly, "We used to take ten or twelve of our best riding horses over there. The first time was the summer after I came to live with my grandparents. I think they hoped it would entice me to join the scouts, but it didn't."

Rea, in turn, was flabbergasted. She remembered that last summer at camp vividly. Her mother had been struggling with chemo at the time but was adamant that she attend. The beautiful, young girl who had arrived with her grandfather and had ridden all the horses into the corral bareback, had been Selina.

"Wow, what a small world. I was there that day. I even spoke to the tall man with silver hair offering to help with the unloading. He'd told me his granddaughter would take care of it. You fascinated me…I mean, your abilities with them did, and I can see they've only grown over time."

Selina quirked her head to the side. "I don't remember seeing you, but I was only paying attention to the horses. It's cool you met my grandfather, though." She smiled. "He could ride, of course, but it was my Great-Uncle Don who me taught to ride and train them."

Rea turned toward the tack room and had just taken a step or two, when behind her Selina said, "If you're up for it, how about riding Dolly bareback to ease the load on her?" The question caused Rea to stutter step.

The thought of having Selina's body pressed up against hers, without a saddle between them was disconcerting, but it would be much better for Dolly. Even with the lightweight one, Rea used, it would be twenty-five fewer pounds for Dolly to carry. With her weight hovering around one-seventy-five, that reduction would make a difference, so she answered, "I'm up for it."

"Great. Then all we'll need are two hackamores and a long lead rope for Jupe."

"I have one that will clip onto the cavesson." Stopping inside the room, she handed both to Selina then grabbed the one she always used for Dolly from the peg.

Selina exited, but Rea stopped long enough to stuff both pockets of her jacket with treats for the horses. By the time she came out, Selina was already buckling Jupe into the hackamore, and he was allowing it. Dolly stretched her neck up and neighed her encouragement. Yup, it looked like they were all just a little excited about the outing.

Chapter Twenty
Hot to Trot

Selina's excitement was running high, but she still approached Jupe cautiously. He'd raised his head with his ears pitched forward and eyed her, but stood his ground. "Ho, Shik'is. You're going to love this. We will be taking a little walk with your girlfriend." She patted his neck then showed him the hackamore. "Now, if you will let me put this on, we can hit the trail." Jupe allowed her to slip it over his head with no fuss, and she had it buckled by the time Rea had reached the stall.

Rea pulled two small cakes out of her pocket, then held them both out to her. "Here are some treats for Jupe. We'll give them both a good breakfast when we get back."

Selina examined one. It was semi-soft and looked like a fruit oatmeal bar. Holding it to her nose, she could smell the distinctive aroma of molasses. She held it out to Jupe, and he lipped her palm, scooping it into his mouth. After he finished it off, Jupe dropped his head and nudged her right hand with his nose wanting the other treat.

She laughed. "Okay, Jupe, you've been such a good boy this morning that I'll let you have the other one."

Selina led him out of the open stall door and paused to watch Rea harnessing Dolly. She skillfully buckled the hackamore, checking the fit with two fingers under the cheek strap, her movements quick and precise. Selina closed her eyes as a shiver rippled through her, imagining those two fingers doing something decidedly more intimate. She fought down the thought and walked Jupe outside. Selina didn't want to get on the back of Dolly with that in her mind, or she'd combust on the spot. By the time Rea exited the barn, Selina had herself under control.

Rea gave her a questioning look, and asked, "I don't have any mounting steps, how should we do this?"

Selina searched the area, but the only thing she could see in the vicinity to use was the paddock fence. Pointing to it, she said, "Why don't I hold Dolly still, while you can climb up on the second rail, then you should be high enough to slide on, and I'll mount the same way."

"That should work," Rea said and led Dolly over to the fence.

Selina followed behind with Jupe, then put a hand on Dolly's flank to keep her steady. Rea clambered up and awkwardly tried to mount several times, but with her short legs, the gap between the rail and Dolly's back was just a bit too far.

"Okay, I can see this is not working out the way we planned. Let me tie Jupe to the rail, then I'll give you a hand up instead."

"I don't know if that's such a good idea, I'm pretty hefty." Rea looked down as if ashamed.

"No. You. Are. Not. I find your plush curves very appealing," she stated unequivocally.

Rea looked at her dubiously but climbed down off the fence. Selina secured Jupe, then she stood at Dolly's shoulder. Bending her knees, she lowered her cupped hands for Rea's booted foot. As she lifted her up, Selina thought she caught the musky scent of arousal emanating from the crotch of Rea's jeans, only an inch or two from her face. Desire coursed through her again. Maybe riding double wasn't such a great idea after all.

On jelly filled legs, she went around Dolly, untied Jupe's led, and handed it to Rea. Selina firmly pushed against Dolly's flank until it was next to the fence again. Climbing up to the second rail, she gripped Rea's waist and gently slid on. Dolly shifted a little but seemed fine with the weight of both riders. Selina inched back, putting a hand's width of distance between them, all too aware of the dangerous effect the woman in front of her had on her escalating libido.

*****

Rea could no longer deny the attraction she felt toward Selina or the possibility the attraction might be mutual. She found it hard to believe, but she'd seen the desire flare in Selina's eyes and heard the conviction in her voice when Rea had made reference to her weight. The look had struck something within her that vibrated through her system like a tuning fork, setting every nerve ending humming. Rea felt an answering pulse in her clit as she mounted, and having the provocative woman settled in behind her was making it worse.

"Ah…Rea, can you give me Jupe's rein?"

"Sure,"—she handed it behind her—"are you ready to go?"

"Yeah. Anytime you are. I'm excited to see more of your farm."

"It's about a mile to the river. The trail passing the orchard is the most scenic, so let's go that way. When we reach the river, we can give the horses a rest there, then head back. Sound good to you?"

"Absolutely. Oh, look here comes Patches."

"Yes, he loves to go out with Dolly. Hopefully, him tagging along won't spook Jupe. He can be a little energetic on these rides."

"I'm sure Jupe and Patches will be fine. Animals can usually sense each other's intentions. As long as it doesn't alarm Dolly, it won't alarm Jupe."

With a soft tug on the rein, Rea turned Dolly, then gave her a slight kick with her heel and guided her away from the barn. It was late enough in the morning that the sun was well over the horizon, and with the clear skies, the chill was gone from the air. She'd have been warm enough, in any case, with Dolly underneath her and Selina's body close behind her. Rea didn't want to let her mind go there, so she asked, without turning around, "How's Jupe doing?"

"Like a gosling following its mother."

"I'm happy. Jupe sure acts like a different horse since you came. He seems to have turned a corner. I was beginning to think he'd never move beyond the abuse he suffered."

"How did you wind up with them both?"

"I got Dolly by paying the boarding fees at a stable where she'd been abandoned by her owners. Dolly's vet, Carol, approached me about Jupe. She works with a rescue group and was looking for a place close by where he could convalesce, so she contacted me." Rea turned her head and eyed Jupe. "He didn't make it easy on me, that's for sure, and several times he tried to bite me. But with Dolly's help, he finally settled in, somewhat, so I decided to adopt him—which was good—because Carol hadn't been able to find anyone else willing to take him."

"I'm glad you didn't give up on him. He's beautiful, and a prime piece of horseflesh." Selina sighed, then steel entered her voice. "There are too many people out there who have no business owning any kind of animal or even having children, for that matter. They have no clue how to care for anything beyond themselves. You are one special lady, Rea."

She felt warmth fill her chest. Selina's admiration mattered more to Rea than she wanted to acknowledge.

"Thank you, Selina, but I didn't do anything all that special. I had the money and space for them. The people I respect are those who don't have a lot of either but still manage to open their hearts and homes for all kinds of orphans. Patches, Dolly, and Jupe saved me as much as I saved them."

Rea's breath hitched when she felt two strong arms slide around her middle, Selina's body firmly compacting her own, blanketing her in a warm embrace. Her chin came to rest on Rea's left shoulder, and Selina's warm breath tickled her ear.

"You're partially right, but here's the key part. Whether rich or poor, people have to have a heart big enough to care, and you have one. Otherwise, since you are financially able, you could have just thrown money at the problem. It takes time, effort, and love to properly care for any living creature, so don't diminish what you've done."

Those words, along with the sentiment behind them, landed deep in Rea's soul. She tried to draw in a deep breath, but the arms surrounding her tightened. Compelled to look into those blue eyes that so mesmerized her, Rea leaned to the right, turned, and swiveled her head. Selina's hands loosened from around her middle and slid down to grip her hips. The eyes gazing longingly into hers darkened, and Selina's bottom lip was caught between her teeth.

Rea could easily read the desire and uncertainty in Selina's expressive features that she felt sure were mirrored in her own. She felt magnetized by a profound need to connect with Selina's lips only inches away. Rea imagined how warm and sweet such a kiss would be. Her breath hitched, and she jerked her head back around, shocked by her thoughts. They barely knew each other, and besides, Rea argued with herself, Selina was her employee.

*****

With every little nugget of Rea's life she uncovered, Selina became more and more certain that Rea was the one for her. She was the whole package. Her nature seemed to encompass the best bits and pieces that had made up the souls of anyone Selina had ever loved. She knew no one was perfect—lord knows she wasn't—but Rea seemed to be the yin to her yang, and Selina wanted a chance for a life with her.

But did Rea feel the same way? Selina questioned herself. As Rea turned and locked eyes with her, she thought the answer was yes, but she could also read the hesitation there. She loosened her grip, sliding her hands to Rea's full hips. Selina was savvy enough to pick up the subliminal cues that things had become too emotionally intense and literally feel Rea pulling away.

Rea turned away abruptly from her intense scrutiny, blew out a breath she'd been holding, and said, "Those words mean a lot, Selina. Thanks again."

Selina squeezed the flesh under her hands to add emphasis to her words. "I meant it. You are one very special lady."

No more was said until they reached the orchard, where Rea started pointing out the different fruit trees, then launched into an explanation of the irrigation system. But Selina could only focus on the soft, warm body cupped against her own. Her interest wasn't on how the thirsty soil got its water but on how her thirst for Rea was growing. Selina's nose didn't register the smell of the cherry blossoms in the air, it was filled with Rea's woodsy scent. Her gaze was fixed on the tiny brown mole on the lobe of Rea's delicate ear instead of the showy white flowers mantling the trees. As they made their way down the trail, her ears didn't register the sound of the horses' hooves impacting the ground—the pounding of her heart drowned it out.

The heat of desire flowed through her, tightening her body. In some ways, things were moving too fast, and in others, not fast enough. Selina felt a sudden need to get off Dolly's back to put some space between her and Rea before she lost control of herself entirely. As if she'd communicated the need to Dolly, she broke into a trot. But the change in gate caused a new issue as her throbbing center bounced gently against Dolly's back.

Selina swallowed hard then asked, "How far is the river now? I think Dolly needs a rest." *And so do I.*

Rea pointed to a small, white structure off in the distance, standing out vividly against the line of trees behind it. "Just on the other side of the shed."

Selina felt she could hold out that long, but no longer. "It would probably be best if I got off and led Jupe through the trees anyway. Why don't we stop and walk them in from there?"

"I think you're right."

Selina thought she heard a hint of relief in Rea's voice, and Dolly picked up speed even more. The last few minutes of the ride were torturous. The second Dolly came to a stop, Selina quickly slid off her rump, and turned toward Jupe, to give herself a minute to gather herself together.

Surreptitiously, Selina glanced Rea's way and saw her leading Dolly down the trail, walking rather stiffly. Patches sat halfway in between them, swiveling his head back and forth as if trying to figure out what was going on with the humans.

Selina would love to have the answer to that one herself. She knew one thing for sure, and she expressed it to Jupe. "Boy, I hope you're ready to let me ride you home because there is no way in hell I can ride back behind Rea again."

Now that her mind wasn't being inundated with arousal, Selina's other senses kicked in. She could hear the gurgling of the river through the trees. The sound further soothed her jangled nerves, then she gently pulled on Jupe's lead and urged, "Let's go find the ladies, Shik'is."

The tall grass that had been prevalent along the trail during their ride became sparse as Selina entered the tree line. Various sized lichen-covered rocks were scattered among the trunks, some captured by knobby roots clinging fiercely to the earth. The smell of damp soil and wet wood suggested the river level had recently subsided.

Up ahead, the trees thinned, and the trail took a sharp turn downward toward the bank. There against the backdrop of the rippling water Rea stood off to the left, holding onto Dolly's reins as she drank, and Patches stood belly deep in the stream. Rea's face was in profile, chin up, eyes closed, as if soaking up some peace from her surroundings. With a single yip, Patches alerted Rea of her arrival, and she pulled Dolly to the side to make room for Jupe.

Selina eased her way down to the water's edge, then stationed herself to the right, putting both horses between them, just in case any of her latent desire still showed on her face. As nonchalantly as possible, she looked around the river. Selina spied a metal pole with wire lines attached to a pulley several yards away, extending to another one impaled on a rocky spit of land bisecting the water. A hose ran along the ground in the same area, then disappeared from view.

Selina turned back to Rea, nodding her head toward it. "What's with the poles and the hose?"

Rea gave her a quizzical look. "Um…it's a part of the irrigation system I was telling you about earlier. The poles, along with the lines, keep our slurpy in place, and the hose carries the water back to the pump shed."

Having no clue what a slurpy was, Selina found herself nodding to hide the fact that she hadn't been paying attention earlier. Of course, she didn't want Rea to know it, so she offered lamely, "Oh, that's what you were describing. Umm…I guess I just wasn't properly visualizing the logistics of it all."

Rea's lips bowed in, and her brows lowered as she squinted at Selina, as if she trying to decide whether to call her out on her fib. With a slight shake of her head, Rea let Selina off the hook.

"There's a nice place downstream,"—Rea said, pointing to her left—"around this bend, where we can tie these guys up for a bit. There is also has a nice sized boulder there to sit on and watch the river for a while."

Selina pulled on Jupe's lead then fell into step behind Rea. When they arrived at the spot, she could tell by the placement of a large rock slab, and the absence of all but a few small trees, the area had experienced a decent-sized flood sometime in the last decade. With the old growth torn away, the position of the boulder had funneled mud and silt into the gap, creating a new flood plain. Selina guessed that Rea stopped here often because the grass where she tied Dolly up was thinner. Securing Jupe's lead to the same tree, Selina went to join Rea on the flat rock and saw that Patches had found a sunny spot to lay down, not too far away.

Trying to be clever, Selina joked with a smile, "Come here often?"

In the same vein, Rea returned, "Why, yes, but I don't think I've ever seen you before. Are you just visiting?"

"No. I am new to the area, but I hope to stick around for quite a while," she delivered sincerely with a direct stare.

A broad smile punctuated Rea's cheeks, bringing out the dimples Selina had come to love, as she replied, "Then I'm sure we'll be seeing a lot of each other."

They spent a pleasant half-hour in general chit chat about the farm and Selina's previous work in the cannabis field as the horses rested. A message alert sounded from Rea's cell interrupting their discourse on pot's medicinal uses.

Rea grinned at the phone. "It's Mia. She's practically ordering me to bring you over to lunch later." She glanced uncertainly toward the horses then stood up. "I guess it's time to head back so we can take care of Dolly and Jupe. They haven't been fed yet, plus I need to spend a little time in my office before lunch."

As they approached the horses, Selina saw Rea's body stiffen slightly and surmised that she too had been affected by their close contact earlier. This reinforced her decision to ride back on Jupe.

"Let me help you up onto Dolly, but I think Jupe is ready for the next step in his recovery and will let me ride him back."

Selina heard the quick expulsion of air and saw Rea's shoulders relax, solidifying her conclusion they were both feeling the same thing. The one question she had left was how best to nudge Rea along, without scaring her off—the answer to that was patience—and she could only hope she would have enough.

Chapter Twenty-One

A Little Space

The ride to the river had been torturous for Rea. The desire she'd felt when they'd mounted Dolly had continued to grow, and Rea had tried to distract herself by giving Selina details about the fruit trees and the pump irrigation system. Rea had even hurried Dolly along—more than she should have—to reach the river sooner, so she could get down. But the increased pace had brought their bodies into close contact, causing Rea's to tense in need. She'd never been so glad to get off Dolly's back before, and hurried away, leaving the tempting Selina behind. Luckily, she had a few minutes at the water's edge to regroup before Selina and Jupe arrived.

Rea had been baffled when Selina had asked about the slurpy. She was sure she'd mentioned it as she babbled about everything…hadn't she? But then she'd seen Selina's guilty look, which told her as plain as day, that Selina had spent at least part of the ride as distracted as she had been.

The quick exchange of witty quips as they'd settled onto the boulder, had diffused some of Rea's tension and brought a smile to her face. Sitting at her favorite spot, with a gentle breeze caressing her face, and the river rippling along, had brought her a true measure of peace. But it had been the harmonious descant of their conversation that had turned the interlude into an enjoyable one.

Rea had been surprised when her phone pinged, and a text popped up. Generally, she didn't have any service out here, but the force of Mia's personality must have assured its delivery. Rea had laughed silently to herself at the message that had come through. Mia always used the voice to text feature, and some of the phone's interpretations were hilarious. The one she'd received was no exception.

Rea drew bring Selena to lunge by noon—but the message had been loud and clear. It was time for them to head home. She wanted a bit of solitude to try and sort out her feelings; so, she'd made up an excuse about having paperwork to do when they got back, to give it to her.

With every step toward Dolly, Rea had braced herself for the ride back. She feared her body would again respond to her increasing attraction to the woman behind her. When Selina stated she was going to ride Jupe home, she was both relieved and disappointed at the same time.

Now that Selina had boosted her up onto Dolly's back, Rea had a front-row seat to what she considered to be an epic moment. She watched in total fascination as Selina faced Jupe. Resting her forehead against his, her lips moved silently, conveying something to him that Rea couldn't hear. Selina patted Jupe's cheek, then tied the end of the long lead rope to the other side of the hackamore and looped it over his head.

In a move Rea recalled from so many years ago, Selina grabbed a lock of Jupe's mane, just in front of his withers, and vaulted onto his back in one fluid motion. She admired the lithe figure leaning forward, running a soothing hand over Jupe's neck. To Rea, one word seemed to fit both this woman's abilities and the woman herself—stunning.

Rea appreciated the breathing room on the way back to the barn but kept turning her head to watch the pair behind her. Jupe's gait was frisky at times as if he wanted to break out into a run, but Selina seemed able to effortlessly hold him in check. The sojourn home was swift. They had both horses cleaned, fed, and turned out into the paddock in short order.

At some point, Selina had removed her flannel shirt, which was now tied around her waist. The well-worn muscle t-shirt left little to Rea's imagination, and she could see the outlines of Selina's pert breasts beneath the thinning fabric. Her response was visceral. A shot of desire followed by a fear chaser had her aquiver, and Rea hoped that none of it had been apparent. She couldn't allow herself to cross the invisible line between fantasy and reality. Turning abruptly, Rea headed away from the barn, desperately in need of some physical space and time away from Selina. As she reached the garage, Rea called out loudly over her shoulder, "Meet you back here at eleven forty-five." Without waiting for a response, she scampered to her back door.

Once inside, she drew in a full breath, but it didn't slow the rapid beat of her heart. Rea slumped down to sit on the floor and intoned to the empty room, "God, Sherry, what the hell is going on with me?" accompanied by the soft thumping of her head impacting the door. "I only met her twenty-four freaking hours ago. Is she even attracted to me? I think she might be, but I could be reading those signals wrong. I have zero experience, after all. I've never been with anybody but you. And need I remind you she's my damn employee."

With a final decisive thump, as if to drive her point home, she muttered, "Things are going too fast for me. If you are manipulating things from the great beyond, you best knock it off right now and let me take things at my own pace."

Exasperated with herself, she rose from the floor and went to her office to get some work done. At least then she could redeem the lie she'd told earlier and maybe find a little peace of mind too.

*****

Selina was thankful Jupe's welfare required all of her attention, so she could focus on something besides Rea. It was effective until they'd let the horses loose in the paddock when she turned to find Rea's gaze fixed on her. Selina was pretty sure she'd caught a flare of longing running through Rea's features before she'd hastily wheeled around, and speed-walked away.

As Selina followed behind, she was wondering what Rea was thinking. When she didn't pause or look her way, and only relayed what time to meet, it became apparent to Selina that Rea was spooked—just like a shy filly would be if approached too abruptly.

She could guess at one of the things on Rea's mind right now because it was in hers as well. They were moving too fast. Selina knew they both needed time to get to know each other better before altering their relationship. There was a lot at stake, between the business and the personal components of their lives, to risk damaging things by being overeager. So regardless of her feelings, that there was something mystical drawing them together, Selina would pull back and trust that when Rea was ready, she would come to her.

At least her morning with Jupe had been productive. Selina had won his trust and, from the gentle way he'd lipped her arm when she'd removed his hackamore, Jupe's affection too. Selina was already anticipating their next ride.

When her booted foot hit the bottom step of the RV, she noticed the dried mud and dust on them. Since Selina didn't have a boot jack handy, she sat down right there and removed them by hand. When she leaned over to set them off to the side, Selina caught a whiff of her shirt. The distinct aroma of horse and sweat filled her nose. Unless she planned to offend everyone around her, Selina needed a shower and a change of clothes before lunch. She had a whole hour and a half to kill, so she decided to get some laundry done as well.

The hot water beating against muscles that had tensed during the ride had Selina groaning in relief. She avoided touching certain parts of her body, afraid if she did, a simple shower would turn into an erotic fantasy session, featuring Rea. Selina definitely didn't want to have that on her mind when they met for lunch.

She spent the rest of the time washing clothes and straightening up the RV—mindless activities—that allowed her to ponder her growing affection for the buxom redhead. Each new thing she discovered about Rea was like a puzzle piece, that when locked into place, revealed an image of her ideal woman, and Selina more than liked what she saw.

Now she stood at the garage and watched as Rea marched toward Selina with a determined look on her face. She was freshly showered, by the wet look of her freshly gelled hair, and she'd also changed clothes. She was now sporting a pair of black jeans, paired with an emerald shirt that deepened the green of her eyes. To Selina, she was simply breathtaking.

When Rea halted in front of her, Selina grinned and said, "You look like you are ready to face a firing squad."

"No, just an inquisition." Rea arched a brow at her. "Are you ready for that?"

"I know the drill. Name, rank, and serial number only." Then Selina offered Rea a snappy salute.

"You say that now, but you'll see. But…maybe since you've just met, Mia will go easy on you this time."

Rea glanced at the shed with a slight frown. "I usually take the ATV over, but the SUV might be more comfortable." Rea's head swung back and forth in apparent indecision on which vehicle to take.

"Why don't you take the ATV, and I'll ride over on Chief," Selina offered. "I was thinking of going into town after lunch so I can get my bearings before Monday."

"Oh good, you can follow me over then."

Selina hadn't missed the sigh or the look of relief that passed over Rea's face, as she opened the door of the shed. Selina hadn't planned to go anywhere besides lunch, but the idea of taking Chief out on the open road was enticing. Selina backed her cycle outside while Rea fiddled with her ATV. She was mounted and ready when Rea drove out. She rode slowly behind Rea, arriving at the charming little house a few minutes later without getting out of first gear.

Mia was already standing on the porch, waving at them madly, with a broad smile on her face. Selina found herself anticipating the meal, figuring she'd have a chance to learn more about Rea through their interactions. Selina had discovered quite a few things already but was looking forward to uncovering more today.

As they stepped onto the porch, Mia threw open her arms and drew Selina in for another one of her big bear hugs. Once Mia freed her, she turned to Rea and did the same to her, accompanied by the endearment, "Cariña."

Opening the screen door, Mia shooed them in, "Rea, ju show Selina to de table, an I go yell to Matty to come." She then took off toward the back of the house in a fast waddle.

She admired the colorful accent walls as Rea led her to the breakfast nook inside the canary yellow kitchen. Selina caught the distinctive odor of molé lingering in the air, starting her stomach grumbling. It had been a long time since she'd had any, and Selina could hardly wait for a taste, especially after having Mia's fresh tortillas and salsa this morning. She knew she was in for a treat.

Mia bustled back in and went right over to the stove. Matty trailed in after her at a more sedate pace, then took a seat across from Selina at the table. A plate was plunked down in front of her with a molé covered chicken breast, traditional rice, and charro beans, followed by a pitcher of opaque liquid with slices of lemon and limes floating in it.

As soon as Mia doled out three more plates, like a Vegas blackjack dealer, she commanded, "Eat, eat, wile I get de tortillas."

Matty started the pitcher around the table, and Selina filled her glass before handing it to Rea. She felt a thrill run through her by merely sitting next to Rea in this quasi-family setting.

Mia came back to the table and set down a colorful round ceramic dish with a red pepper shaped handle on the lid, before taking her seat. Her head dropped, and her lips moved silently, then quickly crossed herself, before deftly launching into a gentle interrogation that Rea had warned her about.

Selina had just taken a bite of a thick corn tortilla she'd been using to sop up the last of the molé sauce on her plate when Mia dropped her verbal bomb.

"So, ju have a gurlfrien?"

Selina sucked in a breath and started coughing when a tiny piece of the tortilla got lodged in her windpipe. Her mind raced back over their interactions, but couldn't recall anything that might have given away her sexuality. So, where had the question come from?

Before she could clear her throat to say anything, Matty spoke up. "Mama, ju need to mine jur own bizness."

As she held a napkin to her mouth, Selina turned to glance at Rea and found her eyes shooting daggers at Mia with a mutinous scowl on her lips. She switched her gaze back to Mia and saw she hadn't been phased by neither Matty's admonishment nor Rea's glare of death, so to defuse the situation, Selina decided to answer.

"No, I don't."

A smug smile graced Mia's face as she rose, gathering up the empty plates. "I get dessert," she said and left the table.

Rea leaned close with a chagrined look and whispered, "Sorry about that, you didn't have to answer her."

"It's okay. I'm not sure how Mia knew I'm a lesbian, though."

"Oh, I'm sure the grapevine informed her, plus she has very good gaydar for an older straight woman. But also, her youngest son is gay. You'll meet him. His name is Carlos, and he owns the garage on the other side of the warehouse."

They finished up their meal with a dessert of rich, creamy flan. Selina's stomach was full and happy. "Mia, this was an excellent meal. Thank you so much for inviting me."

"No hay probelma. I juse to cookin for de family," she added with a wink and a smile.

They all made their way to the door, but Mia grabbed Rea by the arm as she was about to step out. "Ju got a meanit Cariña? I need talk to ju about de lunch wagons for de plantin."

An exasperated look crossed Rea's features before she meekly answered, "Yes, Mia."

"Thanks again for lunch," Selina said to Matty and Mia, then turned to Rea. "My excursion into town won't take long, so I'll be back in time to help you bed down the horses."

"Don't worry, I'll take care of them tonight. But thanks for the offer," Rea replied evenly.

Selina was momentarily confused by the rejection of her aid but got distracted when she caught sight of Mia's lips pulling down into a frown as she shot Rea an exasperated look. Selina was astute enough to figure out there would be some fur flying once she left, so she made a hasty exit.

Selina mounted her bike, and drove down the gravel road, grinning to herself. She wished she could be a fly on the wall in Mia's house right now, to listen in on what was sure to be an incendiary conversation.

Chapter Twenty-Two

Business and Romance

Matty made himself scarce as soon as Selina disappeared from view. With the room cleared, Rea turned on Mia.

"What the hell was the third degree about during lunch? I didn't bring her over here so you could grill her for personal information. And your last question about a girlfriend was completely out of line."

"Now, Cariña, I juss wanted to get to know her un poquito. She has eyes for ju, ju know. Ju need to wake up an smell de roses."

Rea sighed. She knew Mia had her best interest at heart, but she didn't need anyone or anything else pushing her right now. "Mia, you know I love you, but you need to back off. She's been here for one day, and besides, she's an employee. Trying to mix business and romance would be a particularly bad idea, so don't even try to stir the pot."

"What! Ju tink it can't happen dat fass. It did wit me an Mateo. I see de sparks flyin wit ju two. Dis farm is family bizzness so ju can mix de two. Ju do dat with Mateo an me."

Rea closed her eyes, trying to quell the thought of letting anyone get that close to her heart again. Then she felt two strong arms pulling her into a warm embrace. "I only telling ju to give tings a chance. Donn close jurself off. Sherry would wan ju to be happy."

Rea managed to nod around the lump in her throat. She knew Mia's words came from a place of love and caring, but she was still determined to take things one careful step at a time. "I will see how things go, but you have to promise me you won't interfere in any way."

It was a good thing Rea couldn't see behind Mia's back as she crossed her fingers and said, "I promise."

Rea pulled back and asked, "What did you want to discuss about the lunch wagons?"

"Oh…juss to let me know when we need dem," Mia said, with an all too innocent look.

Rea wasn't fooled at all. It was evident to her that Mia had used it as an excuse to have her say about Selina. Well, they'd both had theirs now.

"I'm sure Matty will let you know the schedule for the planting," she said, arching her brow. "But I'm pretty sure you weren't really concerned about that. I'm heading back to the house to get some stuff done. Thanks for lunch, but not so much for…the talk," but Rea said it with a smile.

She left Mia standing on the porch and made her way home. As she put the ATV away, Rea wondered how Selina felt about Mia's cross-examination, even though she'd warned her about the possibility. Selina hadn't seemed to be bothered by it though, except maybe a little over the girlfriend question. Rea knew if their positions were reversed, she would have been less than thrilled with the quiz that had accompanied the meal. Rea still remembered the first time she'd met Sherry's mom. She'd felt stripped down naked by her questions. Thankfully, she now had Mia's promise to stop meddling and needn't worry about it anymore. Rea had enough on her plate right now, trying to keep her growing attraction to Selina in check.

*****

Cruising into town, Selina squinted into the wind, and loose strands of hair from her braid lashed her face. The pulsing vibration of the engine beat against her body like a tom-tom, and the roar of Chief's voice filled her ears. Selina's sole focus narrowed to the cycle underneath her and the road in front, clearing her mind of everything else. Instead of going to the lab, she followed a pickup pulling a boat and soon found herself at Jackson Lake State Park. There was a fee to enter, and since Selina didn't even have her wallet, she turned west, winding along a narrow road at the southern end of the lake, before heading toward Moirai.

By the time Selina arrived back at the farm and put her bike away, she was feeling much more relaxed. That lasted until she rounded the corner of the RV and saw Mia sitting in one of the outdoor chairs on the patio. *Ooooh boy! I wonder what this is about.*

Mia turned and greeted Selina. "Hola. I come over to bring ju some pan dulce."

"Uh...thank you."

"Ju welcome. Sit, sit. I wanna talk to ju."

Selina settled in the chair next to Mia, not sure what was coming.

"Ju like my Rea, sí?"

"Ah…yes. She's going to be a great boss and I'm excited to help her make the farm a success."

Mia rolled her eyes. "No. I mean ju are, atraído por ella, sí?"

Selina felt caught out by the personal question but wanted to be honest with Mia. "Yes, I am attracted to her. I think Rea is a beautiful woman inside and out. I don't see how anyone wouldn't be drawn to her."

"Bueno. She like ju too, but her heart is, asustado…scared. She hide if ju let her, so donn let her. Ju donn need to push, but stay close. Rea, she be lonely for too long. Sherry is gone an she need someone more dan de dog, an de horses in her life. I tink ju be de one." Mia reached out and took Selina's hand. "So, if ju need to talk or advize, ju come to see me."

Squeezing Mia's hand in answer, Selina said, "I will, thanks," then let go.

Mia groaned a little as she rose from the chair. "Dis talk is juss between ju and me, donn tell Rea. She get mad at me. Rea es mi familia y la amo, but she can be hard of head. Ju member dat."

"I will, Mia. Thanks for the talk and the sweet bread."

"Hasta luego."

"Adiós Mia."

Selina noted Mia exited to the rear of the RV, avoiding the possibility of Rea seeing her from the house. She had to laugh a little at the meddling old woman but knew it was driven by her love for Rea. It also helped to know she had an ally on her side. Selina opened the bag Mia had left her, pulling out one of the sweet treats. Grinning like a loon, she took a big bite and made her way inside the RV, feeling as if things were finally falling into place.

*****

Rea wandered aimlessly around the house all afternoon. She started out in her office trying to get some work done but got distracted by Facebook instead. Rea didn't get on it much because, like the news, a lot of the posts were either depressing or full of angst, and she was trying to stay positive. Disgusted, she turned off her computer, then left to gather up dirty laundry instead. Rea set the basket down at the washer, miffed that this chore couldn't be completed because she was out of detergent. When she opened her grocery app to add it to the list, she saw the phone needed to be charged, so she plugged it in. After that, Rea flitted from thing to thing, accomplishing nothing. She just couldn't concentrate.

Finally, she settled down on the couch. Rea opened her Kindle, hoping to lose herself in reading, "Uprising," the newest book by one of her favorite authors, Fletcher DeLancey. She'd always been able to immerse herself in the fictional world of Alsea, and her fantasy lover, Lanaril, but not today. Today her thoughts strayed to the very real woman that had captured her imagination—Selina.

Like her mental image of Lanaril, Selina had blue-black hair, creamy, coffee-colored skin, but instead of deep, brown eyes, Selina's were icy blue. Rea sensed from Selina's meteor story that like Lanaril, she possessed a deeply spiritual side. Selina's belief in the fiery entrance of her talisman as a sign from beyond wasn't that much different from Lanaril's conviction of Fahla's presence in the temple, by the flaming leaves on the Molwyn tree. Rea hadn't believed she could find love again, but maybe like in the books, she would need to take a leap of faith to make it happen. Lord knows she could use a little something magical in her life.

This line of thought wasn't getting her anywhere and she'd already wasted the whole afternoon, so Rea decided to feed herself, then go take care of the horses. She opened the pantry door, and Patches immediately turned up from wherever he'd been snoozing, looking for his dinner too. Rea filled his bowl, then went to the fridge to get out some sandwich makings. She eyed the box of wine sitting on the shelf. No, it was too early to indulge in a glass yet, but Rea promised herself when she finished with Dolly and Jupe, she'd have one.

It was early twilight when she finally made her way to the barn, then stopped short when she saw the doors were open. She looked in the paddock but didn't see the horses. That meant Selina was inside. She distinctly remembered telling Selina she'd take care of them herself. *Shit! Should she go inside or back to the house?* Rea wasn't sure if she was ready for another encounter with Selina yet.

Before she could make up her mind about what to do, the decision was taken out of her hands when Selina made an appearance, pushing a wheelbarrow full of soiled straw and wood shavings.

"Hey, Rea." Selina came to a stop then set the wheelbarrow down.

Rea was immediately distracted by the slight bulge of Selina's muscled arms and the trickle of sweat that ran down her long neck to the valley between her breast exposed by the black tank top she wore. "I hope you don't mind my being here, but I was bored and needed something to do."

Damn, what could she say? Rea was caught between wanting to get closer to this scintillating woman and her need to keep Selina at arm's length. "Well…ah…no, but is there anything left to do?" she offered lamely.

"I haven't fed Dolly or Jupe yet. I wanted to get rid of this dirty bedding first." Selina nodded her head toward the other large outbuilding behind the garage. "I figured that might house the composters you told me about if the mounds outside are any indication. But I need some instruction on those. Can you show me how they work?"

"Sure." Rea led the way, and they were soon at a large access door. When she opened it, the familiar pungent odor in the room assailed her nose.

She stopped in front of one of the large machines and turned to Selina. In a voice loud enough to be heard over the mechanical hum of the composters, Rea explained. "It takes two weeks to process a batch and I started one in this machine four days ago, so just dump your load into this holding bin." She put her hand out and touched it. "They are fully automated, so after we empty out the finished compost from inside, we press the button here,"—pointing at a green one—"and the bin will load this batch into the hopper. The whole process is easy, and it gives us a ready supply of nutrient-rich fertilizer for the greenhouses."

"You're right. Easy peasy, Japanesey!" Selina said with a grin.

Rea couldn't help laughing. "You're a fan of Shawshank Redemption?"

"I may have seen it a time or two…or ten," Selina answered with an accompanying chuckle.

As they walked back to the barn, Rea noticed Selina glancing her way repeatedly with a questioning look on her face and finally said, "What do you want to ask me?"

"Well…since it's legal here, have you ever thought about growing some cannabis? It's definitely a profitable cash crop. Good clean organic plants are needed by medical dispensaries, so you could strictly sell to them if you have a thing about recreational users."

Rea hadn't thought about growing cannabis before, but with Selina's background, maybe she should. She and Sherry had enjoyed it themselves since their time in college. But it had become essential when Sherry had undergone her chemo treatments to help with nausea, then later on to combat the pain. During that time, Rea used it to deal with the stress and anxiety but still smoked occasionally for pleasure. She'd believed, just like with alcohol, it was how a person used it. A stoner wasn't any different than an alcoholic—in her opinion—it was always about balance, overuse of either was detrimental.

Rea realized she hadn't answered Selina and turned to see a rather dispirited look on her face. She didn't want Selina to think she disapproved of cannabis or its many uses, so Rea quickly said, "Let's look into building another greenhouse behind the other, solely for growing it. The upside will be that I won't have to drive into Greely to buy it anymore, and maybe they'll return the favor when I have something to sell."

Selina's eyes twinkled, and a grin broke over her face. "Awesome. I have seeds from a variety of plants I've worked with over the years, and I could develop a new strain exclusively for us. I have some of my special bud with me. Maybe you might enjoy sampling my wares."

When Rea saw a sexy smile directed her way, she felt an old familiar heat expanding inside her as she thought about what she'd enjoy sampling, and it wasn't pot. Damned if Rea wasn't tempted, though, she could use a bowl right about now. But pot tended to loosen her inhibitions, even more than alcohol, and indulging in it would be too dangerous with the way she was feeling.

Instead, she said, "I may take you up on that sometime. Let's go get Dolly and Jupe fed." Rea turned and strolled toward the barn as casually as possible.

*****

Selina had taken Mia's advice to heart and deliberately put herself in Rea's path tonight. She hadn't failed to notice Rea's initial hesitation either, but things had smoothed out by the time they were making their way back to the barn.

When she'd put the whole cannabis thing out there, Selina was happy to find out Rea smoked herself, and couldn't help throwing a flirt bomb into the mix. Even in the low light, from a less than full moon, Selina had caught the flair of desire on Rea's face before she'd schooled her features. Selina decided she may have gone a little too far with the comment, but damn, the woman was hot. Selina wisely backed off and followed Rea's redirection.

By the time they'd finished and closed up the barn, Rea seemed relaxed again. Horses had the same effect on her, so she wasn't surprised by this. Selina was racking her brain for some way to extend their evening when an ethereal howl echoed in her ears. Selina knew that spirit voice but had never heard it when she was with anyone else before.

A startled gasp from beside her made Selina turn to find Rea paralyzed, like a deer caught in a headlight. Without thought, she reached out and took Rea's arm. "Are you alright?"

Rea turned dazed eyes toward her. "I thought I'd imagined it, but I saw one twice now. A white one. But you heard that, right? It's a wolf!"

Selina's head was spinning like a top. *What the fuck was going on?* It was one thing for Selina to see and hear the wolf since it was her spirit guide, but if it showed itself to Rea, that was something else. They needed to talk.

"Yes, I heard it, but I don't believe you imagined it. I think it might have been my spirit guide showing itself to you."

Chapter Twenty-Three

A Turning Point

Rea should have been shocked beyond words by Selina's last statement, but she wasn't. From the moment she spied the wolf on the bank, her life had taken an almost mystical turn.

Selina's voice broke into Rea's thoughts. "I think we need to sit down and talk, but for that, I will need a beer or a bowl. Let's head over to my patio for one or both, what do you say?"

Oh yeah. Rea definitely felt the need for something to help her deal with what was happening, but not a beer. "Grab yourself one and your stash too, but meet me on my porch. I need wine."

Five minutes later, Rea was sitting in one of her rockers, sipping wine, attempting to relax. Patches must have sensed his mistress's unease because he'd glued himself to Rea's side, and took up a watchful posture, gazing out into the yard. When his ears pitched forward, and he let out a welcoming bark, she knew Selina was approaching.

As Selina neared the porch, Rea could see she was carrying a beer in one hand and what looked like a soft leather pouch in the other. She'd brought out her bong, along with a wand lighter, and put them on the patio table next to her. Before tonight Rea couldn't envision sitting on her porch waiting to smoke weed with one of her employees. But as of late, nothing about what had been happening to her was normal.

Selina set everything down on the table, freeing her hands, and she bent down to give Patches some loving. "Well, hello there, dude. Are you guarding your mom? If so, you're doing a good job; you didn't let me sneak up on her."

Selina rose with a sigh then settled into the other rocker. Opening the pouch, she emptied the contents into her lap. She picked up the small pipe and pointed at the bong. "I'm guessing you prefer to smoke that?"

"Yeah. If you don't mind, a bong smokes cooler, and it keeps me from coughing. May I see your pipe though, it looks unusual?"

"Sure," Selina said and held it out to her.

Rea set her wine down then took the pipe from Selina's hand. She turned it over, examining it, while Selina loaded up a bowl. Running a finger over the intricate carvings, she said, "I wish the light were better so I could see the fine details. Is this made from bone?"

"No. Antler. It was a gift from my cousin, Boady. He's making a pretty good living now selling those to shops that the growers I worked for did business with. Since deer and elk drop their antlers every year, he's able to make these cheaply. On this one, the carving depicts a place on the family ranch where a stream runs through it. But I like it because it's small enough to fit in my pouch." Selina offered Rea the bong in exchange for the pipe. "But you're right. Yours will smoke cooler, and it's also a work of art."

Rea held it up to catch a little of the light that was filtering out through the screen door. "Yes, a very talented glass blower

Sherry and I met during a Pride gathering in San Francisco made it. She specialized in rainbow-colored designs."

Rea pursed her lips, then fitted them inside the glass chimney, triggered the lighter, and held it to the bowl. With her thumb over the carb, she inhaled gently. The smoke was smooth, with a slightly sweet flavor she couldn't identify. The last wisps of smoke escaped as she passed the bong to Selina, and the familiar musky scent floated about her. She finally exhaled then took a few sips of wine to cool her throat.

Selina passed it back, but after a second hit, Rea was done. She was already calmer and feeling perfectly buzzed. Anymore would send her right to sleep, and they still hadn't discussed the elephant in the room, but Rea was ready now.

"So, are we going to talk about what's going on with the wolf? As I said, I thought I saw one twice recently. Now you're telling me the howling we heard was from your spirit guide. Honestly, that's a little hard for me to wrap my brain around."

Selina sat up straight, gripping the arms of the rocker. "Believe me, I'm having just as hard a time with this as you are. But let me ask you this. You said the wolf was white. Did it, by any chance, have light blue eyes like mine?"

A shiver rippled through Rea with those words and left a wake of goosebumps along her skin. It was one thing to ponder the possibility there was something mystical happening in her life, but it was quite another to find herself smack in the middle of such an occurrence. If it was indeed linked to the intriguing woman beside her, it was almost more than Rea could fathom.

Selina had remained quiet as she absorbed the implications, but the imploring look, in those earnest blue eyes, that were just like the wolf's, were asking her for confirmation.

"Yes, it did." Rea couldn't help but notice how Selina's body slumped back into the seat. Was it from relief or disbelief, she wondered?

*****

Selina had practically held her breath the whole time, after she asked her question, waiting for an answer she wasn't sure she was ready for. When it came, Selina was stymied. Trying to calm the turmoil in her mind, she set the rocker in motion. Could she explain something so personal to Rea? Selina had never shared or discussed her esoteric notions with anyone besides her Amá sání. Selina had always tried to steer clear of any of those types of talk, not wanting to step on anyone's religious toes. But she wanted Rea to understand that whatever hers were, Selina would honor them.

"I don't know what your spiritual leanings are, Rea, but based on mine, this is astounding." Selina frowned in concentration, trying to think of a way to explain. "One of my grandmother's sayings was, 'There is no one, true way' and encouraged me to find the one that fit me while respecting other people's. I've explored the precepts of many spiritual schools of thought, and certain things resonated with me." Selina nervously licked her lips before continuing.

"What I have come to believe is this—the energy from every atom and molecule that started with the Big Bang—created our cosmos, and we are born out of this celestial soup. In all living things—whether it be plants, animals, or people—this energy drives every part it. When anything dies, it does not cease to exist. It may drift for a time, be absorbed by something else, or be transformed into a new existence." Selina picked up her beer and took a swallow, giving herself another moment to gather her thoughts.

"Specifically with people—I think their residual energy resides in, and around us, and can take on a perceivable form from time to time. What a person discerns depends on their receptivity and their cultural or religious upbringing. Most never experience it at all, while others view it as intuition, or believe that an inner voice is steering them. Some may sense, feel, or even hear a loved one who has passed away because they carry a piece of that person's soul in their hearts. And for a very, very few, this energy may manifest visually."

Selina rose up just enough to turn her rocker toward Rea. She placed her elbows on her knees and leaned forward as if being in closer proximity would reinforce her words.

"The closest analogy I can come up with for my spirit guide would be something like a guardian angel, one that guides and protects a single individual…and mine manifests as a wolf." A wry grin creased her lips. "But since you've seen and heard it, I think I might need to reevaluate my concept."

She looked into Rea's eyes and passionately continued, "But I have a feeling, whatever forces are at work, we were meant to be brought together at this time."

Selina sucked in a deep breath, gathered up her courage, and plunged forward. "I am attracted to you, Rea, both inside and out. I know we just met, and we also have a professional relationship, you need to consider. But I'm asking you to be open to the idea that we might have something more together. If you feel any of the things I do, then give us time to get to know each other and see what develops."

Rea turned her head away, concealing her face in the shadows of the dark porch. She was motionless except for rubbing the pads of her finger and thumb together in what Selina guessed was a nervous habit. Her tension grew as she awaited Rea's answer, feeling like her fate hung in the balance.

Something magnetic seemed to coalesce around them, and she felt her world tilt upright when Rea turned, leaned forward, resting her hand atop Selina's, and simply said…

*****

"Yes." What else could Rea say?

When Selina had started talking, Rea's thoughts had turned inward, but every word resonated with her. After her mother's death, she would speak to her, just like she still did with Sherry, and swore she'd felt them with her on occasion. But then Rea would convince herself it had only been wishful thinking on her part since she hadn't wanted to believe they were lost to her entirely. Rea had never attempted to characterize the experience or stopped to consider they might be spiritual visitations. Selina's idea that she carried pieces of their energy within her, and they were somehow guiding Rea along, seemed to explain it all.

When Selina had asked her to be open to something between them, Rea had felt a subtle power trying to draw them together and instinctively reached out to Selina. But at the same time, her emotional roadblocks and insecurities were getting in the way. To move forward, she would have to find a way to banish them, so Rea had answered, yes.

But getting past her intimacy issues was going to be a struggle. Selina had said she found her physically attractive, but Rea could hardly credit it. With the onset of menopause and her thyroid issues, she'd packed pounds onto her already plump frame, but she'd also added a wrinkle or two. Before Rea could proceed, she'd have to build up her trust enough in Selina to expose her vulnerability.

Turning her hand over, Rea gripped Selina's and squeezed gently. "I've only ever been with one woman, and that was Sherry. We were together for over twenty-four years, and I am out of my depth. So, we need to take things slowly."

Rea watched as Selina rose from the rocker with fluid grace, and gave her hand an answering squeeze before letting go. Then she placed both hands on the arms of Rea's rocker, leaned down, and planted a kiss on her cheek, then huskily whispered, "That's all I ask."

Selina scooped her pouch off the table, turned, and exited the porch without another word. As she faded into the darkness, Rea lifted her hand and placed it against her cheek. She thought she could still feel the warmth of those soft lips. Rea let her fingers trail down to gently rub over her own, and contemplated what their first real kiss might feel like.

Rea was pulled from her daze by Patches' insistent pawing on her leg. "Yes, little man, I know it's time to go in."

She gathered up her empty wine glass and put the bong in the crook of her arm before getting up. Opening the screen door, Patches retreated inside, but Rea paused. She looked up into the heavens, and focused on the glittering stars, and whispered, "I heard you," then went in, closing out the night.

*****

As soon as the inky blackness enveloped Selina and hid her from view of the porch, she turned to gaze back at Rea. There was enough light leaking from around the door of the house for Selina to see her sitting motionless in the rocker. Her night vision was sharp, and she watched Rea lift her hand to her cheek then move her fingers over her lips. Was Rea thinking about another less than chaste kind of kiss? Selina knew she was. When she'd leaned over and inhaled Rea's woodsy scent, it had taken all of Selina's self-control to land that kiss on her cheek.

She continued to watch from the shadows as Rea rose and made her way across the porch with Patches at her side. Pausing in the doorway, she seemed to be staring up into the starry sky, her face plainly visible. Selina saw Rea's lips move briefly, as if she spoke to some unseen listener, before finally turning to enter her house.

Selina tilted her head back as Rea had. Her eyes staring up in wonder at the pinpricks of light that had traveled for millions of years to shine in the night sky above her. It always filled her with a sense of awe, knowing many of those stars no longer existed. Like she'd explained to Rea, their energy hadn't been lost but transmuted into something new—filling the cosmos with endless possibilities.

Tonight, Selina dismissed the physics of the universe from the scientific part of her brain, instead focusing on the mystical side, and said, "Thank you!" Selina was unsurprised when she saw a streak of light traversing the heavens and knew she'd been heard.

Chapter Twenty-Four

Fits and Starts

Selina lay on her side, her head propped up on her hand, while the other played with a button on Rea's shirt. The sun warmed blanket was soft beneath her, and a slight breeze carried the scent of wildflowers in the air. The soothing burble of the river was accompanied by the buzzing of insects that wove nature's song around her.

The setting was idyllic, as was the beautiful woman beside her. Selina leaned forward and gazed at Rea's face, hunting for a sign that she wanted her. Selina had her answer when she saw golden sparks shoot through Rea's green eyes that had dilated with desire. She dove in, sipping the sweetest of nectars from Rea's honeyed lips, parting for her exploration.

Selina's fingers had a will of their own as they slipped several buttons free on Rea's shirt, giving her access to a lace-covered breast—the nipple hardening beneath her palm. The sapid sound of a hungry moan vibrated up through the lips attached to hers but was marred by a burst of angry buzzing. Selina waved a hand, that seconds ago had been holding heaven in it, swatting at a bee zeroing in on her head. The irate droning got even more intense, and she realized she was about to get…

Selina's eyes popped open as she jolted upright, momentarily confused by the blackness surrounding her. The metered tone and flickering light from her cell phone crashed through Selina, bringing with it the harsh reality that she'd been dreaming. The heat of desire was still pumping through her system, accompanied by a rhythmic throbbing in her groin. Selina slumped back into her bed, wishing she hadn't set the alarm for five a.m. so she could have finished that dream. She reached over, picked up her phone, and shut off the app.

Selina was more of a night owl than an early bird—but had started making the adjustment a week ago, when she awoke to the distinctive sound of hoofbeats passing the RV at a gallop. It had been apparent Rea was up and about already, taking Dolly for a morning ride. Selina realized if she wanted to spend any quality time with Rea outside of her working day, she'd have to rise earlier…but this morning, it was doubly hard.

The previous week had been so hectic—doing testing and holding planning sessions with the managers—that Selina had only been able to eke out an hour each morning to be with Rea and the horses. Then another meager half-hour, sitting on Rea's porch after she got home for the evening. Their discussions never straying much beyond things about the farm. The long week had even extended into Selina's first Saturday. She had spent the whole day checking the soil prep in the fields to make sure they were ready to start the planting this morning.

But not yesterday, …yesterday was *perfect*.

They had spent almost the whole day together. By mutual consent, Selina had met Rea at the barn at eight instead of six. She'd appreciated the extra two hours of sleep because she'd been feeling pretty haggard. But then again, so had Rea, as the dark circles under her eyes had become more pronounced as the week wore on.

They'd groomed Dolly and Jupe as usual. But instead of taking them out for a ride immediately after, Rea had suggested they feed them their breakfast first, share a bite themselves, then take a noon ride.

Rea had served Selina fresh blueberry pancakes—instead of eggs—that had only required the addition of some creamy honey butter. They'd spent several leisurely hours discussing their mutual love of sci-fi movies, classic rock, and celebrity crushes, as they'd enjoyed their food first, then drank coffee on the porch.

Then Rea had shooed Selina off to the barn to ready the horses for their ride, while she cleaned up. She'd been surprised when Rea strode in with a pair of saddlebags slung over her shoulder and a rolled-up blanket under her arm. Selina's dream this morning wasn't surprising, considering it played out her fantasy version of the picnic lunch they'd shared down by the river.

However, Selina still felt Rea's reticence keenly, by the physical distance she'd kept between them, even though their conversational topics became much more personal. They'd shared their stories of coming out, then talked about their relationships—hers, being plural, and Rea's singular.

When Rea had spoken of one particular memory, Selina realized their lives had intersected in college too. Rea explained that Sherry would get onto her about her youthful, fiery temper. Then she relayed a story of how one night, it had gotten the best of her, and she'd almost started a riot at a freshman mixer. Selina then volunteered; she'd been there that night but had left just as Rea was getting wound up. For Selina, it was one more sign they'd been fated to meet.

Rea had surprised her by leaving for a few minutes, then coming back with a rod, tackle box, and a net she apparently kept stored in the pump shed. Selina had admired Rea's fishing skill, as she tricked a few nice sized bass into falling for her fly's charm.

Those fish had provided Selina with a perfect opportunity to extend their day into evening, by offering to clean and cook them up for dinner. She'd baked the fillets in the oven with a simple but savory coating of extra virgin olive oil, minced garlic, salt, pepper, and fresh lemon slices. Selina had added some fresh asparagus to the dish, then served it up with two chilled glasses of Chardonnay she'd purchased at the market, that Hank informed her was Rea's favorite.

After dinner, they'd sat out on Rea's porch sharing the last of the wine, while the sinking sun painted the low riding clouds with smears of color. As the darkness cocooned them, Rea had asked her to play more of the Native music from her phone. The trilling tones of the flute, accompanied by the stridulation of the crickets as they sang to each other, added to the romantic ambiance.

Selina would have been content to sit on the porch with Rea for the rest of her life. But all too soon, Rea had called an end to their evening by reminding Selina it was getting late, and they had a long week ahead of them. Then there'd been an awkward moment as they exchanged their good nights'. Selina had so wanted to give Rea a quick kiss or a hug as she departed the porch. But Rea had held the two wine glasses to her chest, as a fragile barrier between them, that Selina hadn't dared to cross.

It hadn't been easy to set her libido aside—but for the first time in any of her relationships—Selina craved the emotional intimacy more than the physical. With Rea's reticence, developing that kind of rapport would take time, and they'd only met ten days ago.

Heaving a sigh, Selina dragged herself out of bed and counseled herself to be patient. She envisioned there would be a lot of cold showers in her immediate future.

*****

Rea woke up this morning feeling immensely guilty for still keeping a certain physical distance from Selina. Since the day Selina had arrived—a little over three weeks ago—Rea had ridden an emotional see-saw. The new morning routine they'd been sharing was enticing, as Rea imagined the care and affection Selina lavished on Jupe, being turned toward her. That had led to daydreams of waking up in those strong yet supple arms.

Selina had immediately taken over the critical working aspects of the farm, and Rea had heard nothing but praise from everyone on her dedicated work ethic. The downside to that was she had way too much time on her hands to think, leaving her hesitant to breach their business relationship. So, by the end of each day, she'd fallen back into her professional demeanor.

Rea had tried to surreptitiously avoid Mia's company, knowing she would want to put her two cents worth into the confusing mix. But that had come to an end within a week when she had to meet with the women running the lunch trucks to coordinate their schedules. The second the last lady had departed, Mia had been all up in her business about Selina.

Since then, every time Mia had caught her alone, she'd lectured Rea to move past Sherry's death, to give herself a chance to find love again, and she'd made an effort to do that. That one Sunday, when they'd spent a whole day together, getting to know each other, she may have been the one fishing, but she was the one that got caught on Selina's hook.

The pure pleasure of sharing meals and conversations with someone so intellectually stimulating had only increased the attraction. Rea had seen indications during the day that her feelings were reciprocated. But as they'd sat on the porch enclosed in the darkness, with the melodic strains of the flute floating around them, Rea's doubts had crept in. When she'd called an end to their evening, and Selina had moved into her personal space, Rea had felt such a physical pull, that she ached inside. But instead of closing the gap, Rea had folded in on herself, afraid to let Selina get any closer. By the time she'd shut the porch door, Rea had lamented the missed opportunity, as she had several times since then.

With the planting well underway, Selina's schedule eased up, and Rea was spending even more time in her company. They'd started taking a few sunset rides together, followed by more intimate evenings, either on her porch or around the firepit on Selina's patio. There'd been several more occasions when Rea had experienced the mystical pull drawing her nearer to the precipice of taking that leap, but still, she'd held back.

It wasn't about Selina being an employee anymore, or even Sherry's memory, or at least not entirely. It all came down to Rea's fear of the physical. Selina was beautiful. She'd also been with quite a few women over the years, and Rea didn't feel like she could measure up. Even with Sherry, it had taken time to move past her view of her less than picture-perfect body before they'd made love. Now here she was at forty-six, fifty pounds heavier, with wrinkles starting to make their appearance, feeling decidedly unattractive. Rea could only hope that Selina would continue to be patient with her as she worked through it all.

Interlude

Once more, amidst the cloudy cosmogenic eddies, the three women gathered together for a meeting of the minds. The sparking aura around one of them was an indication of her agitation and was unsettling the other two.

The old woman spoke up, "You need to calm down, Sherry. The energy you are throwing off is disruptive. What's the problem?"

"I'm sorry, Lily, but Rea is frustrating the crap out of me. I've pushed her as hard as I can, and she's right on the precipice, but she is really hung up on her body image. I think it's going to take something major to push her past that."

"Well you know her best, Sherry, what do you think it will take?"

"I've been contemplating it, and the one thing that really rules Rea is her nurturing attitude. If she felt that Selina needed her on an emotional level that only connecting with her physically could provide, that might be enough to tip the balance."

Lily mulled over Selina's vulnerabilities and could only think of one, but turned to Nita to get her take on it. "What do you think about a big storm? It's the only real emotional weakness I can think of that might trigger what we need."

"Yeah, I think that would do it. Selina doesn't do well with storms, and there is already a big one forming off to the west that you might be able to push south enough so that it passes overhead."

"I can see that, and nudging that storm will take a lot less effort than I've expended tossing those meteors their way."

Lily paused, then tilted her head back while lifting her spectral arms to the side, preparing to impact the storm, when some foreign tendrils of energy swarmed around the three. Lily drew back in, and all of them turned their vision outward to the physical world to see the change in the atmospheric currents had already been made.

All of them were staggered by this intervention, but after a moment, Lily sagely nodded her head and said, "Fate has decided to take the lead on this one. With it in control, the outcome is nebulous, but based on its prior tampering, I think that things will work out in the end. We'll just need to be prepared to stick close to the girls and be there when they need us."

Nita and Sherry concurred, so the three settled in to await fate's hand.

Chapter Twenty-Five
Storm Warnings

Selina jolted awake, feeling as if a tight band was wrapping itself around her head. It was a familiar sensation that started her trembling, her body unconsciously reacting to the drastic change of the barometric pressure in advance of a big storm. Selina bolted from the bed, listening intently as she glanced out the window. She could see distant flickers, painting spidery webs of light across the black canvas of the night. No thunder reached her ears, but Selina knew it was just a matter of time till it did.

She'd kept an eye on the weather reports all week and was relieved when it had been forecast to pass well north of them. Selina didn't do well with thunderstorms and hated to be alone during one. When she lived with her grandparents, they were infrequent, and if they did strike, she had them there to comfort her. As she grew older and moved about the country, Selina was subjected to them more often. She'd learned to hide her distress from others, but usually found someone to hang out with during one.

Now here she was, inside a flimsy RV, and the anxiety was starting to crawl up her spine. She and Rea weren't close enough yet for Selina to go banging on her door at this hour, and she couldn't think of a lame excuse to do so, either. A distant rumbling reached her ears, driving Selina to dress quickly and head to the barn. At least there, she wouldn't be alone.

When she let herself inside, Selina brought up the lights and called out to the horses, "Hey, you two, a storm's coming. How about I give you some breakfast and keep you company until Rea gets here later." They'd been lying down in their stalls but rose to greet her early arrival.

Selina distracted herself from the oncoming storm by giving them both a quick brushing, removing bits of straw from their coats, then gave them both scoops of oats and corn. Enclosed in the windowless structure, Selina couldn't visually track the storm—but she could hear it. The thunder beat out a steady tattoo, and the boards creaked as the wind swirled around the barn.

Selina tried to sit still but soon found herself up and pacing the floor, not realizing her escalating nerves were making Jupe edgy until he jostled up against the side of his stall. Ashamed that her own anxiety had him upset, Selina hustled inside and wound her arms around his neck. "I'm sorry, Shik'is. I'm just being a silly, frightened girl, but don't tell anyone."

A loud boom shook the barn, vibrating up through the soles of her feet, filling her with dread. She tightened her hold on Jupe's neck, as she attempted to console them both with words.

*****

Growling thunder disturbed her planned Sunday morning sleep in, and let Rea know the storm that had been predicted to pass north of them had taken an unexpected turn. She rolled over, checking the time on her clock and saw it was already after six.

Lost & Found

Patches hadn't woken her, and neither had Rory—not surprising since they wouldn't want to be caught outside when the storm hit.

Rea got up from the bed and dressed hastily, wanting to see to Dolly and Jupe's welfare before it hit. She checked the updated forecast on her phone as she went. They were now calling for heavy rain, high winds, and possible hail. She picked up speed, not wanting to get caught out in it. Rea had to order Patches outside, where he quickly peed, then let himself back into the house through his doggie door. He wasn't a fan of storms and always cowered in his kennel or under the desk in her office during one.

Rea's rain cloak flapped wildly on her way to the barn, as a stiff breeze rushed in from the east to meet the boiling black clouds in the west, that was pushing their tops even higher. A flash and crackle of a lightning bolt was followed thirty seconds later by the resounding roar of thunder, letting Rea know the storm was only about five miles away. She broke into a jog, figuring she only had about ten minutes before the storm front arrived.

Approaching the barn, Rea noticed the blades on the wind turbine in the paddock had already feathered, protecting it from the gusts. Instead of using the main doors, she went to the side, opening a smaller one with the echoing rumbles of thunder following her.

Rea entered to the bright glow of the overhead lights and the sound of urgent murmuring coming from somewhere inside. As she came up to the corner of Dolly's stall, Rea paused and peeked around it. Selina was with Jupe, her arms tightly encircling his neck, while his head rested over her shoulder. She could just make out the words, Selina kept saying over and over, in a low, trembling voice, "We're gonna be okay boy, we're gonna be okay."

Drawing back into the shadows by the door, Rea thought furiously about the best way to help Selina. Her behavior clearly proclaimed—she was having an issue with the storm. When Rea reflected on what she knew of Selina's history, she concluded it must be triggering some kind of anxiety or stress disorder due to the deaths of her mother and brother. Unlike her own experience, where she'd been with Sherry till the end, with an opportunity to come to grips with it—Selina hadn't had that. To top it off, she'd found no love or comfort from her remaining parent. Only anger, blame, and rejection.

Was it any wonder, a storm like the one that was about to hit would dredge up her old trauma? The barn wasn't the right place to ride out the storm or try and ease Selina's distress—Rea needed to get her to the house.

*****

Selina felt Jupe pull up slightly against her arm, his posture changing, alerting her without looking that Rea had arrived. She wasn't sure when Rea had entered the barn, and for a second thought about fibbing to explain her stranglehold on Jupe's neck. But if Selina wanted any kind of real relationship with Rea, she needed to be open to sharing all of herself, including her phobia.

Slowly, Selina pulled back and ran her hands along Jupe's neck. With her cheek against his, she whispered, "Thanks for being here for me, Shik'is."

She then turned to face Rea, who was leaning on the post of the open stall door, wearing a yellow rain poncho. Selina could read the concern written across her expressive face. She wasn't sure quite what to say, without sounding like a complete ninny, so instead offered lamely, "Horses are all taken care of."

Selina watched her intently for a few seconds, then Rea's lips pulled back into a hint of a smile, barely showing the indent of her dimples and said, "Unless you want to spend the next hour here, I suggest we head to my house. I bet you haven't had breakfast yet, and I need to get back to Patches. He doesn't like big storms, so he would appreciate our company about now."

And just like that, Rea had offered Selina a safe haven, and a way to concede her own fear. "I don't either. Patches isn't the only one that prefers company during them."

Rea held out a hand to her. "Come on then. We only have a few more minutes before the worst of it arrives."

As if to tack a period onto the statement, a crackle, then a loud clap reverberated around them, propelling Selina forward, to grasp the hand being held out to her. Warm fingers clasp her hand, offering Selina something substantial to cling to as Rea led her out into the stormy morning.

*****

When Rea stepped outside the door, she noticed the wind had picked up, sending the storm barreling down on top of them. She held on firmly to Selina, pulling her toward the house, as fast as Rea's shorter legs allowed. Lightning struck the ground nearby, causing her to jump, and the smell of ozone filled the air. Selina latched onto her arm like it was a lifeline, and Rea could hear her labored breathing over the sound of the storm. They were about fifty feet from the porch when the first large drops of rain hit them like projectiles from a paintball gun, splattering them with cold water—then the heavens opened its flood gates.

Rea was semi-protected under her rain gear, but by the time they'd reach the house, Selina was drenched. She pushed Selina inside the mudroom, following closely behind, and not a second too soon. The pinging on the metal roof announced that destructive globs of ice were being discharged out of the sky like bullets. Rea turned back to look out the screen door and saw marble-sized hailstones impacting the yard. She hoped it wouldn't last long, and the stones didn't get any bigger, or they'd wreak havoc on the crops.

Rea turned to ask Selina about it and saw the panicky look on her face, arms wrapped tightly around her middle, shivering violently. Rea sprang forward, grabbing a large towel off the shelf to wrap Selina in, then removed her poncho and hung it on a peg. Slinging her arm across Selina's shoulder, Rea led her over to the shoe bench, then pushed her down gently onto it. She toed off her own wet sneakers then removed Selina's, who was still quivering, as water dripped off the tip of her braid. Rea wasn't sure if it was from being cold, fear of the storm, or both, but she needed to get Selina out of her wet clothes.

Rea urged Selina up. "Come on, let's get you into a warm shower, and I'll find something dry for you to put on."

Selina didn't say anything but grabbed onto her arm again as Rea led her through the house. When they got to the master bathroom, Rea pointed at her robe that hung on the back of the door. "You can wear this after your shower, then we can get your clothes washed and dried."

Selina seemed reluctant to let her go, but finally unclenched her hands from Rea's arm, then uttered in a sheepish voice, "Alright."

She started edging toward the door and said, "I'll wait right outside in the bedroom until you finish, okay?"

But the lines of tension on Selina's face had Rea pausing. Her pupils were dilated until only a sliver of blue showed in her panicky gaze. Rea was sure Selina didn't want to be alone, as the storm still raged ferociously outside, but might be too embarrassed to ask her to stay.

The alternative was to sit on the commode as Selina showered, only a few feet away, separated by only a tile wall. The thought of being that close when Selina was naked sent a tremor through Rea's body. She drew in a deep breath and offered, "If you would feel better, I can sit out here while you shower."

Selina nodded her head dazedly then proceeded to immediately pull off the waterlogged sweatshirt, revealing an equally wet, and almost transparent wife beater underneath. The shirt clung to her, outlining two pert breasts, with their nipples standing at attention. Rea turned away before Selina could strip any further, but caught movement in the mirror over the vanity. She let her eyes stray toward it, and felt her heart rate escalate, as Selina's magnificent body was uncovered.

The woman was gorgeous. A bronzed goddess! And Rea's eyes roamed all over the reflection. Selina had a rather boyish figure with broad shoulders, long torso, and legs that seem to stretch for miles, but hips that flared out enough to give her feminine curves. Rea's gaze became riveted on the dark thatch of hair, at the apex of her thighs before raising them again, only to catch Selina's eyes staring straight back at her in the mirror. Her face grew hot in embarrassment, and Rea closed her eyes, not wanting to see the look of censure, she felt sure would be there. Some inner force compelled Rea to open her eyes, but the ones staring back into her own, held no reproach, only a fiery desire.

Watching intently, she saw the sexy grin that she'd already seen a time or two spread across Selina's lips, before turning to enter the shower. Rea still hadn't looked away when Selina popped her head back around the tile wall and said, "Want to join me…you'd be welcomed?"

OH MY GOD! Her heart thumped wildly, as Rea watched Selina disappear behind the wall once again, masking the sound of the storm outside with the one now raging inside her.

Rea couldn't deny the desire she'd seen reflected in Selina's eyes was as real and honest as the offer she'd made. It had been so long since Rea had been touched with desire—her body lusted for it—but Sherry had been the only one allowed that kind of intimacy. For Rea, it encompassed being emotionally and physically naked. That took a lot of trust, and she wasn't there yet.

The sound of the shower coming on brought Rea out of her reverie. She realized she could no longer hear the thunder beating against the house, nor the pining of hailstones on the roof—the soft patter of rain had taken its place. With the storm dying down, she felt Selina would be fine if Rea left her alone. She felt an overwhelming need to escape the confines of the bathroom before Selina finished showering. Her psyche wasn't ready for a second visual assault.

Rea put a fresh towel on the vanity and her robe on the hook by the shower door, then quickly gathered up the wet clothes from the floor. Raising her voice loud enough to be heard over the falling water, she said, "Storm's moved off. I'm going to get out of my damp clothes and put everything in the wash."

Not waiting for a response, Rea beat a hasty retreat from the bathroom, closing the door firmly behind her.

*****

Dammit she'd pushed too hard again…hadn't she? Selina couldn't resist making her shower proposition when she'd caught Rea watching her undress in the mirror with a look of arousal on her face. The need to intimately know her had been building since they'd met—but the storm had made the yearning more intense. Rea had seen her fear and wrapped her up in the kind of comfort Selina hadn't known since her Amá sání died. It had opened up a vulnerable part of herself that she'd never shared with anyone else, and she craved the same thing from Rea.

But Selina had literally been shut out when Rea closed the bathroom door and left her alone again. Was it the ghost of Rea's dead wife or something else that kept coming between them, she wondered?

Selina wished she was better with women, but apparently, from her failed relationships, she hadn't figured it out yet. Animals were so much easier—it should be exactly the same, though—they only required love, care, understanding, and some occasional physical exercise. But with Rea, just like with a shy horse, came the complication of trust. The real question was, why hadn't Selina been able to gain Rea's yet when she'd given her own? The only thing she hadn't done was verbalize her feelings for Rea, and maybe that's what she needed to hear.

Selina quickly finished showering, not wanting to let Rea get too far away. She toweled off, then put on Rea's teal robe, admiring the color. Selina bet it looked fabulous on Rea with her red hair and creamy skin. She lifted the lapel to her nose and indulged herself in a scent that was all Rea—sandalwood with a hint of vanilla. Belting herself into the oversized garment, Selina closed her eyes, then rubbed her cheek against the soft cloth, imagining it was Rea covering her. But Selina was never going to get there until she laid her cards out and told Rea how she felt.

When she opened the door, Selina caught Rea with her arms raised getting ready to slide a sweatshirt over her head. She'd barely caught a glimpse of Rea's lace-covered breasts before she hastily dropped her arms and did a one-eighty, presenting her back to Selina. Her eyes immediately zeroed in on something

Lost & Found

black standing out vividly against Rea's pale, ivory shoulder. Selina was almost positive she knew what it was, but had to know for sure. She closed the distance between them before Rea could don the shirt.

Raising her hand, Selina trailed her fingertip along the inked letters, ST, inside one loop of the infinity symbol, and on the opposite side, RT.

In awe, she traced the lines and said, "I've seen this tattoo before." Selina turned Rea, so she could look into her eyes. "You were in my dreams before we'd even met, and I thought those initials were mine. Now I know they must be Sherry's, but it doesn't change the way I feel about them." Now she hoped that one day those initials would stand for her too.

Selina enveloped Rea in her arms, softly swaying, humming the old familiar tune that summed up perfectly the way she felt. Selina dropped a series of gentle butterfly kisses over Rea's forehead, cheeks, and eyes, but avoided her lips. Fearing one sweet taste of those would torpedo her control. Finally, Selina brought her mouth close to Rea's ear and confessed, "You've claimed my soul from the lost and found. You hold my heart, and I need you."

Selina couldn't hold back any longer. She let her lips trail from Rea's ear down along her jaw before capturing her mouth in a hungry kiss. There was enough space between them that she felt Rea's shirt drop to the floor—freeing her arms to wrap tightly around Selina—surrendering to the love song that was becoming a part of them. The motion of their bodies moving in a slow rhythm loosened the tie on the robe, bringing one of Selina's bare nipples into contact with Rea's warm skin. Her desire to make love to this woman, who held her heart, was climbing higher by the second.

Selina broke the kiss, freeing her lips to explore. As they moved down Rea's neck heading for her throat, Selina felt Rea's pulse pounding away like a bass drum. She allowed herself a tiny smile, before moving up to nip an ear lobe. Running her tongue along the soft shell, she heard the hitch in Rea's breathing, followed by a soft moan.

Selina slid her hands lower till they found their way inside Rea's sweat pants. She encountered nothing beneath but two soft, well-rounded ass cheeks. Selina took them in a firm grip bringing Rea's center into contact with her thigh, as her own mound snugged against Rea's hip.

With the woman of her dreams locked in her arms and the gentle rocking motion, Selina felt she could almost come, but wanted so much more. The bed was only a few feet away, so she leaned back enough to drop another string of kisses along Rea's face before ardently whispering in her ear, "I want to make love to you, Rea."

Still swaying rhythmically, Selina started to shuffle Rea toward the bed, but the change in motion had an immediate and detrimental effect. Eyes that had been closed in passion popped open, and Rea shook her head from side to side as if trying to clear it. Rea then pushed firmly against her chest, and Selina had no choice but to let her go.

Rea's head immediately dropped, searching the floor, until she found her shirt and quickly slipped it on, then crossed her arms protectively over her torso. They were only a few feet away from each other, breathing heavily, but the gap between them felt like a yawning chasm to Selina. Bewildered by the sudden change, and a little hurt, Selina took a half step forward, holding out her hand pleadingly.

"I don't understand Rea. I thought you felt something for me." She took another half step. "I've been trying to give you time. But I want…no, I need the kind of intimate connection, that only making love to you will satisfy. Will you let me?"

Another step and Selina was almost within touching distance, when Rea uttered only two words, "I can't!" Then fled the room.

Chapter Twenty-Six

Aftermath

Rea was congratulating herself for her near escape from the bathroom as she hastily donned a pair of dry sweat pants. Audaciously, she went commando because all of her clean panties were in the dryer. But Selina showered quicker than Rea anticipated and caught her half-dressed. Clutching the shirt to her chest, she whirled around, hiding her pudgy stomach from Selina's sight.

From there, things careened out of her control. The touch of Selina's fingers gently tracing her tat, confiding her feelings, and humming the song that spoke to Rea, as no other song did, propelled her into an emotional free fall. But the two strong arms holding her so tenderly, reigning soft kiss all over sent her heart spiraling. But the taste of those hungry velvety lips devouring her own fired Rea's blood. When Selina's hands slid beneath her pants, pressing a firm thigh against her throbbing clit, Rea was caught in a sexual undertow, that she was happily drowning in.

Selina voicing her desire to make love to her, and the shift toward the bed, brought Rea's senses swimming back to the surface, allowing her to push away. As much as her body wanted it, she wasn't ready to open herself up to that yet, and the fear of what crossing that bridge would mean, sent her fleeing.

Mortified by her actions, Rea tore out of the bedroom and through the house, stopping only long enough to don on a pair of boots. When she stepped onto the porch, Rea clung to the post, breathing deeply, filling her lungs with some much-needed oxygen. With her heart still hammering, Rea took off down the steps, her feet crunching on small bits of ice from the thawing hailstones. The rain had tapered off to a drizzly mist cooling her overheated system. Rea had no destination in mind, she just needed to put some distance between her and Selina, while she figured out why she couldn't move past her insecurities.

Before she knew it, Rea was standing at the barn door and quickly entered. Without pause, she let Jupe out into the paddock, saddled Dolly, then left the barn and turned toward the river. Jupe followed along the fence line, whinnying in dismay at being left behind.

The darkest storm clouds had moved to the east, allowing dappled sunlight to glint off the tiny ice shards and puddles of water on the muddy trail. Wanting to keep them both clean, Rea urged Dolly off to the side and into the tall grass. The orchard was in full bloom, and the birds that had taken shelter in the trees were now twittering to each other. If it hadn't rained, she would have been wreathed in their flowery aroma, but the damp earth was all Rea could smell.

The ride soon soothed her frayed nerves so she could think clearly again. Rea didn't know what she was going to say to Selina when she returned. She'd plainly seen the pain in Selina's eyes and heard it in her voice as she'd pleaded for Rea's love. How could she explain her panicked withdrawal, when she didn't understand it herself anymore?

Selina had made her feelings clear this morning, both verbally and physically. If Rea were to head home right now and find Selina gone, she would be devastated. Having Selina in her life, sharing the things that were so important to her, had started filling in the crack in Rea's heart.

Why wasn't she ready to physically return Selina's love yet? Her emotional side was craving it. Rea was starting to believe Selina really did find her attractive. She even allowed for the possibility that there was some mystical meddling going on to try and make it happen. The only thing Rea knew for sure was that she was balancing on a tightrope between love and fear, petrified of the intimate act that would open her soul fully to Selina.

A shrieking neigh snapped Rea out of her trance, but not fast enough to combat Dolly's alarm. The reins were jerked out of her hands, and she was woefully unprepared for the near-vertical reaction that ensued. Before Rea could blink, her body impacted the ground, her head following suit, bouncing against something hard—then all went black.

*****

Selina was stunned into immobility by Rea's sudden departure, and stood in the bedroom, her empty arms outstretched. How had things gone from sublime to shit, in what felt like a heartbeat? She'd opened herself fully to Rea only to be rejected. Had she read the signs wrong? Selina dropped her arms, closed her eyes and swallowed convulsively, trying to keep the hurt at bay.

Flopping onto the bed that only moments ago Selina had hoped to be sharing with Rea, she replayed their interactions. Rea's firm embrace, kisses, and needy moans had expressed her desires plainly. No, she hadn't read them wrong. But apparently, it hadn't been enough for Rea to overcome whatever was holding her back. The look on Rea's face before she fled, had been one of deep longing, shame, regret, and apprehension.

Selina heard the sound of a door opening and closing, indicating Rea had left the house. She needed to go after her so they could try to work through whatever her issue was, together. Sighing over what might have been, Selina opened her eyes, then pushed herself up off the bed. The robe she was wearing gaped open, reminding her that she needed her clothes. She belted it closed then went in search of them.

They were in a basket next to the dresser still wet from the storm. Thankfully, Rea had pulled her cell phone out of the pocket, so at least it was dry. Selina grabbed it along with the basket, then left the bedroom in search of the laundry room. She found it, along with Patches, who was sheltering inside his kennel, still hesitant to come out.

"Hey, dude. The storm you're hiding from has passed, but the one your mom and I created left with her. I'm going to dry my clothes first, and maybe by then, you will feel like helping me find her. Okay?" Patches' answer was a pitiful whine.

Selina put down the basket, opened the dryer door, and found it was still full of clothes. As she moved them to an empty basket that sat on top, Selina stopped to fondle some of the lace and satin underthings, jealous of the simple garments that covered what she coveted. They were mostly tan or plain white, but there was one red set and one black, that made Selina's heart race. It was easy for her to imagine how sultry Rea would look in either of those. She put the kibosh on those thoughts and got her wet things inside the dryer. With so few clothes, Selina set it for thirty minutes then pushed the start button.

Alone in the house, except for Patches, she took the opportunity to snoop a little and started in the living room. Selina browsed Rea's DVD collection and found that along with a few classic lesbian movies, there were also quite a few that fell into the erotica category. That was also something she didn't need to think about right now. Moving on, Selina saw a few photo albums stacked on the bottom shelf of the bookcase and realized for the first time there were no pictures of people in Rea's house.

Curiosity killed the cat, so Selina plucked an ivory-colored leather one off the stack and sat down in the chair. She ran her fingers over the gilded lettering spelling out *Our Wedding* on the front cover, wondering if she and Rea might have one of their own someday.

Selina braced herself. This would be her first view of the woman whose dying dreams were the catalyst for bringing Rea into her life, and whose ghost she felt still hovered near. Selina opened the album, and the first page had their wedding invitation glued on it. Whoever created the card had been an artist. A laser-cut silver tree with heart-shaped leaves created a lacy silhouette over muted sunset colors. It opened down the center, revealing the writing underneath.

Sherry Tyson

and

Réalta Tobin

Invite you to come and celebrate their joining
on July 4, 2008 - 2 p.m.
at the Rosella Winery - Napa Valley, CA

Selina had to smile as she read the date. They'd celebrated their freedom to marry by getting hitched on Independence Day—what a perfect irony that was. Selina knew the winery too. It had been her girlfriend Kim's favorite winery, and they'd always made a stop there when passing through the area. The reason the winery stood out in her memory, was because it was owned by two lesbians, and she'd admired the colorful bird gracing the labels on their bottles of wine.

She flipped to the next page, and her heart skipped a beat. There was a younger Rea, a few pounds lighter but still voluptuous, smiling for all she was worth, at a slender, slightly shorter woman of obviously mixed heritage. Selina studied Sherry's features. Brown eyes with a distinctly almond shape, stubby nose with flaring nostrils, and full lips pulled back over bright, white teeth. Her coffee-colored skin and shoulder-length, curly, black hair were a complementary contrast to Rea's Irish features. Sherry was in a red satin dress with gold dragons embroidered on it, while Rea wore a long, emerald green, silk tunic with black dragons and slit up both sides to her hips over black slacks. They were standing under a white bower with grapevines full of fruit climbing over it. They'd made such a beautiful couple, and their beaming smiles showed they were also very much in love.

On the next page, the two were standing between a tall African American man and a delicate petite Asian woman, that Selina guessed were Sherry's parents. Another one was of a man about forty, with many of Sherry's same features, only taller and more robust, with his arms over both women's shoulders. She surmised it was Sherry's brother, Dan, the attorney, Rea had spoken of. Selina continued to flip through the photos that captured the couple's various wedding activities—first dance, cake cutting, and a double bouquet toss. There was even a picture of Matty and Mia, with a brood of what had to be their children surrounding Rea.

What was absent in the photos was anyone who resembled Rea. Selina knew from their discussions that she lost her father in adolescence, and her mom had passed away when she was eighteen, but from the pictures, it looked like Rea was utterly devoid of any other family members. She wondered if it was because there hadn't been any living, or if they'd shunned Rea because she was gay. No wonder Rea's ties to Sherry were so strong, she'd given Rea a family. After her grandparents had died, Selina at least had a slew of aunts, uncles, and cousins she could depend on. Maybe if they could get past whatever seemed to be standing between them, she could share her family with Rea.

Selina rose from the couch to exchange the album for another when she heard a buzzing coming from the laundry room, announcing the end of the drying cycle. She put the album up and went to retrieve her clothes, so she could go find Rea and make that happen.

Five minutes later, Selina was dressed and putting on her damp sneakers, while Patches waited for her. Suddenly, his ears pitched forward, and he bolted through his doggie door, startling Selina. She jumped up and followed him out the door. She made it onto the porch in time to see Patches disappear around the corner of the garage heading for the barn.

A sense of urgency swamped Selina, telling her something was undeniably wrong. She took off at a dead run, heading after him. The sight of an agitated, mud-splattered, riderless Dolly sent Selina into panic mode. She was positive something awful had happened. Rea was too good a rider, and Dolly too disciplined a horse, to appear without her. She needed to find Rea and find her right away.

With both horses upset, Selina didn't want to take a chance on riding either one of them right now. Plus, if Rea was injured, she might not be able to ride anyway. Selina didn't even stop to unsaddle Dolly, she just opened the gate and herded her into the paddock, hoping that being with Jupe would calm her down. After securing the gate, she raced to the garage for the ATV.

Patches was nowhere to be seen, but Selina guessed Rea might have gone to her special place down by the river. So as soon as the quad cleared the shed door, Selina sped off in that direction. She kept scanning the terrain as she drove, hoping to see Rea limping back toward the barn.

The site of the white wolf standing on the trail brought Selina to a dead stop. When it disappeared into the tall grass, Selina followed but had to drop her speed. A minute later, she saw the trampled grass and Patches lying across Rea's prone body. Selina halted the ATV, scrambled off, and raced to her side.

Rea was unconscious, head pillowed against a rock, with a trickle of blood was running down the side. A few feet away in a flattened patch of ground lay the remains of a dead rattler, its head nearly severed by sharp hooves. Selina immediately looked for signs of a bite and saw Rea's little finger on her right hand was swelling. She was raised in rattlesnake country and knew time was of the essence.

Selina whipped out her phone and prayed she would have a signal. Two bars were showing, so she speed-dialed Matty. As soon as she heard the call connect, she blurted out, "Matty, Rea is hurt badly." Without giving him a chance to say a word, she continued, "She has a head wound and a snake bite. We're down toward the river not too far to the west of the pump house. I can't get her into the ATV by myself, and we need to get her to a hospital immediately."

"Selina, donn worry. I get Doc Dziike to come quick, she have de right medicine an know what to do. We have snake bites before. I call right back."

Selina moved up beside Rea, picked up her uninjured hand, and pleaded, "Hang in there, help is on the way. I need you to stay with me. I just found you, and I can't lose you now." Rea seemed to be barely breathing, and Selina was so afraid help wouldn't arrive in time.

Her phone rang, and she answered hastily, "Matty, what's the plan?"

"Annika is on de way to my place wit de medicine. I bring her on my ATV. She call into de hospital an dey is sending a life copter. I should be dere in fifteen or twenny minutes. Dere is a flare in de ATV. When ju hear me, jues it, so I can fine ju. De Doc say donn move her."

"Okay, Matty, but hurry. Her hand is already swelling, and it's starting to make its way up her arm."

"I will. But ju need to stay calm," he said then hung up.

Selina held on to her hand fiercely, as if that would somehow hold death back if it should try and take Rea away from her. She used her other to gently stroke Rea's face. "See, baby, everything is going to be fine."

Something made her look up, and a few feet away sat Selina's wolf, watching her intently. Relieved to find her guide still with her, Selina addressed it. "Mą'iitsoh nítch'i," she said reverently. "If Rea should journey into the Shadow Lands, please guard and protect her there. She has come to mean everything to me."

It rose, nodded its head at Selina, then shimmered out of sight, and she breathed easier, placing her faith in the divine. Hearing the roar of an ATV engine in the distance, Selina moved to get the flare, hoping the chopper wouldn't be too far behind.

Chapter Twenty-Seven

The Shadow Lands

Rea felt the swipe of a wet tongue against her cheek and pushed against a furry muzzle. "Patches quit licking me, I'm awake. Give me a sec, my brain feels all fuzzy." She pried her eyes open, but instead of the familiar ceiling in her bedroom, she saw nothing but a leaden gray mist.

Closing her eyes again, Rea tried to dredge up her last memory. It was coming back to her now. The catalytic storm had led to the intimate moment in her bedroom with Selina and precipitated her panicked flight from the house. Then she'd taken Dolly out for a ride to clear her head…oh yeah. Dolly had gotten startled, reared, and Rea had been dislodged from the saddle. *I must have gotten knocked out. How long have I been lying out here?* It was so murky that Rea figured it must be close to dusk. Whatever the time was, she'd never in her life seen fog like this.

Rea was sure that Selina would be concerned about her disappearance and come looking for her. Just a month ago, if she'd been badly hurt, it might have been a long time before anyone even knew she was missing—she didn't always see or talk with Matty or Mia every day. At least she hadn't laid out here by herself; Patches had stayed with her. He was such a good dog. Wait! Patches hadn't come with her. He'd been in the house hiding from the storm…then what had licked her arm? Maybe he had followed her, and she just hadn't noticed. That had to be it, Rea rationalized.

Almost fearfully, she opened her eyes and searched the gray mist that didn't seem quite as dense now, but she still couldn't see anything. Carefully, Rea sat up, taking stock of any possible injuries, but she wasn't even sore, which didn't make sense. She should have been bruised from the fall and stiff from laying out on the ground for who knew how long, but she wasn't. Rea rolled over, pressing her hands to the ground, preparing to heave herself to her feet—which at her age and weight, wouldn't be easy from ground level—but it was surprisingly effortless.

The sound of panting reached Rea's ears, through the gloom, making her realize how deathly quiet it had been. She should be close enough to the river to at least hear it, but there was nothing. No birds chirping, crickets singing, nor anything else. Rea squinted her eyes, trying to locate Patches but couldn't see him.

"Patches, come here, boy. Your Mom needs your help to find her way out of this soupy mess," she called out and waited for him to come to her.

Rea was starting to panic a little, but then noticed a softly glowing light, growing stronger, just to her right, that seemed to be driving back the mist. As it thinned, Rea saw the white wolf only a few feet away, gazing at her intently, but everything beyond her was still hidden from view. Things were beginning to feel very surreal, like being inside a dream. Rea remembered what Selina had told her about it being a guide, and she sure needed one of those.

She wasn't sure how to address it and felt a little foolish, but forged ahead anyway. "Spirit Wolf, what is going on?"

"You are in the Shadow Lands. The place between the physical realm and the spiritual one. Selina asked me to guard and guide you here, in this place, after you were injured."

Rea heard the feminine voice clearly in her head. Taking a moment to digest this revelation, her next thought was, *Am I alive or dead?*

"Neither. Ultimately it will be your desires that will tip the balance. Come, there are things to see, and more than one voice, you will need to hear to help you make your choice."

The gray mist pushed back even further, then Rea saw herself lying in a hospital bed, with all kinds of wires and tubes connecting her to machines, but there were no colors. The scene looked odd, like one of those old black and white movies, where the images appeared slightly blurred. She was surrounded by machines, one of which—from the readouts on the screen—was monitoring her heartbeat and blood pressure. Another was emitting a rhythmic whooshing sound that matched the rise and fall of her chest, and Rea realized she was on a breathing machine. Then she noticed her head was wrapped in a bandage, which brought back the memory of her fall from Dolly's back.

"I hit my head, didn't I?"

"Yes, but also, the snake that frightened your horse, bit you, before dying under her hooves. One or the other was serious enough by themselves, but the combination of the two has brought you to this in-between place."

Off to the side, Selina sat erect, looking exhausted with a styrofoam cup clutched in her hands, gazing fixedly at Rea's hospital bed, worry etched in every line of her features. She felt a need to go to her and offer comfort, but some type of barrier prevented it.

"Yes, her love waits for you and is within your reach, but first, there is a spirit that wishes to speak with you."

A thick mist closed in again, blotting everything else out. When it cleared, Rea found herself sitting on her rock by the river. After the slightly blurry imagery of the hospital room, though still monochrome, things seemed sharper and more vibrant. The full moon's shining visage lit the scene, glinting off the ripples of the slowly moving river. Rea's eyes fixed on a reflection of something sitting next to her but was hesitant to turn her head; to find out what ethereal being was visiting her version of The Twilight Zone now. Maybe it was the wolf—it seemed to glow like that.

"Ahem. Aren't you going to look at me, Rea? You've wished for this for quite some time."

There was no mistaking the sound of that well-loved voice. Rea turned her head slowly to see a diaphanous version of her wife sitting next to her, with a knowing smile on her face.

"Yes, ReRe, it's me, or at least the part of me you still carry in your heart. It's enabled me to find form here in this place, where your soul is marking time."

Rea felt tears well up—was she even able to shed them here—at the lovingly spoken nickname that only Sherry had ever used. She'd wished so many times over the years to be able to see and speak to her again. Now Rea didn't know what to say, other than the obvious. "I've missed you so much, sweetheart, that at times, I didn't know if I could go on without you."

"I know, love…but you have, and you should. You've used my memory and our dreams to keep you going, but those are cold comfort compared to having someone who can share a life with you."

"You mean Selina?"

"You know that's who I mean, ReRe. You've talked to me about her a lot recently. You are drawn to her just as she is drawn to you. Your lives have orbited around each other passing close on numerous occasions, only a few of which you are both aware of. Selina was even at the winery the day we got married. You were destined to meet at the right time, and that time is now. The power of fate set this interlude in motion, but the direction it takes now is your choice. We've done all we can, and the rest is up to you."

"What do you mean, WE?" Rea asked, not at all sure she wanted to know.

"You know that answer too. You've already met one, and there will be another after me. You only need to let yourself believe in us, and in Selina's love for you. What's holding you back?"

Even in this otherworldly plane, Rea's voice wavered, "I'm afraid! Afraid of the intimacy, and afraid to risk loving again."

"ReRe, you can't let your fear stop you. You have to believe everything will turn out the way it's supposed to. Take a lesson from the passage in the book "Gone" by Ocean—that you loved so much and memorized because it spoke to you...

"I think it has to do with believing in yourself. You have to believe that, no matter what, you'll be all right. You'll come through whatever it is you need to face. You'll cope with the consequences, life will go on, and you'll be fine. Being afraid is okay. It's normal. It's not fear that's the problem, it's how you deal with or don't deal with it, that's the problem. Someone once said that without fear, there can be no courage."

Sherry's voice took on a pleading tone, "Gather up your courage, ReRe, and don't let your fear stop you from finding love again. You have so much more of it to give."

"I'll try, Sherry, but know I will always love you," Rea said, to the vision as it started to pulse with light.

"I know ReRe, I know. Lay down and rest for a bit. Your energy levels are falling."

Now that Sherry mentioned it, Rea was starting to feel tired, which surprised her. After all, wasn't her body in a hospital bed sleeping or whatever? Her brain was too muddled to think about it, so Rea curled up on the smooth rock and closed her eyes. As her consciousness winked out, Rea thought she felt phantom fingers caressing her temples, soothing her into sleep.

*****

From the moment Rea had been airlifted to the hospital in critical condition, Selina's life had also hung in the balance. They wouldn't let her go in the chopper, and it seemed like an eternity until she could make it there. Selina had taken care of the horses first, then tried to calm the frantic dog, before closing up the house. She'd stopped long enough to change out of her mud-splattered clothes from the wild ride she taken on the ATV, and scooped up her pouch with her talisman in it on the way out. Selina had needed the physical reminder of the promise it presented, that she and Rea, were meant to be together.

It was now Monday, day two of the vigil that she, Matty, and Mia, had kept at Rea's bedside. Rea was in a coma suffering from a concussion and the effects of the venom from the rattlesnake bite, that had made its way into her system, stopping her heart at one point. She was now off the ventilator, and the doctor was cautiously optimistic. But the three of them were a haggard bunch, suffering from a lack of sleep and stress. They were sitting out in the waiting room temporarily while the nurse gave Rea a sponge bath.

Selina wasn't about to leave but thought Matty and Mia could use a break. "Why don't you two go home and get some rest. I'll stay here," she urged them. "Also, the horses and Patches will need to be fed. The weather is warm enough that Dolly and Jupe can stay out in the paddock all night. If you'll open a bale of hay for them, they should be okay for now. The planting is well underway, but if you could check in with the other managers for me, that would be great."

"Ju need some rest too, an food. Ju can't live on juss coffee," Mia said.

"I'm not hungry, and besides, hospital food sucks. When you come back, you can bring me a few of your breakfast tacos, Mia, and I'll nap in the reclining chair in her room if I can cajole the nurse into it. If not, I can stretch out here for a bit, I've slept on worse before. I just can't leave Rea right now."

Mia gazed at her in understanding then turned to tug on Matty's sleeve. "Tal vez deberíamos irnos a casa."

Matty nodded and rose reluctantly to his feet, then turned to Selina. "We go an will take care of de animals, rest, den come back tonight. Ju call if anything happen, we come inmediatamente, sí?"

Selina could see the worry in his eyes, and she shared it. "Yes, I will call if there are any changes. The doctors have told us she is past the critical point, and they have every reason to believe she will recover. They've also said her EEG is good, so her brain is healing. It's just a matter of time till she wakes up," she stated emphatically, not sure if she was trying to convince him or herself.

Once they'd gone, Selina waited until she saw the nurse exit before going back into Rea's room, then over to her bed. She wanted to hold her hand, but one was bandaged, and the other had the IV in it, so she stroked her temple instead. "You rest love. I'll be here when you are ready to come back."

Selina needed assurance in her own mind that Rea would be alright and took her talisman out of the pouch. Her fingers traced the crack in the stone, knowing hers would be fractured the same way if Rea didn't pull through. She cradled it in her hands and offered up a silent prayer.

Amá sání, please watch over Rea and let her know I am here with her. Holding on to the hope that when she wakes, she will be willing to accept this love I hold in my soul for her.

Selina placed a gentle kiss on Rea's forehead then slipped the meteorite under her pillow.

*****

Rea could hear murmuring as her awareness seemed to be returning, but she couldn't quite make out the words. She thought she felt warm lips against her head and remembered Sherry was sharing her rock, but when Rea opened her eyes, she found herself in a vastly different place than her spot on the river.

An old woman was sitting across from her—separated by a small fire—about five feet away. She was plump, her careworn face was lined with wrinkles, and a silvery braid was draped over her shoulder. The glowing wolf lay at her side. The woman watched her quietly as if giving Rea time to absorb her surroundings.

The setting was still devoid of color, but based on the landscape, she guessed she was somewhere in the Painted Desert region, near the mouth of a canyon. With this thought, the old woman cracked a smile and nodded her head.

"That's right, child. You are in the home of the Diné people, a place that has special meaning, for my Lina."

"Lina?"

"Yes, among our family, everyone calls Selina that. She always kept the use of her full name separate from the one she allows only the family to use. Even her previous lovers were not allowed to call her Lina, but I bet she would let you…if you asked her."

"Are you her grandmother? I don't remember what she said your name was, she always spoke of you with a Diné name."

"Yes, I am her Amá sání or Lily, and you may call me either of those, but I prefer the former…" She gave Rea a knowing look. "And I have a feeling you will be joining my family soon."

Rea looked away and studied the terrain, wondering why she had been brought here. She was also uncomfortable with the knowledge that the old woman knew things about her, and could also read her mind.

Giving Rea an understanding smile, she said, "You are right, child, it is impolite, and I will stop now. Do you have questions for me?"

"Yes. Why am I here with you, Amá sání?"

"Look in your hand."

Rea hadn't realized she was holding anything, but when she opened it, there was the meteorite that Selina believed was sent to bring them together.

"Lina is with you, in the hospital, and asked that I come to you in this place, to watch over you, but she also wanted me to intercede for her."

"Intercede, how?" Rea frowned.

"She hoped that I could somehow convince you to allow her to love you." The old woman cackled. "But Lina doesn't know you've already been visited by the one person who has that type of influence with you—Sherry."

Confused about everything that had been happening since the accident, Rea asked, "Sherry told me she was able to come to me because I carried a part of her spirit in my heart, but how are you able to be here?"

"Because whether you are willing to admit it to yourself or Lina yet, you already carry a piece of her soul in yours, and I am a piece of hers, so voila here I am."

Rea was trying to digest this, but the old woman continued on. "You are almost ready to go back and face the world again, but there is one more thing you need to understand."

The eyes piercing hers were full of wisdom as if she had all the answers Rea needed. "And what is that, Amá sání?"

"The shell you wear in the physical plane is unimportant to Lina even though she finds that attractive. She has never judged anyone by it because she, too, has been judged that way before. She only cares about your soul, and that she finds beautiful, as did Sherry. It shines through to the people that count. There is also a very distraught couple sharing Lina's concern for you. I think Mia has almost worn out one of her rosaries."

Rea could almost picture it and felt guilty for having worried everyone. She needed to get home. "I'm ready to return, Amá sání. How do I get back to the physical plane?"

With a mischievous smile, Lily said, "Goodbye, Rea." The shimmering form started to fade before her eyes. "Just follow my daughter, she will guide you." And then she was gone.

Rea hadn't noticed, but the wolf that had been sitting only a few feet away had morphed into a woman. She was a taller leaner version of Lily, but someone who also shared many of Selina's features, especially her blue eyes—the only thing with color that Rea had seen. Shocked at this revelation, Rea asked, "You're Lina's mother?"

The woman's smile held a touch of sadness. "Yes, I'm her mother, Nita. But Selina hasn't been aware of this, though if she'd thought about it, she could have put two and two together and figured it out. Especially after I showed myself to both of you at the same time. My appearances in her life were not like those of a traditional spirit guide. Those types of encounters are usually initiated by deep meditation, and in some instances, with the aid of certain kinds of plant matter. But I am a spirit that could not rest easy when my daughter's soul energy called out for guidance. I've used it to open a metaphysical door, to reach her, and manifest as the wolf."

"How were you able to visit me at the river, before I even knew Selina existed?"

"Because she was searching for something, I knew resided in you. I also had a little help from Sherry pointing the way. Come let us walk, it is time to go."

They rose, and it grew darker as they left the fire. Rea had one burning question she hoped Nita would answer. "What about my mother? Why didn't she visit me here?"

Nita stopped and focused those glacial blue eyes on her. "I'm sure she would have if her soul hadn't already chosen to be reborn. You will meet her again someday. Neither of you will recognize the other, but there will be an instant bond between you."

Nita stepped back, and a thick mist started to coalesce around her. "It was good to meet you, Rea, and I approve of my Lina's choice. You will not remember all of what happened in this place, but you will take heart from your time here."

The dense fog that started Rea's journey here returned until all she could see was the dimming glow of a wolf vanishing into the nothingness that was overtaking her.

Chapter Twenty-Eight

Home Is Where the Heart Lives

Selina had drifted in and out of sleep most of the day, often rousing to check on Rea. They'd come in around noon to take Rea for another CAT scan, and she'd paced nervously until they brought her back. Doctor Uy, a diminutive, occidental man, with his calm and caring demeanor, came in at two to examine Rea. Selina had tried to get answers to Rea's current medical status, but he sadly shook his head. He could only provide the information to Matty, who held her medical POA. He did give her hand a reassuring squeeze, though, before departing.

Matty and Mia hadn't returned, but they had called a bit ago to let her know everything at the farm had been taken care of. They'd mentioned something about bringing her food, but that wasn't important to Selina. What was vital to her, however, was their arrival would mean Selina could finally get answers to the questions that she had a burning need to know.

She was just starting to nod off again when the beeping on one of the monitors increased. Alarmed, Selina quickly went to the hospital bed and depressed the call button, searching Rea for signs of distress. But what she found was Rea's eyes moving under her closed lids and a quiet moan escaping her lips.

Selina leaned over close to Rea's ear and urged gently, "Rea. Wake up, dearling," the heartfelt endearment slipping easily off her tongue. But then again, it fit, since Rea was near and dear to

Selina's heart. "You need to open those beautiful eyes and let me see them. Come on, Rea."

Just as the day nurse, Barb, hustled into the room, Rea moved her head slightly and moaned a little louder. The woman rushed toward the bed, causing Selina to step back while Barb checked Rea's vitals. She then turned to Selina with a smile and said, "She's coming out of it. Stay with her and keep talking. I'm going to go call the doctor." Leaving Rea's bedside, she scurried back out the door.

Selina immediately moved back in. "Rea, you've had me, Matty and Mia, so worried, but you are going to be okay." Leaning over, she stroked Rea's cheek. "Come on, dearling…I need to look into your eyes so I can tell you how much I love you."

She watched as they fluttered open to mere slits. Rea attempted to wet her lips as if she was going to speak, but Selina put a comforting hand on her shoulder and said, "Don't try to talk yet, your doctor is on his way."

Rea's forehead furrowed as her eyes opened wider and locked onto Selina's in mute appeal. Understanding, she continued, "You're in the hospital. You'll be fine, but you've been unconscious for a while."

A second later, the doctor hurried in; the nurse hot on his heels. Selina moved back again so they could take her place.

"Welcome back, Ms. Tobin. I am your physician, Doctor Uy." He reached out and touched her arm reassuringly. "Your throat is going to be sore, so do not try to speak yet, but I need to examine you."

Selina watched from the end of the bed as he checked both wounds. He then pulled out a penlight and shone it in each of Rea's eyes, eliciting a soft groan from her. He finished then said, "I am going to raise the bed a little, then ask you a few questions, but just nod yes or no, alright?"

Selina saw Rea's chin dip slightly. A mechanical hum sounded as the head of the bed rose about twenty-five degrees then stopped, putting her almost at eye level with the doctor.

"Do you know where you are?" Rea's head dipped. "Do you recognize this woman?" he said, pointing at Selina.

A tiny smile formed on Rea's lips, and she nodded. Selina was glad she had a firm hold on the foot of Rea's bed as her knees weakened in relief. When he asked if Rea was in pain, she lifted her bandaged hand and tried to draw her finger and thumb together, then abruptly dropped it, but Doctor Uy understood.

"I can give you something for that now. Are you thirsty?" With another nod from Rea, the doctor made notes on the electronic chart and gave it to the nurse, who then headed out of the room.

"Barb will be back in a few minutes with some ice chips and something to add to your IV for pain, but the best thing for you to do is rest." He turned to Selina. "She's going to get sleepy again soon, but she should improve rapidly now." He then looked back at Rea. "I'll be in to check on you again later when I finish my rounds." Then he retreated, allowing Selina to return to Rea's side.

She noticed that Rea's face already had more color, and her hazel eyes looked a little brighter. There was so much she wanted to say to her, but before she could begin, Barb came back in and handed Selina a small cup of ice with a plastic spoon.

"Give her one at a time. Once she's had some, she might be able to speak a little, but she should limit that for now," Barb instructed, then busied herself at the IV.

Selina spooned up a piece of ice. "Okay, here you go, first one." Rea seemed to savor the cold chunk. Watching keenly, she noticed Rea's face tightened slightly as she swallowed, then changed to a look of relief. After about half a dozen, Rea raised her hand a little with her palm out, so Selina stuck the spoon back in the cup and asked, "Had enough?"

The soft, raspy "Yes," that followed was like music to Selina's ears. Rea wriggled her shoulder a little, then lifted it slightly and whispered, "Something's…there."

Selina gently pushed her hand between Rea's shoulder and the bed, encountering the meteorite, that she'd forgotten she placed under her pillow. It must have moved when the doctor raised the bed. Once she'd pulled it free, she was flabbergasted to see something looking like silver, had sealed the crack in the stone. She stared at it wonderingly, hoping this was another sign.

Selina turned to show it to Rea but saw her eyes had closed, and she'd fallen back to sleep. She gripped the talisman between her palms, lowered her head, bringing it close to her lips and silently offered, *Thank you!*

*****

It was so great to be home, Rea thought, as she lay propped up against the arm of the couch with several pillows stacked behind her back. She was freshly showered and wearing her favorite pair of flannel drawstring PJ bottoms with an over-sized thermal T, which was heavenly after having to put up with those awful hospital gowns that gaped open. Patches hadn't left Rea's side since she'd stepped through the door of her house, and neither had Selina. After almost four days, two of which she had been in a coma, Rea had been more than ready to leave the hospital.

She didn't remember much from her first waking, except the loving smile Selina had worn on her otherwise exhausted face. The next time she surfaced, Mia and Matty were in the room, and that conversation had been memorable.

"Ju scare us haf to death, Cariña. Is so good to see ju awake."

"Where is Lina?"

"Ju mean, Selina?"

Saying Lina's name had instantly brought back hazy memories of her experiences while comatose. No, Rea was not ready to discuss that yet and especially not with Mia or Matty. "Yes, I meant Selina. I guess my head is still a little mussy."

"She go home to ress. She not leave jur side for two days, an I haf to order her to go. She be back later, ju see her den."

By the time Selina returned, Rea had convinced Mia and Matty to go home. She'd seen the doctor again, and he had filled her in on her condition. They'd also removed the catheter she hadn't been aware of, and that experience had been less than pleasant. All the wires that had been monitoring her head and heart had been unhooked, then a pretty, young nurse had given her a sponge bath, which had made Rea a little uncomfortable.

She'd barely finished up with some soup and apple sauce when Selina had strolled in, looking much better than she had hours before, with a smile that had seemed to light up the entire room. Rea returned it, acknowledging to herself for the first time, that she was totally in love with this woman.

The *Hi, dearling* greeting from Selina had warmed Rea from her head to her toes, and fogged her brain enough that she'd let slip, "Evening, Lina."

Rea remembered Selina's quickly indrawn breath at her use of it, accompanied by a questioning look. But thankfully, neither of them was ready to head down that road while she was still in the hospital, so Selina had let it go without comment. From that point on—by unspoken mutual consent—they'd steered away from any serious discussions. But now Rea was home, and the time for that was fast approaching. Even the word had taken on a new meaning for her. Home was where her heart lived, and that now required Selina in it.

Rea heard the beeping of the microwave and could hardly wait to have some decent food. To say the least, the meals she'd had in the hospital were pitiful. A delicious smell accompanied Selina's arrival at the side of the couch, carrying the lap tray. Rea looked up and could read the concern plainly written across her lovely features. "Can you sit up?"

"Of course, I can. No need to baby me."

Selina broke out into a sing-song voice. "B-b-b-baby, you just ain't seen n-n-nothin' yet, brrum, brrum, b-b-b-baby you just ain't seen nothing yet." Selina's slightly swaying hips drew Rea's lustful gaze.

Unfortunately, she wasn't ready for any of that, so instead, she concentrated on sitting up. Some slight pain and stiffness accompanied her efforts, reminding Rea she wasn't completely healed. Doctor Uy had told her the rest of the swelling in her right hand should be gone in the next four or five days, but total recovery from the snake bite and the head injury would take weeks.

Rea acknowledged she'd been lucky in so many ways. The fall itself could have killed her, but instead had knocked her out, keeping her heart rate and respiration low, slowing the progression of the toxin in her blood. Next, was the fact Selina had found her so quickly, and Annika Dziike stocked the proper anti-venom and was able to reach Rea with it before the snake bite could prove fatal. But the one that was forefront in her mind was the mystical intervention that Rea felt certain had played a vital role as well.

Now that she was upright, Selina laid the tray across her lap, then sat next to her on the couch. Rea's stomach rumbled to life as the savory smell of the chicken tortilla soup wafted up from the bowl. She fumbled to pick up the spoon with her left hand and felt warm fingers close over hers to remove it.

"Here, let me do that," Selina offered.

"Thank you. I'm still a little clumsy, and I would rather most of this end up in my mouth instead of down my front," Rea said with a chuckle. "Plus, I've kind of gotten used to you spoon-feeding me."

"Yeah, I've kind of gotten used to it myself." Selina dipped the spoon into the bowl then lifted it toward Rea's mouth.

"Mmmm," Rea moaned at the first taste and noticed a slight tremble in the hand holding the spoon. She lifted her eyes to Selina's and saw a flicker of desire burning in their blue depths.

All of a sudden, Rea wasn't so hungry anymore, at least not for food, but felt drawn to taste the lips that were just a foot away from her own. The tray seemed to levitate off her lap, landing on the table, freeing her to move. Reaching up with her good hand, Rea cupped Selina's jaw and gently ran her thumb over Selina's lips. Rea wanted to kiss her right then and there, but they needed to clear the air first. So, she reluctantly pulled back and said, "Let's go out and sit on the porch. I've got things I need to tell you, and I feel I should do that outside for some reason."

Selina nodded. "Maybe it's a part of my Diné heritage, but being outside is freeing, and it always makes me feel more at ease. But are you sure you're up to going outside? How's your head, any dizziness or pain?"

"No dizziness and just some minor aches. But no more pills, I'm done with those. A couple of Advil will do the trick if I need something. Right now, I'd prefer a bit of pot." Rea smiled. "I need a little something to help smooth out some of my nerves."

An understanding look passed between them and alleviated the tension that the almost kiss had generated. Rea now felt ready to share more than her story—she was ready to share her home and heart with Selina.

Chapter Twenty-Nine

Crossing the Bridge

From the moment Rea had called her Lina at the hospital, she'd been waiting for this moment. She left Rea to finish up her soup while she ran to the RV to grab her stash, and also put the meteorite in her pocket. She'd yet to show the healed stone to Rea, but tonight the timing seemed right.

As she approached the house, she spotted Rea sitting in the rocker, with a light blanket draped over her shoulders, and Patches at her feet, just like they'd been almost a month ago. That evening had signaled the initial turning point in their relationship, and Selina hoped that tonight they might turn another one too. She loaded the bong, and they'd passed it back and forth between them a few times, relaxing as the night closed in.

The silence was broken when Rea began to speak softly, "I never thanked you for saving my life. If you hadn't found me so quickly, I would have died. I owe you big time."

Selina leaned forward, hands on her knees. "No! You don't." She felt her chest constrict. "It was my fault you left the house and took off on Dolly in the first place. It was probably even the reason you fell. I'd bet my bottom dollar you weren't paying attention. You're too good a rider to get thrown unless you got surprised." Selina sagged back into the rocker and thrust it into a gentle rocking motion. "I shouldn't have pushed you before you were ready."

Rea shook her head and said earnestly, "Oh no, I'm not letting you take the blame for what happened. I'm the one who started off the whole fiasco by ogling you in the bathroom mirror..." There was just enough light for the blush to be visible on Rea's face. "And it was just the first time you caught me doing it. Honestly, I've been attracted to you from the moment I saw you on FaceTime, and it only grew stronger as I got to know you. I was simply too afraid to let myself cross that bridge, but now I'm not, and that has everything to do with the accident."

Selina went still in the rocker, almost afraid to breathe as if any movement would interrupt what Rea was getting ready to share with her.

"And it was an accident. You're right, I wasn't paying attention, but I don't think that would have made a difference. I remember Dolly was almost vertical when I slid off, which means she was completely surprised by the snake. Even with a grip on the saddle, I don't think I would have been able to hold on. We weren't on the trail, and nothing was visible in the tall grass. Dolly didn't see or hear it, so it must not have been coiled or rattling, meaning it hadn't been aware of Dolly either. I was startled, Dolly was startled, and so was the snake. We all played our parts." Rea paused, licked her lips, as if her mouth had gone dry, then picked up her bottle of water, taking several sips, before continuing. "I'm not even sure anymore that it was an accident."

Now Selina was the one startled and shoved her hand in her pocket till it closed around the meteorite. "What do you mean?"

"I mean, I was letting my fears get the best of me. I needed to get some sense knocked into me, to push past it, and I got that, but the accident was the catalyst."

Rea turned toward her then leaned forward too. "I know you will believe me when I say, only my body was in that hospital bed while I was in the coma. The thinking, feeling part of me wasn't. I was someplace else...some different plane of existence, and I wasn't there alone."

"The Shadow Lands," Selina whispered, and chill bumps popped up along her arms.

The term seemed vaguely familiar to Rea. "Is that what you call it?"

"It's my name for the place I believe a soul hovers when it is between life and death. I've read many accounts of near-death experiences, what people saw and heard while there, to have faith that such a plane exists. When I found you, you were barely breathing, and I was so afraid you would die. But then I saw my wolf guide and asked it to guard you there, so I am eager to hear your descriptions of it."

Rea closed her eyes, tilted her head slightly, and focused her thoughts. "Your name for the place is apt, everything was in grayscale. At times I felt like I was floating along in a fog. Some of my memories are just as murky. I don't recall everything that happened, but yes, your wolf was there...and she wasn't the only being I encountered."

She? A guide was neither a he nor a she. They were incorporeal beings, taking on an animal form, what did Rea know that Selina didn't?

Without pause, she continued, "My haziest recollection was of sitting in my spot by the river with Sherry." Rea opened her eyes and focused them on Selina. "I don't recall much of that encounter, but whatever transpired, I found closure there. I do know she admonished me to find the courage to move on and open my heart to love again." Rea's forehead wrinkled in concentration. "Maybe that's why I can't feel her presence anymore. I've finally let her go. One thing I clearly recall her telling me, though, was that we were fated to find each other."

The import of Rea's words sent Selina's heart thudding in her chest, but the next revelation sent it soaring.

"My more vivid memories are of visiting with your grandmother, Lily." Rea's green eyes twinkled. "She called you Lina and said only your family was allowed to call you that. But she was sure you'd probably let me too."

"She was right, you can." Selina would have given anything to talk to her Amá sání again, but it was enough to know she'd been there with Rea. "Do you remember anything else she told you?"

"She said something about you asking her to watch over me, and I faintly remember her explaining how all our spirits are connected, but that part is hazy."

Rea placed her hand on Selina's knee. "My clearest memory was just before I came out of the coma, and that's the one I think

I was meant to recall. For you more than me. The wolf is the spirit of your Mother, Nita."

The wind stirred, and Selina thought she heard a wolf howling off in the distance as if to confirm what Rea just said.

But Rea continued as if she hadn't heard it. "To me, she resembled a shorter, stockier version of you, but she had the same blue eyes."

The description was spot on, and Selina acknowledged there were times she wondered about the wolf's visitations. They weren't typical for an animal guide, but she never let herself question it, almost afraid if she did, it might get offended and stop showing up. And she'd needed it. Her guide had been there at every critical junction in her life. Finding out it was her mother's spirit appearing in the wolf's guise made perfect sense.

Selina slid her hand atop Rea's and squeezed it gently. "She never showed her true face to me, but I'm glad to know it now."

"Nita said her spirit couldn't rest when you needed her. She also told me you'd been searching for something she believed resided in me, so Nita found me with Sherry's help. Whether it was fate or our loved ones that brought us together, I'm sending out a heartfelt thank you into the universe."

Everything Rea revealed opened up their future together, one consecrated and brought about by souls of those that loved them the most. Selina reached into her pocket with her free hand and pulled out the meteorite, holding it out for Rea to see. "I put this under your pillow in the hospital when you were in the coma. After you woke up, but before you went back to sleep, do you remember feeling something uncomfortable under your shoulder?" Rea nodded. "You can see the crack is filled now. When I saw this, I hoped it was a sign that your heart had healed. And I, too, am thankful for their intercession."

As Rea rose from her rocker, the blanket slipped from her shoulders and came to rest on the wooden seat. She tugged Selina up by her free hand and pulled her into a loose embrace, with the talisman resting between them. "I have healed."

Selina gazed into eyes that were now a vibrant green, her heart swelling with a love she saw was being returned in kind. "Mom was right. You are everything I've wished for in a life partner." Selina dropped a quick kiss to the lips so close to her own. "It doesn't matter if it was fate or the spirits that brought us together, it only matters that we've found each other."

*****

Rea felt such comfort wrapped in Selina's arms, and her sweet kiss had conveyed so much. She no longer doubted Selina's feelings for her, but she did have one little hurdle still to get over. "Will you lay with me tonight? I'm not up for anything energetic, but I want to sleep close to you."

"I would love that as well. I'll go get something to sleep in."

Rea gathered up her courage. "Clothing is optional. I prefer to sleep in the nude." She felt the arms holding her tremble.

"So do I. Especially when I can sleep next to a beautiful woman like you. It will be such sweet torture, but I promise to keep my libido under control."

Rea smiled to herself and said, "Me too." She pulled back just far enough to look into Selina's eyes. Yes, she could read the unmistakable desire there, barely held in check, and believed fully for the first time, that Selina found all of her attractive.

"Let's go inside then, I'm feeling trashed. It's been a long couple of days."

Rea headed directly into the bedroom while Selina put things away and cleaned up the kitchen. She quickly brushed her teeth, disrobed, then slipped into bed, turning out all the lights but the one in the bathroom.

A shadowy figure moved through the room, and then it grew even darker as the door clicked shut. From the bathroom, Selina called out loudly, "Do you have a spare toothbrush?"

"Yes, look in the top right-hand drawer of the vanity."

A few minutes later, the sliver of light outlining the bottom of the door went out, followed by the slight creak of a door hinge, and she held her breath as the bed dipped slightly. Rea rolled from her back to her side and faced Selina. There was enough light coming in from the window for Rea to see that Selina was lying as still as a statue, her arms clamping the blanket down over her torso, looking nervous. For some reason, this gave Rea's confidence a boost.

She moved closer and raised up on her left elbow, causing Selina's right arm to slip under the covers. The fingers on Rea's right hand cooperated enough to tilt Selina's head toward her, and leaning in, she kissed the soft lips beckoning hers. Rea kept it brief. She didn't want to start something she wasn't physically up for yet.

Rea did a one-eighty and came to rest on her right side then said, "Goodnight, Lina."

A second later, she felt Selina's longer body spoon around hers. "Goodnight, dearling," was whispered against her ear, eliciting a heartfelt sigh. Rea's last thought before she succumbed to sleep was—yes—it was going to be a torturous time for them both.

Chapter Thirty

Lost and Found

Since the first night Selina had spent in Rea's bed, they'd grown steadily closer. She'd learned a lot of little endearing things about Rea. Like that first morning when she'd caught Rea rubbing the edge of the sheet against her cheek, and discovered it was a leftover habit from when she'd sucked her thumb as a child. She didn't know if Rea was aware of it or not, but Selina had noticed her rub the pad of her thumb in circles over her index finger whenever she was anxious as if she had an invisible blanket between them.

Rea was also incredibly body shy. She'd slipped in and out of her robe quickly, giving Selina only the briefest view of her unadorned curves. But in bed, in the dark, Rea seemed to find a level of comfort with their nudity. There'd been some intense kissing and some gentle fondling, but they had yet to make love. It had been the sweetest agony and a testament to Selina's self-control.

Thankfully, she'd been able to distract herself the rest of the week by staying busy. She'd helped Rea catch up on all her paperwork, met with the managers regularly, and took care of both the horses. They hadn't had to worry about cooking any meals as the local women had stopped by to visit, bringing different dishes and casseroles with them. No one stayed long, but she caught a few of them casting knowing looks their way. Selina was sure the grapevine was buzzing with conjectures about them. The upside to all the extra work was, by the time Selina made it to bed each night, her exhaustion helped to keep her ardor at bay.

All that had changed late this afternoon when Rea's doctor had removed her stitches and given her the all-clear to resume regular activities, except for riding, which would have to wait another week. Instead of hurrying back to the farm, they stopped at a tiny Italian restaurant for a decidedly romantic candlelit dinner.

Now coming into the house from bedding down the horses, candlelight was once again setting the scene. They were laid out like a glowing trail of breadcrumbs leading her home. The heady aroma of sandalwood and vanilla, Rea's two favorite scents, permeated the air adding to the ambiance, as did the soft, soulful strains of "Natural Woman" emanating from the bathroom. Selina hoped Rea was using the song to send the same message she had when they had swayed together in each other's arms ten days ago.

The muted sound of splashing water drew Selina toward the bath, like a moth to a flame. She made her way quietly to the open door then had to grab onto the frame, her knees going weak, as she took in the sight of Rea in the tub. Soft, flickering candlelight created phantom ripples on the water that obscured Rea's body from the neck down, and Selina wanted to see that body up close.

"May I join you?" Selina almost pleaded.

A rosy hue, Selina was sure had nothing to do with the water temp, rushed up Rea's neck as she looked down demurely and answered, "You may."

Selina knew one way to combat shyness was with desire, so she took her own sweet time divesting herself of her clothing, and this time it was Selina watching Rea in the mirror. She wasn't wearing much, but drew out the process, as Rea's eyes tracked her every move. She was down to a long t-shirt that covered most of her torso and was timing its removal to the end of the song.

Selina smiled when instead of a new track playing, Aretha's voice filled the space once again, and she realized Rea had set her phone to play on a loop. Selina took that as an answer to her earlier question—Rea was sending the message—that her soul was ready to be claimed.

She turned and faced Rea, whose creamy shoulders had made an appearance above the waterline. Lowering her hands, she crossed one over the other, grasped the hem of her shirt and slowly pulled it up over her head.

The ambient glow from the candles danced about the room, and Selina wondered if her movement or Rea's, sitting straight up in the that caused it. Either way, she didn't care; there was enough precious light to see two full, rosy tipped breasts, emerge from the water, and the sight drew her in.

Selina slowly approached the tub, and Rea scooted forward, giving her space to fit herself in behind. The over-sized tub was deep, but she still took her time easing herself in, her legs skimming along Rea's and watched the water level rise to within inches of the top. If Selina didn't keep her movements gentle, they'd be mopping up water, and that would definitely kill the mood.

She carefully slid her arms around Rea's middle, clasping them just under her breasts. Rea leaned back until she was laying fully against Selina's front. The feel of the soft wet skin against hers caused her whole body to contract in need. Her breath hitched as Rea's head turned, and her hand rose out of the water to tug on Selina's braid. Although no words were spoken, the request was unmistakable, and Selina lowered her head, bringing their lips together in an exploratory kiss. It was both gentle and erotic—their tongues tangled as their lips slanted over each other—sipping the sweetest of nectars.

Selina's hands rose of their own volition and cupped Rea's full breasts, her thumbs circling the turgid nipples. Rea's soft moans punctuated the air, creating a counter-rhythm to the love song playing in Selina's heart. She didn't want to make love to Rea for the first time in a tub. So, Selina pried her lips away, kissing along Rea's jaw, up to her ear, and husked out, "My beautiful Rea, I love you. Let me show you how much." Nipping the lobe, so close to her lips, Selina implored, "Can we take this into the bedroom?" She lowered her hands, holding fast to Rea's hips and waited.

*****

Instead of answering, Rea rose from the tub first, water dripping to the tile floor as she stepped out and offered Selina her hand. "Come, love. Let me show you first."

Over the last five days, Rea had found a new level of comfort, with the thought of allowing Selina to view her chubby body. One conversation specifically boosted her confidence, when they'd shared their celebrity crushes. Selina's top three had been Amy Schumer, Adele, and her first one at fourteen, Rosie O'Donnell. It seemed apparent from this list Selina actually found plump women appealing, but she still had a slight niggling doubt.

Rea had kept her body mostly covered, planning out this first intimate encounter—the slow burn she'd imagined when her hands had mapped out Selina's hidden contours in bed at night—had almost ended at the sight of her nude body. Rea had almost risen from the tub, but the naked look of desire in those blue eyes had held her in place.

The last few minutes feeling Selina surrounding her, kissing and playing with her body, had ramped up Rea's sexual tension. But the whispered words of love and longing that Selina uttered tenderly in her ears pierced Rea's heart and soul.

Now she stood before Selina, bare in both body and spirit, wanting to share everything she was with Selina, in the most physical of ways. When the warm hand slipped into Rea's, she tugged Selina gently from the tub and handed her a fluffy towel. She noted the speed with which Selina dried herself off, telegraphing her own driving need to retreat to the bedroom. After draping their wet towels over the bar, Rea picked up her phone, linked hands with Selina, and led her out, blowing out the candles as they went.

She stopped at her dresser, pausing only long enough to select a new playlist and dock her phone with the mini speaker system. The now-familiar warbling of a flute echoed through the room, as Rea ushered Selina over to the bed.

In one swift move, she swept the comforter to the end of the mattress, stacked two pillows against the headboard, and climbed to the center, never letting go of Selina's hand. Rea drew her in until Selina's head and shoulders lay propped up against the pillows. Straddling Selina's lap, resting most of her weight on her bent knees, Rea was in the perfect position to access the things she wanted to feel and taste the most.

Selina's hands snaked up to grip her hips and firmly brought Rea's center down against her own. She felt the tell-tale moisture there, betraying Selina's desire for her. Rea would get to that, but she planned to ramp things up a bit first. Rea started by tracing the chiseled outlines of Selina's face with her lips, pausing briefly to claim her mouth in a hungry kiss, before moving on to a shell-like ear. Rea traced it with the tip of her tongue then gently nipped the lobe. The hitch in Selina's breathing gave away her arousal, and Rea husked out, "You like?"

"Yes." She felt Selina shiver. "My ears are very sensitive."

"Good to know." Rea gave the lobe a final nip before traveling south along Selina's graceful neck. She could feel Selina's pounding pulse vibrating beneath her lips. Rea made a complete circuit before giving Selina's other ear the same treatment. Selina moaned deeply, her hands moving up Rea's sides until they firmly clasped her breasts, fondling them with nimble fingers. Then it was her turn to moan in Selina's ear.

Things were moving a bit too fast for her liking, and she decided to slow things down. Reaching up, Rea captured Selina's hands and brought them back down to rest on her hips. Pulling back, Rea looked into Selina's passion-filled eyes, and admonished, "Ah, ah, ah, keep your hands where they are. It's my turn first." Eliciting a groan in protest.

"You're killing me here." Selina thrust her hips up and ground her center against Rea's. "Can't you feel how wet you've made me already," she growled.

Rea could. "Yes, but you'll have to be patient. I still have more exploring to do."

In a minor act of defiance, Selina slid her hands around to Rea's backside and squeezed. "Well, get on with it then."

Rea gave her a predatory smile and brought her hands up to cup Selina's small but pert breasts that filled her palms perfectly. Rea's thumbs circled the nutmeg colored nipples that were already standing at attention, before lowering her mouth to suckle one of them gently, tweaking the other with her fingers. The turgid bud grew impossibly firmer as the tip of Rea's tongue mapped out every ridge and bump, then switched sides, giving the other nipple her full attention.

A needy mewling reached Rea's ears, as Selina's hips squirmed under hers. The hands on her ass kneaded her flesh in a matching rhythm, and Rea's clit throbbed in response. Dropping a last kiss on each breast, she pulled away, preparing to move south, but the ecstasy etched on Selina's features made Rea pause. Selina's head was thrown back, with her eyes slammed shut, and her bottom lip was caught between perfect white teeth.

God, she's beautiful! Rea lifted her head and sent out a silent thank you for bringing this woman into her life. She rose up, placed a tender kiss on each of Selina's eyelids, and murmured, "I love you, Lina. You own me, heart, and soul."

Selina's hands let go of her rear and traveled up to take firm hold of Rea's face. The blue eyes opened, capturing her gaze, before replying, "As you own mine."

The passionate kisses that followed spoke clearly to Rea of their mutual needs. In a move that seemed choreographed, Selina nudged her onto her back. Pivoting, Selina lowered her own center toward Rea's mouth. She nuzzled Selina's inner lips, absorbing her unique smell and taste, before snaking her tongue out to flick against Selina's clit. The warm mouth dancing over her own had Rea's hips moving. From that moment on, the dual sensations of loving and being loved so intimately, built to an earth-shattering crescendo, until they both came undone.

Exhausted, Rea managed to turn onto her side, pulling out one of the pillows under her head for Selina. Air sawed in and out of her lungs, reminding her of how long it had been since she'd experienced this kind of intimate joining.

Selina recovered first, swiveled, and dragged the comforter up with her. She rested her head on the pillow next to Rea's and flung a knee over her possessively. She reciprocated by clasping

Selina in a warm embrace. Rea felt replete for the first time in years, and it was all thanks to the woman beside her.

Rea dropped a butterfly kiss on Selina's lips. "Thank you for being so patient with me, Lina," she murmured sleepily.

"You were more than worth the wait. I'm just happy we found our way to each other. Now go to sleep, you haven't fully recovered from the accident yet and need your rest. We have a lifetime ahead of us for repeats."

Rea smiled dreamily at the thought of the days and nights to come. She leaned in for one last soft kiss, then said, "Goodnight, love."

Selina followed with, "Goodnight, dearling."

Rea closed her eyes. As she drifted off, she thought she heard a whispered, "Thanks Mom," followed by the resonating howl of a lone wolf before sleep claimed her.

Epilogue

Selina found it hard to believe her life had changed so drastically in just one year. But here she was, bumping along the uneven rocky terrain, heading toward three familiar boulders with Rea riding shotgun in the other seat. Selina briefly splayed out the fingers on her left hand, where it gripped the steering wheel, for a quick glance at the pink gold wedding band with its silver etching, gracing her ring finger. A huge grin split her face as Selina looked toward her new bride.

The answer to her prayer had stood next to her yesterday, and they were married in the community hogan, by one of the clan elders. Rea had looked fabulous in the teal ribbon shirt gifted to her by Selina's family, and she'd worn a traditional Diné rug dress in red and black. Her family had taken up their positions in the south. While Matty, Mia, Reenie, Emma, and a few others from Moirai that had become family to Rea sat in the north. Since there was no exchange of rings in a traditional ceremony, Rea had waited until after they'd consumed the blue corn mush, to surprise her with them.

They were simple but elegant bands. Rea had taken the meteorite to a jeweler, that smelted the silver from the crack, and used it along with pink gold to artistically design them. The silver infinity symbol with RT and ST in the open loops encircled the rings.

Selina's second surprise had been last night. They'd spent the week apart while she was in Holbrook arranging the wedding.

After the ceremony and reception, they had retreated to a hotel room in Chinle. Selina had removed Rea's clothing like she was unwrapping a gift. She'd paused as Rea's bare shoulder came into view, and Selina saw she'd embellished her tattoo. The black lines of the infinity symbol were now braided with yellow, white, and turquoise. A slightly larger set of initials augmented the originals, with some added shading that made them look two-dimensional.

Both were Rea's ways of acknowledging not only the love they'd found together but the loving spirits that had led them to each other.

Selina was brought out of her musing when Rea pointed at the boulders she was heading for and said, "I've seen this place before. The rocks form a semicircle near the mouth of a canyon."

Selina was shocked but intrigued. She turned her head to Rea and asked, "When?"

A momentary look of concentration crossed Rea's face before it lit up with an ah-ha look. "I was here when I was in the Shadow Lands. It is where I spoke with your Amá sání. I remember now. She said something about me becoming a part of her family like she knew we would marry, and I think I recall the other spirits saying we were destined to be together."

"They probably did know; after all, they with us during our darkest hours. And with all those times we'd almost met in the past—is it any wonder they intervened—to bring the threads of our lives together to make our future possible?"

They arrived at her spot and got busy unloading everything. Rea had fallen silent while they worked, seemingly absorbed in some inner contemplation. It was a trait they shared in common, so Selina stayed quiet, leaving Rea to her thoughts.

As the sun sank below the horizon, they sat side by side near the fire, and Rea asked, "Did you ever watch a TV show called Twin Peaks?"

"No, I wasn't ever a fan of creepy movies or TV shows. Why?"

"I've been thinking about something you said a while ago, and it kind of reminded me of something said during one episode, about coming through the darkness of future past. But instead of a malevolent magician bridging the two worlds, it was the souls of those who'd loved us the most that brought us together, and for that, I will be forever grateful."

Selina turned toward Rea, and the look of love in those green eyes with the gold flecks at their centers had her offering her own silent thanks. The fire popped and crackled as the smell of the wood smoke rose in the air. The night sky was strewn with glittering starlight. The constellation Sagittarius—The Archer—was directly overhead—bridging heaven and earth. A deep peace stole over Selina, bringing with it a feeling that all was right in the universe.

She started to hum what she now considered to be their song, and Selina leaned forward, sealing her lips to Rea's. She poured her heart and soul into the kiss. A soul that was no longer in the lost and found. Rea had changed that along with everything else in her life. There were no more doubts or uncertainties about her place in the world—it was beside this woman. Selina ended the kiss and sat back.

She smiled to herself when Rea started humming where Selina had left off, but then she paused and asked, "Have you given any more thought to passing on our mystic meteorite?"

"Do you really think the magic it holds might bring other lost souls together?" It was Selina's personal talisman, after all, sent by her Amá sání.

"I don't know,"—Rea turned to look deep into her eyes—"but maybe you can do your thing, like you did before and ask for a…Oh my god, look!"

They both stared up in wonder as a streaking object made a transient appearance in the heavens before winking out, and they knew they had their answer.

~The End~

Glossary

Foreign Words and Phrases

Diné (Navajo)

Amá sání - Grandmother

Yá'át'ééh - Hello or said when greeting someone (Literally: it is good) Can also be used when saying goodbye.

Shik'is - my friend

Mą'iitsoh níích'i - Wolf spirit

Latin American Spanish

Cariña - Sweetie

Hola - Hello

Sí - Yes

Hola mis hermosas damas - Hello my beautiful ladies

Ay Dios mio - Oh my God

Adiós - Goodbye

Gracias - Thank You

Buenas tardes - Good afternoon

Es un placer conocerte - Nice to meet you

Hablas español bien, eso será útil - You speak Spanish well, that will be useful

No hay probelma - No problem

Un poquito - A little

Atraído por ella, sí? - Attracted to her, yes?

Glossary

Rea, es mi familia y la amo - Rea is my family, and I love her

Hasta luego - See you later

Tal vez deberíamos irnos a casa - Maybe we should go home

Inmediatamente   - Right away

About the Author

Elle Hyden embarked on a new phase of her life in 2015 when she retired, allowing her to indulge in her favorite pastime, reading. Inspired by the other authors' stories and using what her mother had called, an overactive imagination, she decided to write a few of her own.

She has already begun work on the next book in this series—Evermore.

CPSIA information can be obtained
at www.ICGtesting.com
Printed in the USA
LVHW081321311019
635957LV00023B/191/P